Heavy Duty Attitude

Iain Parke

bad-press.co.uk

Also by Iain Parke

The Liquidator
Heavy Duty People

ISBN 978–0–9561615–3–6
www.iainparke.co.uk

For Pat, for keeping the faith
For richer, but mainly for poorer…

The Guardian

Friday 15 May 2009 – page 11

Security guard stabbing

Police are seeking witnesses after nightclub bouncer Sean Norman (42) was fatally stabbed last night outside the Aurora nightclub in Lincoln. Initial police reports suggest that Mr Norman, who was alone at the time as his colleagues had gone inside the club to deal with a disturbance, was rushed just before midnight by a group of three men wearing balaclavas and immediately set upon. Inspector James Allen of Lincolnshire police said, 'This appears to have been a deliberate and planned attack on an unarmed man and we are appealing for anyone who saw anything that can help us identify these men to come forward and talk to us.'

Avoiding contempt and hatred

A ruler must guard against two kinds of danger: one internal coming from his own people; the other external, coming from foreign powers. To defend yourself against foreign powers you need a good army and good allies. And if you have a good army you'll always have good allies, and when you're secure against foreign powers you'll always be secure internally too, assuming there wasn't already a conspiracy underway. Then, even when a foreign power does move against you, you have only to keep your nerve and you'll survive any and every attack.

The Prince, Niccolo Machiavelli 1469–1527

From the Tim Parks translation 2009 (Penguin Books)

The Guardian

Monday 8 June 2009

Fight night clubbing

In what police fear may be an act of retaliation between rival biker gangs for the killing of Sean Norman last month, the Xanadu nightclub in King's Lynn was burnt down last night in a petrol bomb attack.

Mr Norman was attacked by a group of men and stabbed last month outside the Aurora nightclub where he worked as a doorman and died on his way to hospital. Known by his club nickname of 'Boom-Boom', he was also the vice president of the Lincolnshire chapter of the Yorkshire based regional 'outlaw' motorcycle club Dead Men Riding MC.

The nightclub destroyed in last night's attack however is believed by police to have links to local outlaw rivals Capricorn MC who are based in East Anglia and who have previously clashed with the neighbouring club in disputes over territory in Cambridgeshire and Lincolnshire, both areas where the two clubs are believed to have competing interests.

'We are concerned that these incidents may be linked and may indicate an upsurge in violence between the two groups,' said Inspector James Allen who is leading the investigation into the death of Mr Norman. 'This is certainly a line of enquiry we will be pursuing and we are already in contact with our colleagues in SOCA [the Serious and Organised Crime Agency] for information and assistance in this regard.'

Police sources have however conceded that they are disappointed in the lack of information received to date about Mr Norman's murder. 'It doesn't surprise me at all as the biker gangs operate under a code of silence,' a spokesman for SOCA said, on condition of strict anonymity. 'Even when there is a serious attack on one of their own they will refuse to talk to the police or co-operate with us in any way, and we suspect they have put the word out amongst all their associates that no potential witnesses are to be allowed to come forward. It also doesn't surprise me that this is centred around nightclubs. Both gangs are actively involved in providing clubs with security as control of who can enter a club means control of who can deal drugs inside.'

Speculating about where this might lead, he said, 'The danger is that the clubs will want to deal with this direct themselves which could lead to a prolonged period of tit-for-tat violence between the two, as well as potentially incidents at which innocent members of the public get hurt. After all, it was only fortunate that no one was left in the club that was attacked last night.'

1   RSVP

Tuesday 28 July 2009

'I liked your book,' he said, as we shook hands across the table.

'Well thanks,' I answered guardedly, as I slid onto the bench seat opposite him and sat down. It was around three months since it had come out and so just coming up to about a year since his election.

'You mean the one that just about stopped short of saying that you killed him,' I asked, 'or that you at least had him killed?'

'Yes,' he nodded with a smile on his wolfish face, 'I particularly liked that part.'

Obviously given the history and who he was, I had been very wary when I had taken his call last week at the paper asking me to meet up with him.

No, wary was the wrong thing to say. Scared shitless would be more like it.

So I had my work cut out to persuade myself that it would be safe to go, but eventually and possibly foolishly, I had managed to convince my inner coward.

That he wanted us to get together somewhere in public was some reassurance.

He would also have to assume that I would probably take some elementary safety measures. I would tell someone who I was meeting and where so they could call the cops if I didn't get back in a reasonable time.

I might even, if I wanted to, have arranged for someone to come along to keep a watchful eye on me and raise the alarm if it looked as though things were getting ugly.

Even so, it had taken me quite a while to screw my nerves up to actually come. After all, fear of legal consequences wasn't something that ranked very highly in his world. And the trouble with the all elementary safety precautions I could take was that they still wouldn't mean I was safe.

I knew, absolutely and without question, that these were people who wouldn't think twice about killing me, whatever the situation, if that's what they had decided they wanted to do. It might only take a moment to take me out, and a moment might be too quick for anyone to intervene, while afterwards they would have all the time in the world to persuade witnesses that they might not actually remember what had happened.

4

So I knew I was taking a risk, perhaps even sticking my life on the line. But in the end I had decided I would go. The urge to know was too strong, and we'd agreed to meet at a motorway services, so it was about as public a place as I was going to get. Although, as I was on my way I suddenly regretted my choice as I realised that Heathrow might have been even better. The knowledge that armed police would be expected to be on patrol in the terminals might have given me even more comfort.

It was a summer Saturday afternoon, the road was busy with holiday traffic, and the car park was full as I pulled in and parked up. Families were milling around open cars feeding kids ice creams, and camped out eating sandwiches and slurping cokes at the wooden trestle tables on the grass beside the main block, to the background noise of traffic roaring by. Welcome to staycationland I thought, as I headed inside, the automatic doors swishing open in front of me as two large women in low cut tops that clashed with their orange-glow skin came out past me sucking at straws from Styrofoam cups, brown paper burger and chips bags grasped in their other hands.

I walked through to the eating in area, my eyes adjusting quickly to the relative dimness of the cool interior from the bright glare of outside. As the doors hissed shut for a moment behind me, the noise of traffic faded away to be overtaken by the noise of people echoing against the concrete cave as children ran about and a murmuring susurrus of the noise of people talking and eating competed with the piped musak and clattering cutlery.

Well, here goes, I thought, steeling my nerves.

He was easy to spot.

The restaurant area was crowded as I walked in, the noise level reaching a pitch and all the tables filled, except for across by the window on the far side where a series of booths lined the wall.

The bikers were where you would expect to find them, looking out into the room, backs to the wall, always watching, always wary.

He was sat in the middle of the row, a coffee in front of him at the otherwise empty table. The neighbouring booths on either side of him were each also occupied by a single full patched Brethren with a drink in front of them, and despite the jam packed tables elsewhere, obviously no one had asked them to move, or had even decided that they wanted to sit in the adjoining booths.

He had seen me as I arrived and gave me a quick nod of acknowledgement as I walked across to him, while I could feel eyes following me across the room as people realised I was approaching his table. Was this what it was like I wondered? For them I mean. To always be on show, to always be the centre of surreptitious attention wherever you went?

He had gestured for me to sit opposite him and I did.

We paused while he asked me what I wanted and one of the guys went off to get it, joining the queue to pay like any other law abiding citizen. He wasn't in much of a rush and I guess he was safe enough that no one was going to nick his table while he was gone.

Wibble looked much as I remembered him from the few times we had met. The guys' lids were all with the bikers' Harleys parked up outside the entrance and were being guarded as always by a striker serving his time. Wibble was wearing his summer riding gear, a padded check work shirt which was now open to reveal the black and red hooped T-shirt underneath, with part of The Brethren logo showing just above the left breast. His sleeves were rolled up to his elbows, and over the top of the shirt was his black leather biker's vest which I knew would have his colours on the back.

He looked a bit older that when I'd met him before but then it was what, four or five years ago now? His sharp featured face was a bit more lined than I remembered, his shoulder length mass of wild hair and short cavalier style beard was showing grey amongst the black, but he still looked wiry, whip-hard and very, very dangerous.

But then when you looked at the front of his cut, when you took in the grinning ∬ style skull and crossbones tottenkopf flash on his left breast that was his Bonesmen tab, and the simple red and black embroidered *Freemen* and *President* flashes ranked above it; then that would have told you he was a Menace, in every sense of the word, and needed to be treated as such, whatever he looked like.

Despite what people assume, few of the bikers actually wear any Nazi insignia these days, not because of any objection to it of course, much the reverse in fact as many of them often admire the triumph of the will image of the Nazis. An aura of disciplined ranks, marching as a body and a strength through joy reliance on violence has an atavistic and strong gut appeal. But in practice any of the clubs which has a presence in Germany has dropped anything with a swastika from its flash as their German charters simply can't wear it without going straight to jail. The Brethren's bonesman patch with its ∬ style skull and crossbones was unusual in that in its red dyed variation, so far, they had managed to get away with it.

There was a plain diamond shaped black and red patch on the opposite side of his cut. It was a new tab, one I'd not seen before, for obvious reasons.

6

It simply read *In memory, Damage. RIP* and underneath, *LLH&R.*

So why the hell I went and blurted out what I said next, I'll never work out. Did I have some kind of death wish?

'Well,' I said, 'now I'm here, do you mind if I ask you a question?'

'Naw, feel free mate,' he said, lounging back, 'What do you want to know?'

'Alright then,' I said in an in for a penny, in for a pound moment of madness, 'can I ask, did you kill him?'

His smile seemed to stay fixed, but he leaned forward, resting his heavily tattooed arms on the table and bringing his face closer to mine as though he was going to say something in confidence and I couldn't help but tense, wondering with a sudden mix of what – terror or regret? – if I'd just blown it with the first remark out of my mouth?

'Of course,' he answered steadily, the smile still on his face but nowhere near to touching his eyes which were boring into mine, 'but just because you can ask anything you like, doesn't mean that I have to answer, does it?'

'No,' I quickly surrendered.

'Well I didn't really expect an answer to that one anyway, but I've got to try,' I said making an effort to recover the situation.

He left me on the hook for a moment or two, his expression not changing a bit, as though he was silently and deliberately calculating whether to have a problem with what I had said, or not. But, he was also saying in his silence, he didn't need to calculate what he would do if he decided to take it that way. We both knew what he would do, crowd and CCTV or no crowd and no CCTV.

Then he let me go.

'I suppose so,' he agreed, leaning back again and looking a little more relaxed after that demonstration of his power.

'How are his wife and kid? Are they OK?' I asked, partly to change the subject a bit, and partly out of genuine interest, 'It's been a while since I saw them.'

'Shaz and Lucy? Oh they're fine, they're being looked after.'

'Good,' I said and meant it. I had liked Sharon; Damage's petite and pretty wife was a talented artist, and Lucy had seemed a great kid.

'So,' I said, a bit more nervously but relieved that he still seemed to want to talk to me, 'can I try asking you another question?'

'Sure,' he said, the smile wider now, 'Christ, you really are a nosy bugger aren't you? Beats me how Damage put up with you for so long.'

'Sorry,' I shrugged, 'it's just the job, that's what I do for a living, quiz people.'

'And then you write it all down?'

'Well, some of it anyway,' I said, a bit more defensively than I had intended. 'You always have to leave some stuff out as a journalist, and of course you can't reveal your sources.'

'Yeah, I get that and that's good,' he said looking up and back over my shoulder, 'Ah here we are.'

'There you go,' said the full patch man-mountain of a Brethren as he arrived back at our table to serve me with a skinny latte and a couple of sugars. Not something that I had ever really expected to happen.

'Thanks,' I said automatically, 'that's great.'

''Salright,' he shrugged and slid back onto his bench in the booth behind Wibble.

'So,' I said ripping open the paper spills of sugar and tipping them into the tall glass, 'if you don't want me to ask you questions, what can I do for you?'

As I dipped the spoon into the drink and absentmindedly watched the white milk and dark coffee swirl together as I stirred, I heard what he wanted to talk about.

And much to my surprise, for obvious reasons in some ways, but equally as the most obvious topic in others, what he wanted to discuss was Damage. And I was interested to know why.

'Like the man said, the evil a bloke does lives on after them, the good that guys do gets buried with them.'

Now it was my turn to smile.

'What is this?' I asked, 'Friends, Brethren, citizens, you come not to praise Damage, but to bury him?'

'Something like that,' he agreed.

'Well then,' I continued, in a bit of a mock declamatory tone, 'so let it be with Damage. The noble Wibble hath told you Caesar was ambitious.'

His eyes narrowed a bit as he looked at me.

'Are you taking the piss?' he demanded.

'No, I said hurriedly, 'I'm just thinking about your quote. I was trying to remember how the rest of it went.'

I was dredging it up now, from a year sitting there at school in Mr Majewski's English class. How did it go now I asked myself? And then I remembered that it ran something like, *if Damage was ambitious, it was a grievous fault and Damage has paid for it grievously*. It just seemed appropriate really, but possibly not one for sharing with Wibble just at this moment and bearing in mind how our conversation had started.

'Did you tell anyone you were coming here to meet me?' he asked from out of left field.

I shrugged in acknowledgement. There didn't seem to be a need to say anything else.

'Sensible,' he nodded, 'to take precautions I mean.'

I knew straight away what he was referring to.

'So did you like it?' I asked. I had always wondered, and I had never heard anything from the club since it had come out. For months after publication I had half expected, half dreaded the bikers turning up at my door one day to wreak retribution. Knowing what they were undoubtedly capable of, in some ways the silence had been as unnerving.

'Personally?' he asked.

'Well, yes I suppose so, but I really meant the club.'

'Yes,' he said after a moment's consideration, 'I guess I did.'

'Even with what it was saying?'

I was conscious that the autobiography I had helped Damage to write hadn't held back from discussing how some of The Brethren made their money and what sort of business they conducted to get it. And I was very conscious as I sat there in front of him, that Wibble had been talked about specifically. In fact, in some ways when I thought about it, Wibble had been the sole living member of The Brethren who could in any way be implicated in a crime from what Damage had told me. I had always wondered exactly why

Damage had told me that when he had always been so careful about what aspects of business he had been prepared to discuss.

'Yeah, even with that.'

I was curious now. I had never expected to have this opportunity to talk about it with someone like Wibble, who was after all, as high up in the club as you could go in this country. 'Why?' I asked.

His answer surprised me a bit. 'It took us seriously I suppose,' was his considered judgement.

'It treated the club with respect and wasn't full of the usual crap about biting the heads off chickens, or weird gangbang sex shit. At least it gave Damage a chance to talk straight about who we are and why.'

The way he had asked me to, I thought.

'Oh don't get me wrong,' he said as he saw the expression on my face, 'a whole lot of the guys were seriously pissed off at it, so don't make that mistake. There were a load of them that just wanted to stomp you on principle for writing about us, but I squashed that.'

'Well thanks for that,' I said a bit weakly.

'Mind you if we really hadn't liked it, we wouldn't need to be getting you here for a chat,' he continued matter of factly, 'so don't make that mistake either.'

He pointed a finger at me and mimed shooting me in the head.

'If you were going to be hit, we wouldn't be meeting up like this, you'd just be dead mate. Bullet in the back of the head in a car park. Bomb under the car. There's all sorts of ways.'

As well I knew from what Damage had told me.

'Besides which, we live in a surveillance society you know,' he carried on conversationally as if discussing how I might be murdered with me was the most natural thing in the world, and waved around him, 'CCTV everywhere, and everyone you meet carrying a camera all the time.'

'You know,' he said turning away to gaze round the room at the crowded tables before coming back to stare at me, 'I bet at least someone in here is filming us even now on the sly.'

'You reckon?' I asked.

He shrugged. 'Yeah, sure. Here we are, three Brethren having a meet with a civilian. It's quite a sight if you're some drone out with the wife and kiddies and just popped into the services for a burger and fries, and yet, look around you.'

I glanced around the room myself. Then I looked back at him. 'So?'

'So, did you see how everyone is so studiously not watching us,' he laughed quietly, 'and failing miserably?'

He was right of course. I had felt the duck and flick away of people's eyes, terrified to accidentally make contact, as soon as I had looked around from our table. Not surprisingly it would make sense that someone amongst the crowd had their mobile out, video running and pointed awkwardly, and they hoped discretely, in our direction to capture a wavering image of two men leant forwards together in a booth while his bodyguards watched the crowd either side. If it was me and I was a civilian, I'd have been filming it too, so I could show it to my mates.

'Is that why you guys have become so much more relaxed about photos?' I asked.

The time was, not so long ago, when no Brethren wanted to have their photograph taken at all and any request would be met with the brusque refusal *because we aren't poseurs*, if the asker was lucky. But these days The Brethren, in common with some of the other big six clubs had become open to pictures, and charters all around the world had their own websites with crew pictures emblazoned on them. As ever with a lot of these things the Angels had led the way with a book of photographs becoming a best seller and had even produced a calendar featuring members, each pictured with their bike and a tasty model just to keep the punters' interest levels up.

'Yeah, we just have to work with it these days.'

Which I guess meant having to take it into account when doing *business*. It was definitely time to change the subject I decided, but to my surprise, Wibble got there first.

'Hey then, let me ask you a question.'

'OK,' I said, 'what?'

He sort of hesitated, as if working out the best way to phrase what he wanted to say. 'If I said I hadn't,' he started finally, 'killed him, I mean. Well, would it make a difference? Would you really believe me?'

There was no hint of any emotion in the question at all. He had asked it completely flatly, as if it was a simple matter of fact query, the answer just to be filed away somewhere for information.

And I really didn't know how to answer that one. Just how safe would an honest response be?

I had written a book about Damage. But only because Damage had been speaking to me in the months before he was killed, which I had always afterwards assumed was on the basis that he knew he was going to be hit.

Wibble was the only living member of The Brethren that Damage had in any way implicated in a crime in what he had told me, and after he had been murdered, Wibble had taken over his role as President of the Freemen, effectively the top spot in the UK Brethren.

You could never prove anything, it was all circumstantial, but there was quite a chain of events there.

And I couldn't quite work out whether he was trying to tell me something or just being curious. Confused, I filled what could rapidly become an uncomfortable silence as he sat still and potentially deadly across the table from me, waiting for an answer, with a question of my own.

'Well if you didn't, who did?'

He nodded slowly at my response as he evaluated it. 'Now that,' he said at last, 'is a very good question.'

'And do you know the answer to it?'

'Well,' he said, effectively shutting the topic down again, 'that's another thing that you can ask, but I might not answer.'

'But you know stuff don't you?' he asked changing tack.

'Stuff? What do you mean?' I replied. It wasn't feeling exactly like a verbal fencing match, not yet at least, but it was starting to feel like a bit of a warm up to one, a wary arms length circling, sword tip to sword tip, with an on edge feeling that at any moment a sudden lunge could come.

'Damage told you a lot didn't he? A lot more than went into your book I mean? Not everything went in, did it?'

There didn't seem to be any point in denying it so I shrugged. 'Yes. I spent a hell of lot of time interviewing him, we covered a lot of ground, talked about a lot of things but when you come to do a book like that, there's only so much you can put in. You have to edit, make decisions, leave bits out.'

'Makes sense,' he nodded, 'did you tape all of it?'

'Yes, it's the easiest way. Much better than just relying on making notes if the interviewee's up for it. That way you can make sure you've got everything.'

'And he didn't mind?'

'No, he was cool with it.'

'I bet there's some interesting stuff there.'

'Could be,' I said more warily now, unsure now as to where this was heading.

It was definitely time to change the subject, I thought.

'So, getting back to my question, I said, 'what can I do for you? I take it this isn't just a social call or the start of a book club?'

'You ride don't you?' he said unexpectedly, 'Damage said you did.'

There was no getting out of that then, 'Yes I do,' I admitted cautiously.

I had ridden as a kid, in my early twenties I had even constructed the world's worst chopper out of an old Z400 twin, a peanut tank and a pair of six-inch over fork extensions, rebuilding the engine in my bedroom, which had really done for the carpet. These days I still had an old Guzzi 850 sitting in the garage. It was more a toy now than the all consuming passion it had been, and one that in truth I admitted to myself, I hardly ever used, but I still had it and it was insured for the odd weekend blast when it was sunny and I felt like a breath of fresh air. Even though I was such a fair-weather biker these days, at least I understood something about riding that had given me some point of contact for talking to Damage.

'Well then, come for a ride with us.'

I could hardly believe my ears.

'You want me to come on a Brethren run?' I squawked.

'Yeah. You can tagalong at the back,' he said dismissively, although of course that was where I would have to ride given what my status as a civilian would be on such an outing.

I was still trying to process the bizarre idea of The Brethren inviting a journalist along on one of their runs, and what's more inviting me as someone who had written what I had about them.

'But why do you want me?'

'To see for yourself what we do, what we're about.'

'But why?' I asked, in danger of starting to sound like a broken record.

'PR.'

'PR?'

'Yeah,' he shrugged, 'we want to start to generate some good PR.'

It seemed from what he told me that The Brethren had decided that they wanted to polish their reputation. As a club they already did a lot of stuff for PR purposes; charity runs, bike shows and so on, but now he told me they were looking to move on from this. They wanted to open up a bit, become more public about who they were and what they did. They didn't want to drop the mystique, and they didn't want to be fucking poseurs, but they had decided that it was time to be less secretive than they had been in the past and it was time to actively put a positive spin on what the club was and what it did.

Given their reputation and history, it was going to be a pretty tall order, I thought.

'We've got a run on this Saturday, a weekend bash,' he concluded, giving me details of the time and the place they were meeting.

'Be there,' he said, in a serious, but not threatening, tone, 'come out with us. See what we're really about.'

I nodded to confirm that I would at least think about it.

'There's just a couple of things,' he added, by way of an afterthought as he began to stand up.

'What's that?' I asked.

'Well first, when you come, remember you're going to be riding with The Brethren. So don't be a fucking wanker, don't wear anything fluorescent.'

I looked up in surprise and he was grinning from ear to ear as though this was the funniest joke in the world.

'And second?'

'Pack a teddy. A fucking big one, you know, like the ones they have at the funfair? Put it on expenses.'

We shook hands. And with that and a 'see yah then' he was up, gathering his guys behind him with a nod and off out of the café with a hundred pairs of eyes once again surreptitiously following him, before not quite swivelling back to me as people leant over the tables in whispered conversations.

I sat back and sipped my previously untouched coffee.

Gradually a few more lines from back in my O-level days came to me.

> *But Brutus says he was ambitious*
> *And Brutus is an honourable man.*

Perhaps it was just as well that we'd dropped that line of discussion before we'd got too far into it I decided. I doubted that Wibble would find the reference flattering.

Should I take him up on his offer I wondered? Would it be safe? Meeting him here in public was one thing. Riding off with him and the whole crew God knows where was something else. Talk about exposed, I thought.

But then as he said, I was exposed anywhere really if they wanted me badly enough.

And after all, I thought, as I swirled my coffee around in its mug.

> *For Brutus is an honourable man*
> *So are they all, all honourable men –*

Honourable, I remembered Mr Majewski saying, now that was a double edged word.

I sat for a while after I had finished. I don't know why, other than that it seemed right to let them have a chance to ride off before I got up to go.

It was a while before anyone new came into the restaurant and sat down in one of the free booths either side of me.

The Guardian

Wednesday 29 July 2009

Leeds shooting

One man was killed and another injured in a shooting in the Chapeltown area of Leeds yesterday. The victim was named by police as Jeremy Arnold, aged 42 from Huntingdon, however, the injured man is understood to have given a false name and to have discharged himself from hospital before police could question him.

According to eyewitness reports, the two victims had been confronted by another group of men outside a snooker hall. They had just returned to their car when a lone figure approached and fired a handgun through the driver's side window at point blank range.

Mr Arnold was shot twice in the head and was declared dead at the scene of the attack. Police are appealing for witnesses.

2 The run

Thursday 30 July 2009

I had been a crime reporter on the paper for over ten years now. It was how I met Damage and The Brethren in the first place. I had been to talk to him when he'd first been elected President of The Freemen, and then later when he was inside I'd interviewed him extensively in the last few months before he'd died. The publication and success of the biography that had come out of those sessions, *Heavy Duty People*, had made my reputation as a writer on both crime and biker clubs. So nowadays I often talked to both the police who specialised in this field, and other clubs who spoke to me with varying degrees of wariness or enthusiasm about the prospect of publicity.

On the police side of the fence, it helped that I'd known someone who was now one of my key contacts from way back when we were both teenagers. Bob and I had been at the same sixth form college together, had both been into bikes and so almost inevitably we'd both been part of the same small town social scene of pubs, discos, parties, bored suburban kids and girlfriends for four or five years or so. All normal teenage stuff, and one of my abiding memories of him was a night when we had cycled away at the end of a party we'd gone to on our tredders so we could get pissed; and him pulling away from me into the darkness while over his shoulder all I could hear was the sound of him fondly imagining he was imitating the noise of the black and gold Ducati 900SS that he had his heart set on as the perfect bike. Which would be quite a step up from the Wetdream he had at the time.

I'd moved away after university, up to London to follow my career and I'd lost touch with the crowd as I drifted away. I'd known vaguely that he'd joined the force and every so often heard a bit about his progress; off the beat and across into plain clothes, sergeant's exams, marriage to a Woopsie, inspector's exams and a posting as what he apparently described to one of our mutual acquaintances as the Sherriff of Uxbridge.

And then one day about six months or so ago, out of the blue we'd just met up again. I was at a SOCA briefing, the Serious and Organised Crime Agency that seemed to fancy itself as nascent British FBI, and there he was, up in front of me on the platform being introduced.

So I made a point of grabbing him at the end of the talk before I could miss him to say 'Hi', and we had snatched a coffee and a catch up for an hour or so in the canteen before it closed for the evening.

It wasn't surprising given the background we shared that biker crime was one of his areas of interest, and yes, he'd read my book. Useful background he called it. He had been particularly interested in asking what links I still had with The Brethren, and seemed disappointed when I'd told him, 'None, and given what was in it, I probably won't be having any anytime soon.'

Which at the time I thought was true.

We'd done some more social 'Do you remembers?' and 'Whatever happened tos?' and a bit more mutual professional quizzing and probing about 'What do you know?' and 'What can you tell me?' and that was it at the time. We were back in touch and we parted on the 'keep in contact' promise, which of course we both would. It was easy to see that we could be useful to each other in what we were doing.

So ever since then we had been dealing reasonably frequently. Telephone chats here, emails there, the odd meeting every now and then. Of course there was a tricky balance to be maintained on both sides in this kind of set up. For a crime reporter a link into police sources, and particularly SOCA was vital, but while he could give me background, there was a limit on what he could say about the detail of any ongoing investigation, certainly for the record. From my side of the house, not only did I have a duty to protect my sources, but I knew full well what some of them might think if I started gossiping to the cops about everything they had said.

But we were both professionals, we had both been here before and we both knew the rules of the game. We knew what we were doing, and as importantly, what the other could and couldn't do.

So Bob was the obvious person to call once I'd got back to the office.

'Well,' he said once I'd finished, 'so are you going?'

'I don't know,' I admitted, 'I guess it depends on how safe it feels.'

'Do you think it might be a set up?'

'It's a possibility I suppose, but no,' I said on reflection, 'I don't think so. Like he said, if they wanted me out of the way they could easily have done that by now. They don't need to lure me out on some run to do it and to leave such a public trail.'

'I think you're probably right. If it was just a question of them wanting to settle business with you, then I'm sure they could arrange that without all this fuss.'

Well thanks, mate, I thought, that was comforting to know.

'Unless they want to get you somewhere to do it as a group thing,' he continued, 'to make an example of you as sort of a public spectacle within the club.'

Jesus, he was a cheery bastard.

'What about the cops? The Brethren wouldn't want to do anything with them around would they?'

'What cops?' he laughed, 'There won't be any on site. Never are. The Brethren police their own event. There's never any crime. Well, reported that is.'

'Christ.'

'So are you worried about going?' he asked.

'Yes of course I am,' I exclaimed, 'even before your jolly shit. Just because I'm invited by Wibble what guarantee is that? How can I be sure that one of the others won't just tee off on me on sight? Wibble said there were some pretty pissed off guys in the club about what I'd written.'

'But Wibble said he'd squashed that didn't he? And if it's Wibble who's inviting you, then I guess the first question is, do you trust what Wibble's saying?'

And it was odd but the answer to that, despite everything you might think or read about The Brethren, was yes. I think I did trust him and what he was saying. With my life? I reminded myself. Well possibly. And anyway, I thought to myself, I didn't have to stay long. If I didn't like the look of how things were shaping up I could always make my excuses and leave.

'And the second question is, do you think he can really control his guys?'

Well, having dealt with Damage for so long and learnt through him how the club ran, I thought I knew the answer to that one, and I was reasonably comfortable with it.

'Is it all peaceful now as far as your mob know?' I asked.

'Yes, about the big boys at least,' he said, 'there's nothing serious on the radar at the moment as far as we can tell, but that's only because they've got it all sewn up.'

'What about the stuff going on up in Lincoln?' I asked.

He seemed relaxed about it. 'Like I said, it's nothing to do with the big boys. Dead Men Riding and Capricorn have both got interests in the club trade out that way. There's been a bit of turf rivalry between them for years, there always is when you get a couple of clubs rubbing up against each other and there's business to be done. I don't know why it's flared up just now but I doubt it's anything too serious and nothing for you to worry about in terms of The Menaces, they won't be involved. A beef between two smaller clubs won't be on their radar, it's too small scale stuff for them.'

So Bob was confirming what I understood from my contacts as well. With the deal that The Brethren under Damage had refined with their main rivals The Rebels over turf and dealing, all was still quiet between the senior clubs at the moment. Everyone got on with making money and each generally kept their local, more junior, clubs in line in their own territories, albeit in the regions where there wasn't a senior club presence, like around Lincoln and the Wash, there could still be trouble brewing between the local boys. But while it might make for a potential follow up story, that wasn't my main concern just at the moment.

It was a bit odd this call just the same I thought, as I put down the receiver. Bob was a cop after all, and what's more, one with SOCA as well. Whatever anyone else thought about The Brethren and the other outlaw bike clubs, SOCA's view was crystal clear. The MCs were simply organised crime, full stop. So how come Bob seemed to be reassuring me about going on their run rather than warning me off, I wondered?

You would have thought a cop would only have one response to someone telling them the equivalent of 'I wrote a book which drove a cart and horses through the rules of omerta, and now I've been invited to a Mafia party,' which would be, 'don't go.' But it sounded as though Bob almost wanted me to be there.

I guess he must really think it'll be reasonably safe and he'll be hoping I might gather some intelligence for him, I decided. After all, I knew The Brethren were one of his key targets.

Well, we'd see. It would be useful to have some bargaining chips to trade with him if I could pick anything up on the day.

Saturday 1 August 2009

Of course it was their Toy Run. I had realised as soon as I thought it through while properly drinking my lukewarm coffee after Wibble had left.

An annual event, the Toy Run was one of The Brethren's main charity dos and an opportunity for them to present a positive face to the public who were always invited in for an open day and to see the bikes on show, and as much media as they could get to turn up. The local Brethren charters each took turns in hosting it on some kind of rota, with all the other charters

20

riding in bringing toys with them as donations that then went to children's charities. There would be beer tents and fairground rides during the day, a bike show and prizes, and then bands and decidedly more adult entertainment going on into the evening, as the rally turned into a more hardcore bikers' party which would go on through the Saturday night and well into Sunday morning.

I checked on the web. There was a booking site for tickets and to register for the run campsite for those who were going for the full on experience. This year I saw it was the Cambridge charter's turn to host. I wondered about going up into the attic and seeing if I could dig out my old tent to pack and then decided against it. I would take my sleeping bag just for show, but I didn't have any intention of using it. I was nervous enough about being there during daylight as it was. Sticking around until after dark when the beers would have been flowing all day just seemed to be asking to push my luck that little bit too far.

The meet for the run was in West London. I followed the instructions that Wibble had given me and so I rolled into the street in Wembley at about ten to ten the next Saturday morning. The Brethren clubhouse was the end pair of a row of shabby Victorian two-up two-down terraces a little way north of the Hanger Lane gyratory. The windows were covered in steel plates painted with The Brethren's black and red club colours, as was the front door of the further one, above which nestled a cluster of CCTV cameras covering the approaches from the front. The other front door had been bricked up so I assumed the houses had been knocked through inside somehow. A high brick wall topped with broken glass enclosed the yard to the rear which was accessed by a set of double steel gates, again in the same paint scheme, and which were, unusually I assumed, open, so that as I drew up I could see there were at least half a dozen Harleys there, parked but loaded and ready to go.

Not that The Brethren would be worried about security too much this morning. A further couple of dozen Harleys in various states of customisation were drawn up along the curb outside the yard and along the front of the clubhouse, all facing outwards, with their riders hanging around in groups, smoking and chatting as they waited for the off. The club's strikers had put out some police cones along the road to reserve space for themselves. Someone had nicked them, I guessed.

I read some bollocks somewhere a while ago, some journalist who had been fed a line that bikers always parked up so the bikes were backed against the pavement and facing away from the road so as to conceal the registrations from police observers. I had almost wet myself laughing. How the hell the pillock's informant had managed to keep a straight face with that one was beyond me.

It was just practical. If you were going to leave it on the side stand the bike was generally safer if you parked it that way so it couldn't roll forward. Christ, I despaired sometimes at the crap some people would believe.

Faces turned to check me out as I pulled up at the far end of the line where there were a couple of anonymous large Jap bikes tucked away as if out of sight. The nearest full patch guy turned away from a youngster he was talking to and fixed me with a wary glare.

'Yeah?' he demanded as I swung off my bike and he eyed the large teddy bear bungeed to the pillion seat of my bike, which I had indeed put on expenses for the day, 'And who the fuck are you?'

And a good morning to you too, I thought, but obviously didn't say.

As he'd turned I'd caught the flash across his chest, *Sergeant at Arms* above the blood red dyed tottenkopf tab. The head of club security. Shit, just the sort of guy you wouldn't want to have a problem with at the start of something like this.

'It's OK Scroat, that's the writer guy Parke. He's with Wibble,' growled a voice behind him that seemed slightly familiar, as I saw the man-mountain from the meeting at the service station walking across to where we were standing.

'We'll be off in a few minutes so you just fit in here at the back with us and the tagalongs and Wibble'll see you when we get there, OK?'

That was OK by me.

Scroat grunted and abruptly turned his back on me to resume his conversation with the kid he'd been talking to.

That was OK by me too.

The order in a club run is always the same. The club's officers would be at the front, the president and the road captain first, followed by the sergeant at arms and secretary, full patch members next, then strikers and finally the lowest of the low, tagalongs and very, very occasionally, a stray civilian like myself. Sometimes there would be a full patch tail end Charlie to keep an eye on the back of the column and a support truck if there was one bringing up the rear. The pack would ride close together in pairs and with this number of bikes on the road, a couple might take it in turns to ride ahead as shotgun so as to block traffic coming out of side roads while the column passed to prevent the pack getting split up by intruding traffic.

The only variation today was that it seemed as though Scroat and the man-mountain were fixing to ride at the back with me and two young looking guys.

I looked around and caught the eye of the kid standing next to the bike beside mine. From his unadorned jacket he was presumably a tagalong and I assumed also the owner of one of the Jap bikes. The other one must belong to the other lad I decided. After all, no self respecting full patch Brethren would turn up for a formal run of this importance on anything other than their hog.

It was the slickback's first time I guessed and I wondered if he realised how much he was giving off waves of pure nervousness, as though he was trying to look tough, pleased and serious all at once. It wasn't working. And it was the sort of thing I thought that someone like Scroat would pick up on like a shark smelling blood in the water.

He smiled at me, I think in recognition of someone who was less of a threat and introduced himself as Danny.

They would call him 'Danny the Boy' I thought, I could see it now.

'Hi,' I said and nodded at him, 'Iain.'

He had obviously heard what man-mountain had said and he was a bright kid. He immediately put two and two together.

'Hey,' he asked, 'are you the guy who wrote that book? You are, aren't you?'

'*Heavy Duty People*?' I asked.

'Yes, the one about Damage.'

'That's right,' I admitted quietly, looking around to check out any reactions. It really wasn't a subject that I was very comfortable with him talking about right now thank you very much. I guessed that Scroat for example might not be much of a fan.

'Hey it was a great book.'

'Thanks,' I said, wanting to shut the conversation down, 'Glad you liked it.'

'I've read it loads of times. It's one of the reasons I wanted to ride with the guys.'

Oh God, I thought.

'So how come these guys are at the back with us lot?' I asked him as a way of changing the subject, but also out of curiosity. 'Shouldn't they be up front with the others?'

'Don't know,' he said, 'this is my first time out with the guys and Bung's my sponsor so I guess he's going to keep an eye on me.' He gestured in the direction of man-mountain, so now at least I had a name.

'And Scroat?' I said nodding in Mr Surley's direction.

The kid just shrugged. 'Guess he's Charlie's sponsor,' he said nodding at the other kid who was now standing off to one side, quietly watching what was going on and ignoring us completely. Given that he looked as though he couldn't be more than twenty or so I was shocked to see that he already had a bottom rocker marking him out as a striker, someone working his passage and on track to be voted on for a full patch after a year or so. It seemed extraordinarily early. The Brethren was a very adult organisation, in all senses of the word. Most of its active members were in their thirties, forties, even fifties, with a few grizzled veterans even older than that and still riding and rolling with the crew. While one of the byelaws said that no one under twenty-one could become a full member it was almost an irrelevance since in practice no one ever got put up for membership until they were in their late twenties or early thirties anyway. The Brethren wanted solid guys, people who had done their time, in various ways, who had proved themselves. So what was this kid doing on his way at this age I wondered, filing it away in the interesting-things-to-follow-up-at-some-time category.

Danny the Boy didn't look as though he was about to introduce me and given Charlie's attitude I decided that I didn't think that was looking like any great loss.

Just then there was a sudden wave of anticipation and movement that swept its way down the crowded pavement as fags were dropped and riders started towards their machines. An instruction had plainly been given from up at the top of the line and we were about to move off.

As I turned back to my bike it suddenly struck me that there was something odd about the crowd mounting their bikes this morning. The Toy Run was a charity gig and a major club party event. But all of the guys here were single packing. Why was no one planning to take their old ladies today? Yet another thing to file away in the corner of my mind marked things to worry about. Perhaps the girls were making their way over separately, I wondered?

That would be good, I thought. But it seemed unlikely as I started to worry.

There were only two reasons to single pack on a party run that I could think of. The first was because it was going to be the sort of a party that you didn't want to take your old lady to as she might cramp your style. But on the annual Toy Run, as a semi public event, that seemed unlikely.

And the second was because you thought there was going to be trouble.

The kid next to me hadn't clocked any of this, I could tell from his attitude. I wondered why he was here. The kid was worried about how he would hold up in this crowd, he hadn't picked up on the vibe that there was something going down here at all. He was an innocent who just smelled of wannabe and that was never going to wash with this crowd. The other kid, Charlie, the one who'd blanked me completely when I'd arrived; he felt more right, watchful, arrogant, unfriendly. He already had the air of apartness that characterised some of the guys. Despite his age, you could immediately tell that he was right as a striker. He'd fit straight in, I thought, if he stayed the distance. Damage had talked once about recognising, not recruiting, and with these two I could see just what he meant.

'Hey,' Danny the Boy shouted across from astride his bike as he did up his helmet, 'Are you writing another book? About the club I mean. Is that why you're here?'

That was a very good question, I asked myself. A very, very good question. So as I pushed the bike upright off its stand, turned the key and pressed the starter button for the bike to crob into throbbing life, I smiled back at him and shouted across the honest truth to the kid over the roar of the engines firing up all along the kerbside.

'The thing is kid, I really don't know.'

*

The run, the ride there, wow that was something else, like nothing else I had ever experienced.

I'd ridden with other bikers before of course. As kids my mates and I had hung around together and ridden together as we graduated up from our fizzies and AP50s onto our first real machines, our two-fifties, Bob on his Dream, me on my GS250T, Cliff on his RS. We'd all taken our tests and ridden these throughout our student years, blasting up to town to the Hammersmith Odeon for Sabbath gigs, or to the Marquee for Girlschool, racing each other round Surrey lanes and south west London's streets, or cruising down in a group to the west country to join the rest of the lads, with their assortment of second hand minis and parents' cars borrowed for the week, at Croyd or Perranporth for our drunken surf and zider holidays.

And then as we'd each got jobs, the first purchase had been the bigger bike, the seven-fifty, the real thing.

'It's like falling in love with motorcycling all over again,' Bob had told me when I first got mine, and he was right, it was.

And for the next few years we did all the same things on them as we'd done on the two-fifties, only bigger and better and faster. The trip to Devon or Cornwall was a complete thrash, one which cost me my first three points somewhere on the A303. The biking holiday one year for three of us was a seventeen hour and fifty-six minute blast leaving from Lands End at just gone five-thirty one beautiful July dawn and pulling into John O'Groats just before midnight that evening having realised as we zoomed past Carlisle and headed to the border that we were only half way.

And when we headed down to Box Hill on a sunny weekend we needed to be careful to dodge the speed cops on the dual carriageway.

I'd ridden on MAG demos in London, we'd joined in semi organised runs from Box Hill to Brighton on an August bank holiday.

Courtesy of Bob, I'd even been out a couple of times years ago with his local police motorcycle club, and fun rides they were, mind the speed limits in town and don't cross solid white lines but once out onto the unrestricted roads, it was every man, and one woman in skin tight leathers riding a bright yellow café racer Kwacker special, for themselves.

But none of those was ever anything like this.

Damage had talked to me about the discipline, the presence of an outlaw pack. But hearing about it and being part of it, even in such a tangential way at the back, was such a different thing.

Wibble had been right about one thing though. There was no need to wear anything fluorescent, not riding with this mob.

No one, not even the blindest Volvo driving twat, was going to do a sorry-didn't-see-you-guv-pull-out on an outlaw convoy like this.

The lights were red as we came to the junction with the North Circular so as I pulled in at the back of the pack behind the two staggered lines of slowing bikes in the column, I was just bathed in the noise washing over me of the clattering and banging rumble of the overruns as The Brethren braked.

The Japs had copied the look of the Harley, they'd even produced some fantastically close looking clones, but it was all surface. They had never managed to capture the souls of the machines, the feel, the heart, or most gloriously, the noise. That indescribable deep melodic throaty booming rumbling burbling growl emanating from the mouths of the slash cut shotgun exhausts.

Ahead of me I could see rear mudguards shaking and juddering from the Harleys' tick overs as we waited at the lights, a sound that at idle always seemed to clutter almost to a ragged dying halt, before tumbling over in its cycle again, the inimitable uneven mechanical heartbeat of the big V twin.

I was the only one in a leather jacket. The Brethren didn't tend to go in for the traditional British biker uniform, distaining its practical safety aspect. Black bomber jackets or donkey jackets were their riding outfit of choice underneath leather waistcoats bearing their sacred patches.

So the riders ahead of me were a contrast of black, red and steel. The high widespread handlebars of the big bikes putting the riders into a wide shouldered stance that flew their colours in an arrogant and open challenge to the world, while below the fat bulbous chrome steel dome of the primary drive cover hanging out low down on the left side of the bike, shining proud behind the riders' feet and hanging ponderously low, close to the rolling tarmac beneath, giving the bikes and riders that classic Harley profile from the rear.

Then the lights turned green and the noise picked up into a full throated roar as the heavy machines launched forward again in pairs and swayed in a heavy curve through the corner and out onto the main road.

*

A couple of hours later we swept through the high street of what would otherwise be a quiet Cambridgeshire fenland town like an invading army, the bikes' reflections flashing in the windows, and the harsh bark of the exhausts bouncing between the buildings, heads turning at the approaching guttural noise, the bikers' eyes fixed rigidly ahead, ignoring the everyday Saturday morning shoppers as they stopped and turned to watch the convoy rumble past like some kind of fearsome pageant.

Our destination was a rugby club just on the outskirts, where once through the gates we rode along a tarmaced track through a small orchard and then out at the edge of an open playing field with the sets of posts at either end, and a reasonable sized red brick built club house behind which the first bikes were pulling in.

We were here.

As we parked up at the back of the pack, Wibble was already striding straight across towards us, pulling off his lid as he did so.

'Alright?' he asked with a friendly grin as he reached us where I was settling the bike down onto its side stand and swinging myself off it. 'Enjoy the ride?'

'Yeah, it was great thanks,' I replied honestly, grinning right back. It was true. There was nothing like riding in a pack like that and feeling the world's eyes on you. It just did things to you. It was like an old biker saying, *If I had to explain, you wouldn't understand.*

'OK then,' he said, as I hurriedly stuffed my gloves into my lid and clipped it to the lock on the bike while he pulled his gloves off and quietly surveyed his dismounting horde before turning back to see how I was getting on.

'Well at least it's a V-twin I suppose,' he observed looking at my bike, 'even if it's an Eyetie one.'

'And at least he doesn't ride it like a twat,' the big Brethren chipped in from behind me to my surprise. 'Can't stand these fucking "born again bikers" wobbling round the corners like they're a thruppenny bit.'

It was an old Guzzi California, one of the original ones, with the black barrel shaped tank and huge creamy white trimmed buddy seat. I don't know why but its semi CHiPs styling had always appealed, I had just always wanted to ride a bike with footboards for some reason. I'm quite tall and lanky and I'd worried before I'd got it if it would be comfortable or whether I'd find myself banging my knees on its pots but it had been fine. Long legged and easy to live with had been the strapline on the gloriously sexist bike mag ads back in the eighties that I had ripped out and bluetacked to my bedroom wall, as long haired models in drapey slit-sided skirts lolled languidly and suggestively in front of the gleaming bike. And it wasn't a half bad choice of description either, the torquey 850 shaft drive was easy to live with and with plenty of grunt made for a comfortable, if a bit squishy long distance cruiser, ideal for those summer trips over to France with my mates in my early twenties, boys abroad with tents bungeed onto the rack with one gallon plastic cans for red wine en-vrac at what seemed like pennies a time.

'Looks in good nick though for its age,' Wibble added approvingly.

Nowadays, it wasn't as sexy or as urgent as it had been when I was younger, it was an older affair, comfortable and relaxed, it felt like an increasingly middle aged reminder of a freshness and youth I'd never recover.

His ride, when he showed me later, was a very different proposition indeed. I guess someone who didn't know bikes, and I guess quite a few who did, would have taken a glance at it and just assumed it was a mildly customised Harley. But they would have been wrong. From its 2000cc S&S motor with RevTech coils, single-fire ignition, carburettor and pipes, its hand built frame, twin cap mustang style tank and classic chopper chrome Bates headlight, right down to its hand laced chrome spoked wheels and billet forward controls it was an entirely custom built, purpose filled machine. He told me the only original Harley components on it were the gear box and the traditional tombstone taillight, and afterwards I wasn't even too sure about that. Not that I could really tell all those details either. I was too long out of the serious bike scene to be able to pick it apart like that, but I only had to ask Wibble a single question about the bike to get the full ground up build and spec run through.

Mine was a comfortable old classic and well worn, but off the peg number.

His was a sharp edged, tailored high spec machine.

It was country tweeds suit versus hardnosed city slicker.

It was casual versus very, very serious.

'Ready?' he asked. I nodded.

'Come with me then,' he said, 'there's some people we need to meet first,' and turned away to walk off.

Well I thought, since I was here today, it was obviously time to go to work.

The kid who was standing next to me looked awestruck.

'See you round,' I nodded to him as I left and headed to catch up with Wibble.

'Yeah see you,' I heard from behind me.

*

'Where are we going?' I asked.

'We're here, so we need to meet the locals,' was his cryptic reply as we strode out, with some of the other Freemen falling in behind us.

The show cum rally cum party ran over the weekend. It wasn't in the same league as the Big Two's events, the Hells Angels' Bulldog Bash or the Outlaws' Rock and Blues Customs Show and Ink and Iron festival, the premier events in the UK biking calendar, but even so, The Brethren were determined to put on a good show.

Round the front of the clubhouse was the show. To the right of the pitch was a street of tents. Looking down the lines along which a small crowd of bikers and apparent tourists were drifting, I could see from the signs that the closest were hosted by a friendly support club, the local Harley dealer, a T-shirt seller, a Triumph owners club and traders in leather jackets and helmets. Beyond that the line curved round in an arc that lead back to the top end of the rugby pitch where there was a small cluster of other stands which from this distance looked like some kind of autojumble.

Ahead of me a giant beer tent and a row of burger vans from which I could just about smell the frying onions, marked the far side of the pitch; while behind them ran a hedge beyond which were the camping fields where a mass of tents of every colour, size and design had sprouted like a forest of demented toadstools, interspersed with parked up bikes and fluttering club flags.

The pitch itself had been cordoned off with a waist high screen of portable metal railings since it would be being kept clear for the day's events. At the moment the half to my right was being used as a showground for a guy doing unbelievable tricks on a trials bike, his commentary booming across the field from speakers on poles at each corner as he rode up and over seemingly impossible obstacles without bothering to ever actually use the front wheel of the bike.

Early in the afternoon there would be the formal ride in by The Brethren, followed by the other clubs and independents in order of precedence, up onto and across a stage that had been organised at the far end of the pitch on my left, to present their toy donations to the charity. Those bikes that were being entered for the 'show what you rode' would be parked up on the pitch for display and judging while the stage would be set up for the evening's bands.

Show awards would be at six, the music would kick off at eight and go on into the early hours. It was one of the reasons for holding it well out of town.

Should be quite a night.

And then further off to the left, behind the stage and beyond the pitch itself, was a single large marquee. There were two flagpoles outside the entrance each flying The Brethren's colours and even from here I could see a cluster of what were obviously strikers on guard at the entrance, one of them striking in the other sense of the word from the bright white sling his arm was in. He'd obviously had some kind of a shunt but as a patch, striker or tagalong, you'd have to be pretty fucked up and totally bedridden to miss today I knew. Still, I wondered how much slack, if any at all the sling would get him as a striker? Not much, was my bet.

This would be the members only tent.

Wibble headed straight towards it.

'Locals?' I asked, although I'd guessed what he'd meant.

'The Cambridge crew.'

I had been wondering whether he was going to take me into the marquee but as it happened we didn't need to get that far as a small posse of Brethren emerged from within as we approached and came forward to meet us.

The two groups stopped, facing each other a few feet apart as Wibble and Thommo, the local charter president, stepped forward to embrace in the usual formal backslapping bearhug and expressions of solidarity, while their respective crews eyefucked each other across the gap.

'So who's this?' Thommo said looking at me with an openly hostile stare as they broke apart again.

'He's a journalist,' Wibble replied calmly.

'You brought a fucking journo here? This weekend? What the hell for?' Thommo demanded.

'PR,' Wibble answered simply, 'He's here to see how nice we are right? So treat him nice yeah, you hear?'

It didn't look as if this news was endearing me to Thommo any more than before. Then Wibble really twisted the knife, 'You might have heard about him. He's the bloke who wrote the book about Damage.'

'Oh it just gets better doesn't it?' Thommo said, giving a surly snarl towards me.

Well thanks a bunch Wibble, I thought, that's just fucking great. Are there any more psychopaths you want to wind up and set on me?

'Yeah sure,' Thommo said, the edge of sarcasm obvious in his voice for all to hear. 'Why don't you just feel free to snoop around, just see what you find to write about?'

*

'What the fuck was all that about?' I whispered, as we walked away again towards the food stops, Wibble looking pleased with himself.

'Ah, just winding Thommo up.'

The subtext was clear. Thommo hated journos so Wibble imposing one on the party on his turf was really just Wibble rubbing Thommo's nose in his authority.

'Tell me, he's not a fan of yours anyway is he?'

Wibble raised eyebrow at me. 'What was it Damage used to say sometimes? You might very well think that, I couldn't possibly comment?'

Despite everything I laughed. That was Damage alright, from one of his favourite shows.

But still I wondered, if Thommo wasn't a fan, why make him mad? Surely Wibble already had enough to do watching his back, without provoking Thommo's hatred. Wasn't that just making unnecessary trouble for himself?

'So was that just a pissing contest then? Showing him who's top dog?'

'Could be. Does him good to be put in his place every now and then.'

Great, I thought, with me as the post to piss on. Thommo didn't look like the kind of guy to let it lie and if he couldn't get back at Wibble directly I reckoned he'd have no qualms about getting at me if he could. I'd need to be very careful about keeping away from him and his guys, I decided, both today and in the future.

But as it turned out, it seemed as though Wibble had thought of that too as the next thing he did was to organise me a minder.

'OK, so what happens now, what do you want me to do?' I asked.

'I've got some stuff I need to do first, so how about Bung shows you round?' he said, indicating over his shoulder with a jerk of his thumb to where The Brethren I had already recognised was standing. Even if Danny hadn't already dropped his name, I couldn't miss who Wibble was talking about, it would be hard not to. At six foot two or so, in most directions as far as I could see, he was the man-mountain who'd got me coffee at the services, and so presumably was one of Wibble's personal bodyguard.

'Bung, come over here for a minute willya?' Wibble shouted over to him.

'Bung?' I asked Wibble quietly as he ambled towards us.

'Short for Bungalow,' he answered.

Wibble introduced me with a, 'You've met.'

I could see why the nickname had stuck, although looking at the sheer size of him, Brick Shit House might have been closer to the mark.

'Stick with Bung here for a while will you? He'll show you round, let you meet some of the guys, keep an eye out for you, and then we'll talk.'

That was OK by me again, and so I headed off with the lumbering giant.

Over the next hour or so Bung walked me round, introducing me to The Brethren as we went, although I couldn't help but notice that the ones he took me to talk to were mainly the other Freemen and some of the ride ins from other charters. I didn't really do any interviews as such, more just a bit of chit chat. There was a bit of a tense atmosphere and for a while I couldn't put my finger on it.

At first I thought it was just me. After all, Thommo was hardly alone within The Brethren in what he thought about writers and so I thought the hostility was personal, not helped by who I was specifically and my history.

Then I realised how separate Thommo's local charter and some of the other ride ins were keeping from the Freemen and those that were hanging with them and so I decided that the tension I could feel stemmed from some animosity between these two groups. But after a while that simple explanation didn't feel right either as the tension seemed to be ratcheting up as the day wore on, without any noticeable interaction or overt incidents between the two clusters who simply seemed to be keeping themselves to themselves.

There was something else going on. But for the life of me I couldn't work out what.

As a civilian I knew I wouldn't be particularly welcome riding in after the patched clubs to make my donation, so after checking the form with Bung we made our way back to where I'd left the bear on my Guzzi.

As Bung and I wandered back past the clubhouse and the rows of parked bikes I spotted the two kids I'd ridden in with. They had obviously been told to stay with the strikers guarding the bikes as the start of their long apprenticeship ladder that might one day lead to a Brethren patch, and after a morning that felt a bit as though it had been spent bothering smiling tigers in their cage for interviews, I decided it was time for some light relief.

'Hey,' I said as I freed the stuffed toy from where it had been riding pillion and handed it to Bung who was gathering up a three foot high panda from one of the other non-club ride ins, 'do you two fancy talking for a bit?'

Danny smiled at the approach, but gave a slightly uncertain glance at Bung as if for approval that this was OK. The other kid just shrugged as if it wasn't worth making the effort to open his mouth.

As I began to talk to Danny, Bung roped in first a striker and then a grumbling Scroat to complete the collection and then, having made sure I was ensconced for a while, marched them off to deposit the toys on the stage, Scroat still moaning about 'Fucking teddy bears,' as he went, the three foot girth of mine edged under his left arm.

At first I tried to include the other kid in my questions as well, but all I got was a glowering look and occasional grunts so eventually I thought, well screw you chum, and concentrated on Danny.

I felt uneasy at how proud as punch he seemed to feel to be there. A bit of guilt perhaps that I was a little bit to blame, that I'd helped to glamorise The Brethren, although God knows it wasn't as if they were famous or infamous enough before I'd come along, after all they had a string of newspaper headlines stretching back since the early seventies in this country that had given them their public reputation.

I asked him anything and everything I could think of. Why was he here? How had he first met The Brethren and got involved? What did he think about The Brethren now he'd met them? What did he think about their reputation? What did he think he was getting himself involved with? Did he think it was worth the risks? What did his family think?

I suppose I was asking him the questions I would want him to ask himself before it was too late. Before he got too committed to something from which as far as I could see it was very difficult to back out of later.

With a heavy heart I realised that whatever I was saying, I wasn't getting through to him. And as I looked up from where we were sitting on the grass to see Bung bearing purposefully down on us, I realised I had run out of time.

'Well, if you ever want to talk kid, about all this I mean, come and see me.'

'Hey yeah, will do. Listen, but like with all the questions, you are working here aren't you? Writing I mean? That's what this is all about right? Isn't it?'

I could see how his mind was working. None of my question had done any good at all, had raised no doubts. The only thing he was thinking about was that he might end up being in a book about The Brethren and wasn't that going to be just cool.

That was the only time that the other lad decided to get involved. He could see it as well and he didn't like it.

'That's not what it's about. It's not about being a poseur,' he dismissed the prospect with barely concealed hostility and contempt, 'and you don't talk to anyone about the club without the club's say so. Club business is club business you understand? Because if you don't get that then you're never gonna make it.'

Danny fell silent and his face flushed red.

'Time to go,' said Bung, and I stood up and walked away.

*

Wibble wanted to see me. 'You're staying the night,' he said bluntly. 'Don't worry, Bung here'll look after you and I'll sort you out properly afterwards.'

He must have seen the look on my face.

'No, not that sort of *sort you out*. Protection I mean.'

I didn't know what he meant by that, but I didn't much like the sound of it.

It seemed as though I was free to come and go as I liked around the site, but given what had happened with Thommo, straying too far from Bung and the Freemen didn't seem too smart a move. Still it wasn't as if we were joined at the hip so I had a chance to think as we took a stroll round the site.

Bring a sleeping bag Wibble had instructed me when he'd given me the details of the run, so I had, just so as not to piss him off. So it gave me an excuse to head back over to where they were all parked up although what I really wanted to do was surreptitiously check out the situation by the bikes again. Of course, there were strikers on guard. If they had been told I wasn't to leave, there was no way I was going to be getting my bike back out the gates, and anyway, there were strikers on them as well under the control of a quiet watchful pair of patches, collecting the ticket money from the faithful as they arrived and stuffing it into plastic carrier bags that every so often would be collected by a posse of full patches and carried off back to the members only tent.

'So where are you guys sleeping?' I asked Bung as I unhooked my bag from where it was bungeed to the bike's buddy seat.

'Crash tents. Some of the strikers have come in a transit and they're busy getting them up now.'

'The ones behind the beer tent?'

35

'Yeah, it's all TA gear, Widget and his lads have borrowed it for the weekend.'

So that explained the gang I'd seen laying out a row of large green army tents.

As we made our way back across the showground so I could drop my gear off, I was still keeping my eyes open for possible escape routes.

There was a fence around the rest of the site facing onto the road and hedges and smaller fences elsewhere. Even if I gave Bung the slip, I'd be seen if I tried climbing over any of them during the day so if I wanted out, I resigned myself to the fact that it looked like the best bet might be to wait for dark anyway.

While Bung stopped to meet and greet a posse of bikers from some support club that he seemed to know and want to chat to, I took the chance to wander out of sight for a moment and whip out my mobile.

Thank Christ, Bob answered on the second ring. Breathlessly I filled him in on my situation and asked what he thought I should do.

'Nah, you'll be safe enough I'd think,' he said, 'It's the Brethren's main public event of the year, a big money spinner and a shop window for them. They aren't going to want to compromise all that with a murder. Not when they could do it any other time. Why have the hassle?'

So it looked as if my chances of rescue from the outside weren't great either.

'OK?' asked Bung as he caught up with me as I chatted with the guy at the next stand about his charity which involved getting disadvantaged kids to build ratty but working bikes.

'Yeah fine,' I said cheerfully, but I remember thinking as I did so, show any fear and you'll never going to fucking get out of here alive.

But as it happened, as the afternoon wore on, despite my misgivings, I did start to feel safe enough in the Freemen's company to unwind a bit and begin to enjoy myself.

The sun was shining. People, by which I meant The Brethren and their cohorts, were, in the noticeable absence of the Cambridge crew who it seemed had taken themselves and their grudge off to a beer tent on the other side of the field, relaxed and friendly.

I supposed there must have been some underlying issue with Thommo's charter that the Freemen had thought might lead to trouble, but now that seemed to be off the agenda they just seemed determined to bask in the crowd's attention and have a good time.

There'd been no mention of The Brethren in connection with the local punch-up between Capricorn MC and Dead Men Riding MC or any suggestion of a link that anyone had made to me so far, so I didn't think it had anything to do with that, although I supposed perhaps Thommo and his boys were under a bit of pressure from the rest of the club over it. It was clear that part of the reputation of a senior club like The Brethren rested on the expectation that they would keep the more junior clubs on their turf under control. After all, no one wanted any unnecessary trouble since trouble was bad for business, and a war, even between two junior clubs was trouble since it could lead to all clubs, senior and junior, coming under the spotlight. So I guessed The Brethren would be looking to Thommo and his boys to get this thing under control which might explain the obvious needle between Wibble, as president of the Freemen, and Wibble as the local charter P.

'Spliff?' Bung asked.

'You want to roll up here?'

'Nah,' he said, before adding in best Blue Peter fashion, 'here's some I made earlier,' surprising me when he flipped open a pack of cigarettes from his cut's pocket to reveal half a dozen or so tailor-mades and a handful of twisted doobie tips, and tugged one out.

He cupped his hands around his lighter as he flicked the wheel with his thumb and sucked in a deep breath to draw it into life. They were huge hands I noticed as I watched the performance, darkly tanned with the blurred and faded blue-green of old tattoos dark against the skin under the hair on the back, the fingers encrusted with a selection of heavy and ornate silver skull and patch themed rings that probably did well as an impromptu set of knuckledusters when needed.

Then he all but disappeared in a huge puff of acrid white smoke as he exhaled and took a second toke. He looked around the field approvingly as he held it in for a moment, giving an air of complete contentment.

'Lovely,' he said as he exhaled slowly and proffered it to me.

I had to take it. There was nothing for it but to do what I had to do.

I'd smoked a lot at uni, In my day it was resin, eighths of hash, gritty but soft and crumbly Leb black, or rock hard nodules of Moroccan red that needed to be melted with a match before you could sprinkle it onto the baccy; or so our little league dealers told us. Grass was a rarity and anything else was an occasional experiment as and when it presented itself. That was how I had first actually spoken to any of The Brethren, when a trio of them were selling ten quid wraps of speed outside the doors of a Motörhead gig at uni. Not that I remembered much after that other than borrowing a fiver from a mate to roll up and heading straight to the bogs to do the lot. It was evil fucking stuff I have to say.

But I'd been a reasonably regular stoner as and when I could catch it, right up until I'd had a bad trip while under the influence; panic attack, hallucinations, shit it shook me up. And then I left uni and suddenly I wasn't around the people I knew who could get it and so I just sort of stopped. It wasn't that I gave up as such; it was just that I wasn't bothered. And then I'd given up smoking period.

And much to my surprise I'd beaten the habit, at least other than the odd guilty fag or café-crème once in a blue moon and nowadays I didn't even smoke ordinary smokes really anymore, let alone joints.

I lifted it to my lips and took a hit.

'Jeeeezus!' I swallowed a cough as I concentrated on keeping the smoke down to get the full hit, even as the harsh hotness of the raw weed caught at the back of my throat. Then I let it out again in a long stream as a definite buzz hit me. 'What the fuck are you smoking?'

Bung just grinned as I spluttered and gasped while I handed back the joint.

'It's good shit isn't it? Our local Cong's sensei special.'

'I can see why they call it skunk,' I said, 'Christ it stinks.'

The Cong were the growers, I knew that already from Damage. Cannabis farming had become something of a Vietnamese gang speciality with rented houses gutted to make way for intensive cultivation under hot lights by trafficked peasants using stolen electricity until the smell, the heat or the occasional fire when someone got careless with the wiring gave them away.

But with the plants cropping in batches every few months and continuous cycles of batches coming through, the occasional lost crop was just a cost of doing business as far as they were concerned, while intensive cultivation was inexorably raising the strength of the weed's THC.

What the Cong didn't have was the distribution networks to retail the gear or the muscle to control dealing territory which was where other operators, like the bike clubs, and others, were a natural fit.

And if you were dealing in the shit and had a taste for it the way Bung obviously did, naturally you would keep some of the best stuff for your own personal use.

Whether it was the strength of it, or whether it was just that I was now so unused to it after all these years, after only a couple of tokes I realised that Christ, I was actually pretty bloody stoned already.

'Shit, I need a beer,' I said.

'Now you're talking,' agreed Bung and together, the man-mountain and I shambled across the field towards the bars.

As we went inside and a path opened up in front of Bung towards the bar I slipstreamed in behind pulling out my wallet as I did so, it was my shout I reckoned; I had a brief moment of clarity. Probably one of the last for the day if I'm honest looking back.

Advice or no advice, thanks to taking that first spliff, it was pretty bloody clear by now that I wasn't going to be leaving. I would be staying the night with The Brethren and if I was going to be under Bung's protection from whatever Cambridge's beef was, then I needed to stick to him and keep him onside.

And then I plunged on in before the crowd could close in behind him and separate us.

*

So for the rest of the day and into the evening I tagged along with Bung, meeting the other Freemen and those of The Brethren who were attaching themselves to Wibble's crew. As the day wore on I was introduced to a generally friendly parade of names that I tried to keep track of, from the Bills, Steves, and Mikes of various descriptions, to the Smurf, Gollum and Viking.

It was a tricky balance to try and pull off. As a reporter my natural instinct was to observe, learn and record. But as the beers flowed and the spliffs circulated during the afternoon that ambition became more and more impossible, while I also knew that having notes taken about them wasn't exactly a favourite activity as far as most Brethren were concerned and so if I was too obtrusive I ran the risk of changing the atmosphere fast in the wrong direction.

And since it seemed as though my health and safety depended on these guys' goodwill, discretion very rapidly took the part of valour and I stuffed the notebook away early doors, promising myself that I'd write up some notes when I crashed for the night.

Some hope.

As a result, looking at the scrawls in my notebook it was true when I wrote at about midnight: *As it is, all I have are some very fragmentary notes and increasingly fractured memories of the night.*

Cambridge crew are keeping themselves to themselves, but Bung and the other Brethren, with me tagging right along after them, are mingling with visiting clubs. Patch, side patch, MCCs. Come to show their colours and/or pay their respects? Even a women's patch club, The Psyclesluts MC. Very scary crop haired women with ears that looked as if they'd been in a nail factory accident. Why should the guys have all the fun?

Seems they've all read Heavy Duty People. *Bung at pains to tell me that he'd nicked it, not bought it. Long surprising discussion with two Brethren, nicknamed Eric and Ernie, about twentieth century English novelists, a dismissal of D H Lawrence as really just an Edwardian writer and an appreciation of the oeuvre of Virginia Woolf. Astonishingly well read but then a real surprise. Open University English degree. BA Hons, the both of them. On the road and inside, Eric explained,* Not a lot to do inside but read. *Ernie:* He waited 'til he got out to graduate y'know, so he could go up on stage with his colours under his gown.

Impressive camaraderie and self assurance. People who trusted each other bond of brothers. Explanations of their philosophy. We're not called The Brethren for nothing. The name wasn't picked by chance you know? These are my brothers, my family. *Then more serious.* Our trouble is we make good villains. *The lament on the proffered business card,* When we do good no one remembers, when we do bad no one forgets.

Bad munchies. Mars bar, chips, and a coke from a van.

Bonfires of tyres from neighbouring field after dark. Party atmosphere, faces emerging from the black, lit up by the fierce yellow stinking blaze. Laughter as one of the strikers rips the arse of his jeans on the barbed wire of the field as they struggle back over the hedge bearing a dead tree for the bonfire. Ribald and very concerned inspection reveals that the family jewels are intact.

The music from the sound system in between bands. A cracking set. A lot of stuff I don't recognise, some stuff I do. Anti Nowhere League's driving rasping gargling version of Streets of London *running straight on after John Otway's* Beware of The Flowers, *Dumpy's Rusty Nuts,* A Burn-up On

My Bike, *Christ, not heard that in years, and then ZZ Top,* Blue Jeans Blues.

Roaring noise in my ears. Stagger out of main tent, not sure if it's the skunk, the generators, the booze or the bands. I'm sodden. Around midnight, Bung had had Wurzel and one of the others wrestle me down into the mud amongst the press of the beer tent towards the bar. My first Brethren party so he said I had to be baptised. Half a dozen of them pouring pints over my head, laughing while I buck against the weight and grip of the bikers and call them bastards!

Back at the huge roaring bonfire, all red, orange and white heat against the blackness of the night, Brethren and others sitting and lying around the upwind fringes to avoid the driving acrid thick smoke coming from off the burning tyres.

People increasingly wrecked. You need to write this down all about how we came together as a band of brothers to ride free and go out righting wrongs. *Laughter from further round the fire at the bullshit. Protests:* no I'm serious!

3   The show

Sunday 2 August 2009

Shit I felt rough. I just lay there unmoving for a few moments after I'd woken up, just to let the nerves that were jangling from this unexpected and rash decision to regain consciousness, recover.

After a minute or so, the bursting need to get out for a piss finally and reluctantly convinced the rest of my body to begin negotiating the process of extricating myself from the coils of my sleeping bag, which seemed to have me trapped like an anaconda after a good breakfast. I fumbled with the zip having untangled my feet slowly and somewhat unsteadily levered myself upright. Thankfully I'd abandoned my boots close by and so I shucked them on and staggered as carefully as I could through the bodies and over to the tent flap.

Peering outside, the world was grey and misty damp. The bonfire out front was a blackened charred mess, steaming gently where coals still glowed red in the centre amongst the ash, while a swathe of soot blackened field stretching out to my left where the smoke from the burning tyres that still gave it a rank sulphurous smell had soaked everything in a clinging coat of sticky ink.

As I trudged over towards the ground's clubhouse and the relative civilisation of their indoor bogs, I saw there were other survivors. Amongst the field of tents a few bodies were moving about quietly. It felt like the start of a bad zombie film.

Bladder emptied and cold to the bone, I headed over to the burger vans to join a few other souls, my fellow living dead, their voices no more than a murmur if they did speak, their hands grasped around their first hot coffee of the day, and bleary eyed I wondered whether I could face a greasy bacon roll.

Thank God for bacon sandwiches. That's all I can say.

By my second roll and strong sweet coffee, the grease, caffeine and sugar combination was starting to do its work. That and the fact that the sun was staring to break through and burn off the dank morning mist, was gradually making me feel more human. From where I sat at a wooden picnic table I could see there was a promise of blue skies emerging any time now. It could be a scorcher of a day, I thought.

All told, by this stage, I wasn't feeling too bad at all.

Well I'd survived for one thing. No one had shown any sign of wanting to stomp or murder me, Cambridge excepted, and I got the feeling that even that wasn't particularly personal about me. There was something else going on that I didn't know enough about yet I decided.

Gradually as the sun came out the rest of the bikers began to emerge. Bung sat next to me and I couldn't look at him as he put away a full English off a paper plate and then lit up.

'You look as though you fancy another one of those,' I observed.

'Yeah, maybe I will,' he said, 'You offering? Nothing like a good fry-up to set you right for the day.'

I'd walked into that one I realised with a resigned smile. Well I could do with one more brew I decided.

'OK you're on,' I said getting up. 'I owe you for last night anyway. The works?'

'Great.'

So I watched him put away another piled high plate with undiminished speed and equal apparent satisfaction.

'So,' I asked as he finished up, 'what happens now?'

'Well Wibble wants a chat with you a bit later but hey it's a sunny day so it's just kick back, relax and enjoy the show I guess,' he said expansively.

By this time it was gone ten and Bung announced that he wanted to check out the bike show entries and so for an hour or so we wandered along the rows of parked up, primped, painted and polished entries.

To start with it felt much like most of yesterday afternoon. Again I was careful to stick with Bung and the Freemen since I guessed that show or no show, I didn't fancy running across any of the Cambridge crew on my own.

But then as the morning wore on the mood seemed to change. It was imperceptible at first, to be honest to start with I thought it was just me and my hangover kicking back in as the baps and shots wore off. I was feeling rough, but then as the knot of Freemen and their brothers began to coalesce around Bung as we made our slow way through the show field I began to realise that it wasn't just me. They really were becoming increasingly distracted, and closed off. By the time one of the strikers found me to say Wibble was ready to talk there was little or none of the relaxed chattiness of yesterday. They were changed, quiet, tense even, as though through some silent telepathy that I as an outsider wasn't privy to, the pack had become aware of some danger on the horizon and I was glad to get away.

Which seemed odd, since the evening was billed as the really big bash of the weekend, the point to which the club's premier party of the year was supposed to be building.

*

And so it was around noon by the time I managed to talk to Wibble. We camped out at a trestle table with yet more coffees and some more half decent bacon rolls.

'Well how'd you get on?' he asked, 'Speak to the guys?'

'OK I guess, but your blokes didn't really seem in the mood to be chatty this morning. I tried to quiz those two kids I rode in with for a while yesterday.'

'Oh yeah?' he said sounding genuinely interested, 'so how did that go?'

'Well Danny's OK, he was happy to talk. But the other one, Jesus.'

'What, Charlie?'

'Yeah, I think that's his name. That kid's a natural for you guys though isn't he? Christ, what an attitude.'

Wibble grinned, 'Yeah well, I guess it's just in the blood.'

I was tempted to ask him what he meant but decided I'd leave that for the moment. It didn't seem that important. Instead I'd get on with the interview.

We sat and talked for about an hour and for some of it I got what I regarded as the standard biker pitch.

Looking at my notes, to start with it was all very much the usual stuff I was expecting to hear.

We're just bikers and we do our own thing. People have always got a downer on us because we live by our own rules.

Sure there's punch ups, sometimes people have a go, and we have to defend ourselves.

It was funny. According to The Brethren it always someone else's fault that the violence started. As they saw it, they were always the provoked ones.

Sure some of the guys have done time. It doesn't mean the club's a criminal outfit.

We get a bit tired of the cops talking about us like we're some kind of international organised crime mafia. We ride around with patches on our backs so we stand up for who and what we are, we've got websites up with our photographs on it, we do events like this. How much more fucking visible could we be? We stand out from Joe citizen a mile. Is that really what organised criminals would do?

Sure we've got some tough guys; sure we've got a bad rep. But individuals aren't the club. Look at the cops. How many bent cops are there? But whenever there's a bent cop people don't say that the cops ought to be disbanded? Well mostly no one.

Look at what's happened recently. You haven't seen any of our guys on film killing some newspaper seller by clubbing him to the ground from behind for no reason have you? Let me ask you what would have happened if that had been one of us that shoved that bloke Tomlinson after that demo in London and not a cop? What would have happened then?

It was when I asked him the 'why?' question that he got serious. As he spoke over the next few minutes, even though I recognised in what he was saying a philosophy that Damage had espoused from time to time, I felt as if I had touched, almost for the first time, the heart of it. What it meant to be a Brethren.

The government, the cops, the status quo, they don't like us. Most people are scared and the government likes to keep it that way. The government says do this, do that, or don't do this, don't do that, or we'll punish you, or society will disapprove.

Well fuck the government and fuck society. What right has anyone got to tell me how to live my life?'

I caught a glimpse in what he was saying of a fundamental rage lurking under the surface, a fury against any sensation of powerlessness driving a fierce elemental rejection of ever, ever, allowing that to happen.

And people do run scared, they knuckle under, they obey the rules, they live their lives within the boundaries that the system has set for them.

Well not us. No fucking way.

We're the ones who won't just knuckle under, we're the ones who won't just go along, and we're the ones who won't just obey.

And that's the reason that they all hate us.

Because we stand up for ourselves.

So if you want to try to tell me what to do, then you'd better fucking watch out. Because we won't just not take it, but we'll come right back at you with every fucking thing we've got. If you start it, then you'd better be prepared to go all the way because from our side it's going to be total retaliation, no fucking mercy.

Why? Because it's the only way to make sure they learn the lesson and next time they'll leave us alone.

Can we defeat the government? No.

Can we keep it out of our space?

Yes we can, but only by defending that freedom tooth and nail. The only defence is all out war. That's what people need to get if they want to understand us and what we're about. Freedom's not free. If you want it and then want to keep it, you have to be prepared to fight for it and to guard it every second of the day.

Damage had been a fan of something he'd called the anarchist alternative to NATO, which as far as I could make out from what he'd said seemed to involved dismantling the state and letting everyone have their own M16 assault rifle to keep in their wardrobe instead.

'Extremism in the defence of liberty is no vice?' I had suggested, as we came to the end.

'Yeah, something like that. And it's why we are so loyal to each other. We all know that we're in this war, we're all fighting on the same side, and it's a big fucking enemy we're facing and if we don't all stand absolutely shoulder to shoulder against it, it's going to take us all down.'

It was simple really. In defence of their freedoms as they saw it, The Brethren under this philosophy had taken the line of logic to its ultimate conclusion. They saw themselves at war with any authority, whether government or society, that attempted to infringe their freedom.

Then I got it. When it came to the outside world, they were their own NATO. And an attack against one was an attack against them all.

'So what's the problem with the local crew then?' I ventured, 'there seems to be a bit of an atmosphere.'

'They're hurting a bit,' he said matter of factly, 'they lost a guy earlier this week.'

'Did they?' I asked in surprise. 'I hadn't heard anything about that?'

'You should have, it was in the papers.'

And then I made the connection and remembered the striker with his arm in a sling. 'The thing in Leeds? That was one of your people?'

Just then Bung stepped over and interrupted. He'd obviously caught the Tomlinson reference.

'And at least if one of our guys had done it, he wouldn't have been hiding behind a fucking balaclava or have taken off his colours so he couldn't be identified,' he said. 'We stand by what we do.'

'Have you noticed how cops around the world these days are always wearing balaclavas so they can't be recognised?' he continued.

'No.'

'Well they are,' he insisted, 'Just watch'em next time on the news. You'll see.'

Wibble cocked his head at Bung expectantly.

'Yeah,' said Bung, to the unspoken question that had obviously just passed between them. 'I've had the call. Five minutes or so they said.'

Wibble nodded gravely, as though lost in thought for a moment as to what this might mean.

'OK, thanks,' he said as he stood up.

'Looks like we're going to have to wrap this up here for a bit,' he said to me.

'Why? What's happening?'

Then he just smiled at me as if he was tremendously pleased with some secret surprise that he was about to pull off.

'Well I guess it's showtime baby,' he announced, 'Just wait around a few minutes. You'll see.'

*

As word spread through the pack, The Brethren quickly began to gather together for whatever was about to go down. As we waited I was aware of a continuing undercurrent of aggro from the local charter who had formed up as a separate bunch a little way apart from the Freemen charter and most of the other ride ins who were stood behind them.

Wibble seemed to either be oblivious to it, or to be letting it slide off him as if it was beneath him. That seemed to me to be a dangerous game to play. If you were really secure, distain could be a powerful weapon against your enemies, something that said to them and others that they were of so little account that nothing they could say or do was worth notice or action.

But on the other hand, ignoring insolence, insubordination and indiscipline in the ranks could easily be seen as a sign of weakness. That Wibble was too insecure to take action and that the local charter was flexing its muscles.

But before I could think any more about it I felt a stiffening of anticipation sweep through The Brethren around me as they fell completely silent at the first distant sound of an unmistakable noise.

It was the rumble of a large column of approaching outlaw Harleys.

What the hell was this? I wondered to myself as out of the corner of my eye I saw Brethren hands freeing for action. The UK Brethren were all here I knew, so unless it was a big overseas contingent coming in, this wasn't going to be more of their brothers who were turning up.

Suddenly the single packing made sense. Oh God I thought, they've been expecting something, as nervously I started to compute likely escape routes from what was now clearly a Brethren welcoming committee waiting for these new arrivals, whoever they were, and wondered how easily I could fade backwards into the crowd if the bikers made a rush forward.

Because if it wasn't more Brethren then it had to be someone else, some other club.

And in the sort of numbers that seemed to be coming from the rapidly growing noise it wasn't any small local club coming to show their respects.

This was going to be a large pack. From one of the other majors, it had to be.

Was one of the other big six coming to gatecrash one of The Brethren's flagship events?

If so, this would mean only one thing.

Trouble.

People would get hurt, I thought. And that could very well include me.

*

There was a collective gasp of breath as the first of the approaching bikes crested the lip of the site and pulled in through the gate.

A blue and white painted Harley.

I and everyone else on this field immediately recognised those colours and what they represented. And what this meant, right here, right now.

The Rebels, The Brethren's sworn enemies amongst the other senior clubs, were riding in to The Brethren's flagship event.

And The Brethren were standing there, arranged in a rough semi circle with Wibble out front towards the centre.

And me beside him.

Jesus, I thought. The Rebels? The number one enemies, invading The Brethren's number one event. This was going to be serious trouble, civilians were going to be in the firing line and I was right in the middle of what was going to, in the next few minutes, turn into a war zone.

The Rebels were all single packing as well I realised, as their bikes pulled up in a rank parallel to the row of Brethren Harleys. There were no old ladies along for a party day out with them either. This was a group here about serious business.

As their engines coughed and died and the dismounting Rebels began to arrange themselves beside their bikes into a line facing the two packs of Brethren, there was absolute silence all around me.

I recognised Stu, The Rebel's president, from a photograph. I'd never managed to get him to agree to an interview. If anything, The Rebels were even more tight lipped when it came to journalists than The Brethren.

Stu took off his gloves and calmly stuffed them into his lid which he perched on the end of his handlebars before he turned to face the waiting Brethren. He was tall and slim, with sharp, swarthy, almost French looking features, a neat clipped goatee beard and dark grey hair pulled back into a ponytail that streamed down his back to between his shoulder blades.

I had a sudden vision of how he must have looked to Billy Whizz, what, fifteen years ago now or so, appearing at the door of a hotel room in Glasgow like an angel of death. All eyes were on him again now as alone, he stepped decisively forward from the line and towards the Freemen group of Brethren.

At his approach, Wibble stepped forward as well, until the two men were standing face to face a few yards apart in a small no man's land separating the rival gangs.

It seemed as though everyone was holding their breath as I began to slowly sidle backwards to mingle in with The Brethren crowd. I didn't want to get hurt, I knew riots could become very ugly situations very quickly but I did want to have my camera handy in case I could get a chance to use it so I snuck my phone out of my pocket and flicked open the lens praying that no one would notice.

I needn't have bothered. All eyes were on the dramatic standoff unfolding in front of us.

At last, as if they had both made some kind of final decision at the same time, Wibble spread his arms and advanced towards Stu who did the same. Was this some last parlay before the mêlée I wondered, some last posturing exchange of insults and threats before the first punch was thrown and the riot began?

They were now face to face, standing in silence, about a foot or so apart.

I held my breath and broke my gaze away for a second or so as I swiftly looked around me, scoping the exits and calculating and recalculating at lightning speed my likely escape routes. The two sides would rush each other I decided, swinging with whatever weapons they had to hand. I would just let The Brethren sweep forward either side of me I decided, fade backwards until I was at the rear of the pack and then turn and bolt. So long as none of The Rebels reached me in their own rush and none of The Brethren went into such berserker rage that they began attacking anything in sight, I thought I might just have a chance of getting out of this alive. I knew I might have to negotiate more Brethren heading towards the fight from elsewhere on the field but they wouldn't be interested in civilians fleeing the scene. They'd be too intent on piling in to help their brothers with whatever implements they had snatched up on the way.

Christ, so long as I don't run into Thommo's crew, I thought.

Then came a sight I never thought I would see.

The two of them, Wibble from The Brethren and Stu from The Rebels, came together for a slow and solemn back slap hug. They stayed clasped together for what seemed like an eternity but could really only have been a matter of a few seconds and then broke apart again, hands and forearms clasped together in a rock steady biker handshake.

It was Wibble who broke the silence.

'Welcome to our event –' he announced quietly so that everyone in those circles could hear, 'brother.'

'Thanks – brother,' replied Stu, never breaking Wibble's gaze, 'we're glad we could come.'

Christ, I felt a whoosh of breath as if I'd only just remembered how to do it, and a surge of both relief and realisation at the same time. So this was what Wibble had been planning, I thought. And of course, now they were here, it all made perfect sense. In many ways it was the natural culmination of the trading links that Dazza had first set up and Damage had then consolidated between the clubs. From being bitter enemies in a long running war, the two rivals had gradually been mutating into being strong, if still mutually suspicious, trading partners across the patch divide and with engagement, as is the way of the world, eventually would come the start of diplomatic reconciliation.

All around me I could feel the tension easing. It hadn't gone altogether by any manner or means, but its nature had changed. Neither Stu nor Wibble would think this was easy, or any kind of a done deal. Long held enmities and grudges between the two clubs weren't going to be made to disappear overnight. There were too many years of feuding and too much bad blood had been spilt for that on both sides, so both leaders were going to have to keep their troops on a tight leash to start with to make it a success. But it was definitely détente, if not glasnost.

Wibble walked Stu across to the Freemen to introduce him to his officers. I was still there, hemmed in by the big men in the crowd around me. Stu had obviously clocked me from my lack of a patch, and I can only assume that Wibble had let him know that I was going to be there as Stu stuck out his hand towards me, and with surprise I shook it.

'Here to cover the big event, eh?' he asked.

'Err yeah, something like that,' I mumbled.

Was there more to it though, I wondered for a second. It seemed more than just reporting, it was as though I was here witnessing. I was obviously known to both clubs. Had one or other, or both, wanted me here as a sign of good faith on both sides?

But before I could think more about this and what it might mean, I noticed that Wibble was looking hard at the local pack who were off across to my left. But it was more than just looking, he was staring them down.

'Problem?' asked Stu conversationally following his line of sight.

'Nothing I can't handle,' said Wibble equally calmly.

I could sense the seething hostility coming off the local charter, barely being kept in check. The urge to pick up an iron bar and swing it was still running strong.

But the Cambridge crew were separated from Stu and the cautiously advancing Rebel contingent behind him, some of whom still not sure they weren't simply walking into an ambush and were preparing to deal with whatever came, by a screen of Freemen and their loyal ride ins.

Now I understood why there were so many Freemen here today. Wibble had arranged it. They were there to keep the peace and ensure that The Rebels were not attacked. And I guessed that Wibble must have been checking on security arrangements when we had first arrived. Making last minute checks with his officers and crew so that everything was going to go down the way he wanted it to, and making sure the local chapter got the message to behave themselves or else. And Thommo hadn't liked it.

The locals knew they were outnumbered. Thommo spat on the ground and turning on his heel, led his troops back away around the clubhouse.

Was that also part of the reason he'd been sure to show me off to Thommo?

'Ah well, you can't win everybody over at once can you now?' said Stu which seemed to take Wibble by surprise.

'How about a photo?' I suggested breaking in and lifting up my phone, 'for the paper?'

Stu and Wibble looked at each other and laughed. Stu shrugged, 'Why not? I'm game if you are?'

Wibble was up for it.

So they staged a cheesy photograph for me, the two leaders of what had until just now been clubs at sometimes deadly war, smiling and shaking hands for the camera while their troops fraternised around them.

'Peace in our time,' said Wibble as he walked Stu past me.

So that's why he wanted me here, I thought. To see this. Wibble wants me to write about peace in our time.

'So how's Toad?' he asked Stu.

'Oh don't worry about him, he's fine,' said Stu smiling broadly, 'the boy's are looking after him. They've fixed him up with the run of the bar and some honeys so I guess he's enjoying the hospitality...'

Then it happened.

With a whoosh and a roar, all hell broke loose.

The Guardian

Monday 3 August 2009

Peace Party Gets A Rocket

Six deaths as bikers' party attacked with anti-tank rockets and automatic weapons

The Brethren MC's annual charity Toy Run is the highlight of their year and their premier public event. Even more so on Sunday as this year it had been chosen as the venue to announce a historic burying of the hatchet. The Rebels, The Brethren's main rivals in the UK, had been invited to attend for the first time ever to formalise peace between the two clubs. But someone obviously had other plans, as shortly after The Rebels' arrival at lunchtime on Sunday, the event was attacked with three anti-tank missiles, before the showground was raked with gunfire.

Police believe the attackers were lying in wait in woods to the east of the site at Little Framlington Rugby Club, from where the firing took place, and then escaped using getaway vehicles parked in a lane behind.

The area has been sealed off while forensic specialists comb the area for clues and it is understood that two stolen vans which may be linked to the attack have been found burnt out some five miles away but no weapons have been recovered so far.

The police have appealed for bikers present at the event to provide any information they may have which can help with their investigation but they are reporting that few have yet done so.

Inspector Treaves of Cambridgeshire police who is heading the investigation said 'We know that traditionally so called "outlaw" motorcyclists have always refused to co-operate with the police, but we would urge all bikers who were at this event and who might have any information that could be of assistance to come forward.'

At an unprecedented joint press conference, the presidents of both The Brethren and The Rebels, until yesterday widely thought to be two of the fiercest rivals in the outlaw motorcycle club scene, denounced the attack as an assault on the freedom of bikers everywhere and spoke about their 'dead brothers'. But they both declined to comment when pressed by reporters on whether their members would be co-operating with the police in their enquiries.

The names of the dead were released by police today. Adrian Christianson (42) of West London, Jonathan Hodge (30) from Northumberland, and Nigel Jones (51) from Birmingham, are all believed to have been members of The Brethren. Richard Taylor (46) from Liverpool is understood to have been a member of The Rebels, while local people Martin Gillingham (45) from Ely and Mary Woods (26) from Wisbech are not believed to have been connected with either club.

Over 60 people were injured with 27 requiring hospital treatment. Ten remain in hospital and two are described as being in a serious condition.

Police are refusing to speculate about the identity or motives of the attackers at this time.

'It's too early to say,' commented Inspector Treaves when asked whether the attack might be connected with the announcement by the two clubs, 'Although we would not want to rule out any line of enquiry at present.'

He did however call on both clubs to exercise restraint. 'Emotions will obviously be running high after this unprovoked attack but we in the police warn members of both clubs not to think about taking the law into their own hands.'

Incoming!

An eyewitness account and analysis from our crime correspondent Iain Parke

Amongst the biker world, it was billed as 'peace in our time.' Instead it turned into one of the worst days of violence and death that the UK biker world has ever seen.

Following an invitation from The Brethren MC, known as the 'Menaces' from their black and red colours, to attend their Toy Run, I had ridden there on Saturday morning at the back of the outlaw convoy. It felt a perfect weekend for the event, sunny and peaceful.

The Brethren hadn't given any warning of their intended meeting with The Rebels so the arrival of a contingent from the other club at the event just after one o'clock on the Sunday took most onlookers by surprise and for a moment observers feared serious trouble was about to erupt as the two clubs have a long tradition of vicious rivalry.

But this was quickly dispelled as the two clubs' presidents greeted each other and even posed to allow me to photograph them shaking hands.

Members of the two clubs were beginning to mingle, perhaps for the first time ever when in the words of one biker, 'All hell broke loose.'

The first indication that anything was wrong was a whooshing sound followed by the roar of an explosion as what we later found out was an anti-tank rocket hit a group of parked bikes near to where I was standing.

Someone amongst the bikers yelled 'Incoming' and we dived for cover as a second rocket hit the brick clubhouse behind us. Beyond that, a third rocket struck close to a tent that was acting as a bar for The Brethren and their guests, following which there was the clattering noise as a burst of automatic rifle fire swept the site.

Near where I lay, Brethren and Rebels had hit the ground together and were now rising up to see where the attack was coming from.

The firing died away as quickly as it had started and as some members of both clubs raced across towards the woods from where it had seemed to emanate while others, together with a visibly shocked team from St John's Ambulance who had come expecting to see the odd case of heat exhaustion or at worst perhaps a broken limb from a bike prang, began desperately tending the wounded.

Three of the dead, The Brethren Adrian 'Shady Aidie' Christianson from the London charter, Jonathan 'Greasy Fingers' Hodge from the North East and Rebel sergeant at arms Richard 'Ric' Taylor from Liverpool, had been standing together discussing the bikes and took the full force of the explosion when the first rocket struck.

Elsewhere, Nigel 'Nugget' Jones, a Brethren from Birmingham, was killed by flying shrapnel.

As the smoke cleared and a fleet of cars and vans were commandeered to ferry the injured to hospital pending the arrival of ambulances for the most seriously wounded, the club members gathered in grim-faced quiet conclave. Those who had reached the woods had reported back that the attackers, whoever they were, had fled the scene.

Most of the bikers who were in a position to do so then rapidly saddled up and rode off, ignoring the arriving police to whom, despite everything that had just happened, they had nothing to say.

So, the concern for police is whether the UK is now facing its first ever biker war.

These levels of violence and even the use of sophisticated military hardware are hardly unknown amongst biker gangs elsewhere in the world. Eleven people were murdered, with over 70 attempted murders, during the so-called Great Nordic Biker War when from 1993 to 1997 the Hells Angels and Bandidos fought for control of the Scandinavian drugs trade using machine guns, hand grenades and rocket launchers; in Canada the police attribute up to 69 deaths, including those of innocent passers-by, to a similar war which ran from 1994 to 1999 and which involved numerous car bombings; while in Australia a single confrontation at a motorcycle rally in Milperra in 1984 between members of The Comancheros and members who had defected to patch over and form an Australian Bandidos charter, left six bikers and a 14-year old girl dead.

Until Saturday's incident however, while there have been a number of shootings involving biker disputes, including some fatal ones, this type and scale of violence has not been seen in the UK.

The first question both the police and the bikers will be asking is, who was responsible for this attack?

It would have to be someone with the capability and interest in attacking a biker event and in practice police specialising in the biker clubs at SOCA, the Serious and Organised Crime Agency, clearly believe this means other outlaw bikers.

This raises three main possibilities, each of which will be worrying the police in their own way.

The first, and in many ways the simplest explanation, is that another club had decided to attack The Brethren. In this scenario, The Rebels, who the attackers may not have expected to be there given the historic grudge between the two clubs, would just represent collateral damage. If this is the case, police fear that the two clubs may now seek to join forces to hunt down the attackers.

Assuming however, that the attack at this point was not a coincidence but was linked to the Brethren and Rebels' peace process, then this means the attackers would have to have been in the know about the planned meeting.

Again, it could have been another club which may have felt threatened by the two linking up. Police speculate that the intention may therefore have been to cause casualties on both sides in the hope of sinking the peace deal. However this scenario would require the attackers having advance knowledge of the planned meeting, which whilst known about by officers in both clubs, was otherwise a quite closely guarded secret.

While not ruling this out, given the fierce degree of loyalty that outlaw motorcyclists have to their own clubs and the rigid codes of secrecy, the police are therefore discounting this as a possibility.

There is a third possibility however, which is that dissident factions within one or other club, The Brethren or The Rebels, arranged to stage the attack using either their own members or those of so-called support clubs, as a strike against their own leadership in an attempt to derail the clubs' rapprochement.

If this is the case, the strong joint response of the two clubs suggests that it has not worked, at least so far. However it does raise the possibility that some kind of internal dispute may be breaking out within one or other club.

The implication of any of these scenarios for the outlaw biker scene in the UK is one of uncertainty and possible trouble, and so both the police and bikers are already turning their minds to what happens next.

The first concern is obviously whether there will be further attacks and if so, when and where. Both clubs now have members to bury and while outlaw biker funerals are always significant events within this community, attendance at these particular occasions is likely to be at an all time high. The police will already be considering the security implications of covering each of these runs.

There is obviously also concern about the potential for revenge attacks as and when the clubs believe they have identified those responsible. The police believe that the clubs are already mounting parallel investigations of the attack using their own channels and whilst they will not admit it for the record, there is serious concern at high levels that if the outlaws establish the guilty parties before the police are able to arrest them, there may be an outbreak of serious violence in retaliation.

4   Hostilities

That piece was front page, above the fold, with my by-line.

Pages two and three covered in text and pictures some of my shots, some of the aftermath, police crawling through the woods in white overalls, and abandoned outlaw Harleys being lifted in slings onto recovery trucks to be taken away for examination.

This was the major story on Monday, and one I was right in the thick of whether I liked it or not. The editor had been pleased with the scoop of having an eyewitness account but now he wanted to know more. Who had been behind this, and where was it going to go?

Someone somewhere out there had to know.

I had called Bob first on the Sunday. It was a quick call to his mobile, very much on the fly from the newsroom as I raced to pull together and file my copy. It was the weekend but given what had happened I guessed he'd be working.

But he was no bloody use at all.

'Hi,' he'd answered the phone cheerfully, 'I see you had a fun weekend then.'

'Jesus. Nothing on the fucking radar. Your Intel is crap!' I accused.

'So help us then,' he suggested quickly.

I was instantly suspicious, my natural journalist's instincts aroused, 'What do you mean *So help us then*?'

'Give us information on The Brethren. You're in seeing them.'

*

Naturally it was The Brethren rather than the cops who knew what was going on as I found out with a simple call on Monday morning to the mobile number Wibble had given me.

'Hi,' I said, 'it's me.' I knew they didn't trust talking on mobiles as a rule. Too easy to intercept. Sure enough he kept the conversation short.

'What do you want?'

'I want to speak to you.'

'What for?'

'To find out what's going on, what you know.'

He thought about that for a moment and then said, 'OK then, come over.'

'Where?'

'It's OK, you don't need to know. You at work?'

'No, at home.'

'Fine. Stay there. We'll send someone to collect you.'

'Great, it's at...'

'Don't worry,' he said using an ominous phrase before he hung up, 'we know where you live.'

Of course he did, I thought uneasily. Why didn't that come as a surprise?

*

It was Bung who turned up outside my flat about an hour later. He was driving an ancient Astra and he didn't come in. Just stopped outside and beeped his horn like a taxi waiting for a fare, then sat there waiting behind a pair of dark sunglasses until I appeared. It was the first time I'd seen him not wearing his colours.

I slid into the passenger seat and he pulled away without a word as I tugged the seatbelt down around me and clicked it into place.

We drove in silence for about twenty minutes, Bung juggled his way through the late morning traffic towards Chiswick and up onto the elevated section of the M4 so soon we were heading west out of London.

Then he was indicating and pulling into Heston Services where he headed over to a corner of the car park away from the buildings and stopped beside a battered looking parked up despatch bike equipped with well stickered top box and panniers. A rider started to walk towards us as we climbed out of the car.

'So,' I asked, 'are we meeting him here?'

'Nope,' he replied, without looking at me.

'So what's this?'

'End of the line mate,' he replied turning to me as the other biker reached us. 'All change!'

The biker opened the bike's top box and pulled out a full face helmet with a shaded visor which he handed to me.

'What's this about?' I asked.

60

'We're going the last bit of the way by bike,' said Bung, pulling on an open faced lid that the biker had also produced, 'So get this on first.'

He handed me the sort of black balaclava that dispatchers often wear during the winter against the cold.

'But…' I was going to tell him I was fine when he growled, 'Other way round.'

I understood what he meant then. Wearing the balaclava back to front I'd be effectively blindfolded while the darkened visor on the full faced lid would mean that no one would be able to tell this was the case. They were serious about me not wanting to know where I was going and they didn't want to draw attention to themselves. The bike was an oldish, ordinary, naked, and knackered looking Kwacker, a classic dispatcher's slab sided GT750 shaftie with a lot of miles on the clock and a radio set bungeed across the tank. It was The Brethren equivalent of mufti. In his worn leather jacket and scuffed jeans, on this bike Bung just looked like a bit of a burley despatch rider. Every day and anonymous.

He fired up the bike with an asthmatic roar from its rusty four into one and the other biker guided me with his hand as I climbed blindly onto the back.

Bung had left the keys in the car's ignition so I guessed the other guy would take care of that.

As we rolled out of the car park I realised both that the whole exchange had only taken a couple of minutes, and that the other biker had never said a word.

Bung blasted down the motorway to the next junction and then I felt the familiar sinking sensation as he slowed slightly to enter the roundabout and dropped the bike into the corner before a boot of acceleration in the small of my back tugged my shoulders backwards as it lifted the bike back out again and we were on our way to wherever our destination was going to be.

It was a strange feeling, riding pillion without being able to see. There was nothing to it but to just try and relax, to just go with the interplaying rhythms of the ride; the tugging backwards of acceleration, the sliding forwards of braking and the jinking and yawing swoops to left and right as we took the bends or hopped the traffic, the back wheel juddering over the cats eyes. Without the visual clues it was very difficult to judge how long we were riding or how far we might have come. I'm sure he went round a couple of roundabouts twice just to ensure any sense of direction I might have had would be confused but frankly he needn't have bothered. By the time we got wherever we were going I wasn't going to have a clue anyway.

61

Eventually the wind and exhaust roar died as we slowed almost to a halt before, with a bump of the suspension, we were heading down some kind of a ramp, the exhaust noise echoing back at us as we rode into the cool damp of what had to be some kind of underground car park where we pulled up. Bung kicked out the stand and let the bike settle; steadying it as still in blackness I climbed off and stood surrounded by the acrid smells of hot oil from the bike and old piss from everywhere else.

Bung led me to a lift, in which if possible there was an even worse smell of piss and the doors closed.

The elevator rattled its way up slowly until with an institutional 'ping' it juddered to a halt and the steel doors sighed open.

My guide directed me along a corridor until at last we stopped and he knocked on a door. We waited outside for a few moments, I assume while we were being inspected from inside, before the rattling sound of bolts being drawn came through the door and then it clicked open. At a prod from Bung I stepped forward and into the space beyond.

'OK, you can take it off now,' instructed a familiar voice.

It was a normal flat I saw, as I pulled the balaclava off my head. Up on one of the top floors of a block it had an anonymous view out over what I assumed was somewhere in north London but I really couldn't be sure. Inside, the living room was sparsely furnished and quite ordinary, apart that was from the steel backing to the door and type of secondary internal security cage behind it of the type beloved of drugs dealers looking to avoid being taxed by the clientele.

Wibble was leaning casually against the doorway through to the kitchen, his arms folded across his chest.

'Nice,' I said, setting the lid down next to the ashtray onto a cheap veneer coffee table and pulling off my gloves, 'your place?'

He grinned at that.

'Nah, just a safe house we use,' he said, stepping into the room and indicating I should take a pew.

As I sat on one of the small wooden armed sofas, Bung made himself comfortable, flopping onto an armchair beside the cage. He was going to wait for me and take me back I guessed, noticing he'd not bothered to take off his riding gloves. It occurred to me that Wibble might only just have got here as well since he was wearing riding gear and a pair of thin black leather gloves.

'Drink? Coffee?' Wibble asked and without thinking I said, 'Yes, that would be great please.'

'Bung?'

Bung declined with some comment about needing to get a striker up here to take care of this sort of shit which Wibble warded off with a query whether Bung thought Wibble was too grand to be making a cuppa or two? Besides which he knew this wasn't the sort of place that they brought strikers to now was it?

Wasn't it, I wondered? Why not?

So I sat there and fiddled for a minute while he ducked back into the kitchen and clicked on the kettle. It must have boiled already since with a rumble of bubbles it tripped off again almost immediately and I heard the clink of a teaspoon as he doled out the instant and then poured the water. A fridge opened and then closed with a pop of its seal and he reappeared bearing two mismatching mugs, thrusting one out for me to take before he plonked his onto a spare ring-stained space on the table in front of us beside a pile of bike mags and sat down opposite me.

He made his coffee strong, much stronger than I liked it I noticed, as I found a clearish spot to put the mug down in front of me. Dark brown-black smuts of undissolved granules were still swirling on the surface where he had stirred it. I decided that I wasn't going to ask for more milk. Not now that he'd sat down anyway.

But the odd thing which was starting to make me very uneasy, as I nerved myself and took a cautious sip of the scalding dark brew, was that even now, throughout this process, he still hadn't removed his gloves.

The reasons they might both want to keep gloves on were obvious of course.

I wondered if I could remember exactly which surfaces I had now touched that might have my fingerprints on them since they sure as hell weren't going to have Wibble's or Bung's.

And that was the good scenario.

The bad one was that they were going to protect their hands while they did something else, despite the smiles and the relaxed atmosphere. And the only other person who was there that they might be planning to do that something to, was me.

*

'So?' I asked, taking another brave sip and wincing a bit at the heat as I peered over the rim of the mug at Wibble who had settled back into the sofa with his mug in his hand, 'what's up?'

'It's the goat fuckers,' he said simply, 'them and the zombies. They've gone over. They're now squaws.'

Mentally I translated this news to myself.

Capricorn MC owned East Anglia above some ill-defined border somewhere on the edge of Essex and across into north Cambridgeshire and then up into Lincolnshire. They had been big in the acid trade in the seventies and eighties, and moving with the times to take full advantage of their distribution networks, they were now heavily into the E business, bringing it over direct from the producers' labs in Holland.

What Wibble was telling me was that not only had they joined up with The Dead Men Riding MC who owned Yorkshire and Humberside, so that between them they now controlled a big swathe of eastern England, which was bad enough. But that they had swapped their own colours for new ones in the old Harley brand scheme of orange and black was worse still.

Both clubs had patched over to become Mohawks.

This was big news, I knew immediately that The Mohawks had established a mainland UK charter for the first time. And I knew something else too, that The Mohawks had a long history elsewhere with both The Brethren and The Rebels.

'But I thought...' I started.

'That they were at each other's throats?' Wibble asked calmly.

'Well yes. What about the stabbing and stuff...'

'Well whatever that was about, it obviously isn't a problem between them now.'

Bob would be interested in this, I decided. Now at least I would have something to trade, assuming of course he didn't know already from the cops' sources in other clubs. For all I knew the cops might have had grasses in either or both The Capricorn or Dead Men Riding. But then if he had, surely he would have been better informed before the attack. A question to file away to think about.

But then how long had Wibble known, I wondered? But that also seemed like a question to keep to myself.

'It's a bit too much of a coincidence that the attack took place then wasn't it? Just as your peace with The Rebels was being announced?' I asked.

He glared at me.

My implication was obvious, even if unstated, and he didn't like it. But all the same he couldn't avoid it. If the attack was aimed at spoiling the peace deal's coming out party then someone had to have let The Mohawks know.

'So who is it?' I continued.

He shrugged as if trying to shake off an irritating detail.

'Someone who wants to split the clubs apart again.'

'But who could that be?' I pressed.

'I don't know. Yet. But when we do…' he left it unfinished and I thought it best to leave it there as well and not to risk my luck any further.

But the 'who could it be' was easy to answer. I could do that for myself straight away.

There wouldn't have been that many people who would have known what was about to go down, and all of those would have had to be at least full patched members of either one or the other clubs, if not amongst its top officers.

There would be plenty of guys in both clubs who might object to the two of them cosying up like this. Everyone in and around the outlaw biker scene knew there were hatreds that ran long and deep from what had been twenty or thirty years of virtual war between the clubs.

Or then again, it might be someone with another agenda. Someone aiming to embarrass the leadership of either club perhaps, for reasons of their own.

And that was before you started to think who outside the club might want to attack. But then how could anyone outside have known? I checked myself. No, whoever had actually pulled the triggers, they had to have been operating on the basis of information from within one or other of the clubs.

'So what happens now?'

'We'll leave it to the local guys. They were hosting the run, it was their turf, they were responsible for security and they fucked up. So it's up to them to deal with it or to ask for help if they need it.'

With the serious loss of face that would involve, I thought. Given how Thommo felt about Wibble and his crowd I guessed it would be a fairly chilly day in hell before that happened.

I gathered from his tone that was about all I was going to get for the moment. I could sense, without saying a word, he was drawing our discussion to a close, but that was alright, I didn't need to fight it, I had enough for what I wanted at the present.

Then just as I was getting ready to go, Wibble had a last surprise for me.

'Here,' he said handing me a small cloth embroidered badge, 'Before you go, I've got something for you to take. Put that on.'

I looked at what he'd given me quizzically. It was a smaller stylised variation of The Brethren's patch than the one they all wore between their rockers, with the word 'Support' on a tab above, Wibble's name on a flash across the centre and the initials LLH&R woven on a tab at the bottom.

'Get that sewn on your jacket. Have it on the front or the side somewhere and it'll give you protection, no one will lift a finger against you,' he instructed, 'But don't put it anywhere on the back or you'll get filled in sharpish.'

I understood and nodded as I slipped the token into my pocket. Having it on the back of my jacket would look too much like an outsider claiming some kinship, some entitlement to the Menace colours, and whatever my status no Brethren was going to tolerate that sort of infringement for even a moment.

But by the same token, a Freemen named support patch would be my ticket to the inside. It marked me out as someone who was trusted to work with and for The Freemen, someone on the inside and in the know. It would be a critical pass that told Brethren that they were free to speak to me. And it would be my safeguard, telling any Brethren that decided to take me on that I was under the protection of The Freemen and that they would have to answer to my sponsor if they did so.

'I said I'd sort you out didn't I? Well there you go.'

It was weird, I thought, as I slipped into blackness behind the balaclava again for the trip back. With this support patch, without asking for it or seeking it, I now found myself in a unique position. I was a journalist still, but now one potentially 'embedded' on one side for the duration of what was likely to be a bloody biker war.

I wasn't at all sure how comfortable I was at that as a prospect.

As we rode back I had nothing to do but think in the darkness as I jerked and swung about on the pillion behind Bung.

And try as I might, there was nothing that I could think about other than the immediate aftermath of the attack that day. And out of all the fractured images of the burning bikes, and the screaming of wounded people, there was one fragment that kept coming back to me, playing itself out endlessly again and again like a loop of film projecting against the back of my eyelids.

It was a vision of Wibble. Wibble standing, a picture of cold, calm and collected fury, his lieutenants, and The Rebels guys as well, gathered round him.

It was stuff I hadn't put in my piece for the paper. He might not even know that I had seen and heard it from where I was sitting on the clubhouse steps, still deep in shock at what had just happened.

'It's your shit,' I heard Wibble say forcefully, his face set like stone and all but prodding a fuming looking Thommo in the chest.

'You want to be a P in this club? Well then it's your responsibility to take care of these local cunts, unless you need us to come in and do it for you?' he demanded, backing Thommo even further into a corner.

Of course Thommo couldn't do anything but say he would handle it, take care of business on his turf. The idea he would lose face in front of not just the gathered Freemen, but also The Rebels, by saying he couldn't tackle some local second string club was simply unthinkable. Thommo just had to stand there and suck it up.

And I was sure that Wibble had deliberately done it, putting a Brethren on the spot in front of Stu and The Rebels as well.

Snapping his ferocious gaze from Thommo, Wibble turned to speak to Stu who had been standing by his side.

'Well,' he asked him, addressing him formally in Stu's capacity as president of the assembled Rebels, 'we know you guys have skin in this as well. It not just Brethren that have been hurt here today, but Rebels as well.'

'So this,' he said waving his arm to indicate where bodies were still being tended by the bikes, 'was an attack on both clubs, which means you have your rights here as well, we recognise that.

'But you're our guests here and it's happened on our patch, on our watch, so we have to take responsibility. The question is, are you happy to have these guys here,' Wibble indicated towards the fuming Thommo and his skulking crew, 'handle it for both clubs, or do you want a piece?'

Stu considered this for a moment, glanced across at his guys and then turned back to Wibble with his decision.

'We'll let them handle it,' he announced, but then laid down his condition, 'so long as it gets handled right and quickly enough.'

Wibble nodded. He obviously felt that this was fair enough and honour would be satisfied on both sides.

'Understood,' he answered. 'We'll keep you posted and if these guys need any back up both clubs will step up,' he proposed. 'Agreed?'

'Agreed,' said Stu, and then grim-faced they shook to seal the deal. Again it was a strong biker handshake, clasped forearm to forearm, but this time it denoted something much grimmer. They wouldn't want to pose for a photo of this one.

Wibble had backed his own local charter into a corner. The onus was now solely on them to hold up The Brethren's reputation in front of not only the other charters but also The Rebels by finding and dealing with the attackers. And quickly.

And Wibble had known, I realised, putting my finger on it for the first time. Even back then, as the bullets had only just stopped flying, Wibble had known it was a local club that had attacked.

The problem with that I pondered, as we swayed to a stop again back in the services' car park, was that it was either bloody good guesswork or it was something else on Wibble's part.

And he didn't strike me as the type to be a psychic.

*

The support patch lay on the desk next to the phone where I had dropped it as I came in. I really wasn't sure how I felt about it and the bargain it implied.

Despite my misgivings, I picked up the phone and dialled Bob's number.

'The answer's still no,' I said, when he came on the line.

'Is that what this was about?' I had asked him, what, only this morning. 'You want me to spy on The Brethren for you? I'm a journalist not a grass, you know I can't do that.'

'So tell us what's going on then,' he'd insisted, 'Give us some background, whatever you can. We've got a fucking murder case on here now you know. The chiefs are screaming to know what's going on and where it's going to end and I've got fuck all to tell them at the moment. So help me out here. What do you know? What are they thinking?'

So I told him.

Some, not all.

That I'd seen Wibble.

That he seemed to know somehow that it was Capricorn and The Dead Men Riding.

'It's like their coming out event he says.'

'Coming out event? What do you mean?' Bob asked.

'They've joined forces and patched over.'

'Patched over?' he demanded, 'patched over to what?'

I gave him the one word answer.

'Mohawks.'

It was all I needed to say. There was a moment's silence on the other end of the line. Somehow I felt I had to fill it so I repeated myself.

'He said they've gone over to the Mohawks.'

'I heard,' he said.

It was just about the 'Oh shit' reaction I had been expecting.

'Mohawks?' he checked, 'you're sure he said Mohawks?'

'Oh sorry, my mistake,' I said sarcastically, 'I'm only a journalist so I'm not used to listening to what people tell me, you've just reminded me, actually he said the brownies. Of course I'm sure.'

'OK, OK! Keep your hair on. It's just it's quite a bit of news to take in…'

'Problem?' I asked. 'What do you think? Is this as big a problem as I think it is?'

'Oh no problem,' he replied, 'it's not what you'd call a problem as such. Just more like all out fucking war, that's all.'

It's what I had thought too, but now I was hearing it from the police.

'That serious?'

'Yes it's that serious. The Mohawks have had a Manx chapter for a while now, but them having some bods stuck out on the Isle of Man was something the other senior clubs might not like but could tolerate.'

'Why there?' I asked.

'There was an available club to patch over and besides, it's a useful place to have a base.'

I was about to ask what the hell for since I didn't see that The Mohawks would be interested in fishing, tourism and the TT, when Bob filled me in anyway.

'It's an international banking centre, lots of offshore financing and money management.'

On the face of it the idea that an ambitious up and coming outlaw biker gang would have a great interest in international bankers seemed funny at the outset, but then given recent financial history you might think they probably had more in common than at first appeared. And of course The Mohawks' interest in international banking would be a purely business one in terms of what it could do for them when it came to moving and laundering money. As I'd found from talking to Damage, the bikers could be quite sophisticated when it came to the intricacies of dummy companies, offshore trusts and the attractiveness of bearer bonds; all a long way from the popular image of having no interests other than stripping down and rebuilding a knucklehead while drinking crates of booze, eating handfuls of pills and looking forward to the next shag or fight, whichever came first.

But Bob was still talking. 'Patching over a couple of serious regional firms like Dead Men Riding and Capricorn to give them a mainland presence and territory, now that's something different. That lobs a huge fucking rock into the local pool and all sorts of shit is going to wash up as a result.'

'Does it make so much of a difference if these two have the same patch now?'

'Of course it does. Listen, The Brethren and The Rebels have had their slots for years now, and since your bloody *pax Damage* they've been getting on with business with territories sorted out. They may not be best buddies still but they've had an increasingly good working relationship for years.

My *pax Damage*, I thought?

'But add the Mohawks into the mix and who knows where it will end? What was a two way national carve up at their level is suddenly up for grabs as a three way one. And how do you think it looks to the yanks back in the mother clubs who authorise their local charters? Part of the deal with the local guys over here will have been a quid pro quo. You get your charter and your patches but you have to prove you are top dog locally at your level. Now another senior club shows up, it's up to The Brethren and to a lesser extent The Rebels, as it was an attack against a Brethren event, to show they are still top dog or…'

'Run the risk of having their charter pulled? The yanks wouldn't do that would they? Could they?'

I could just about hear Bob shrug his shoulders in the tone of his voice, 'Who the hell knows what the yanks could or couldn't do?'

Or what the implications would be, I added. It was incredible to think about it. I knew The Brethren had pulled individual local clubs' charters before, setting in train vicious dogfights as the remaining charters' members hunted down the offending ex brothers to reclaim the patches for the club. But never so far as I was aware had they ever done it to a whole country's charter. Christ alone knew what would happen then. Expulsion from the worldwide Brethren network would be a stunning blow for the local charters, not just from a personal and standing point of view but also for the disruption it would cause to their existing international business arrangements and networks. Would it be an open season, I wondered? Would you see Brethren and their allies, associates and hired guns from around the world converge on the UK to do battle with the guys here? And what would the local guys do about business? They would have to get alternative supply routes and contacts set up in double quick time, which would in all probability mean looking to take existing ones off someone else. And whoever that would be, would be unlikely to want to give them up easily. So you could end up with the UK Brethren fighting a three way war, versus The Mohawks, versus the rest of the Brethren world, and versus other gangs whose livelihoods they wanted to take over. Christ, no wonder it looked like bad news to Bob.

'Your book,' he said, much to my surprise changing the subject suddenly, 'all those guns. The ones Damage said they had dropped in from Eastern Europe. Do you think that was true?'

How the hell should I know, I wondered? I just took down what he was telling me when I interviewed him. You're the bloody cops, if you want to go digging for guns why doesn't SOCA find out?

'It's just we've never seen any sign of The Brethren having access to that sort of automatic weaponry,' he was saying. 'Handguns yes, but not AKs and stuff. I was wondering whether it might just have been Damage bigging it up. You know, using you to put a bit of a scare into potential rivals. *Don't take on The Brethren, they're seriously tooled up*, that sort of thing.'

'Yes, as far as I know.'

'Any idea where they would be now?'

'You're joking aren't you?' I asked. He really was clutching at straws now if he thought anyone in the club was ever going to tell me stuff like that.

'Oh yeah, and Wibble gave me something.' I said picking up the small piece of stiffly embroidered cloth from where it lay.

Like a lot of other clubs, The Brethren sold support gear to raise money for the club. It was a bit of a cottage industry, with each local charter producing its own designs of T-shirts, badges, stickers and for the girls, knickers, but these would never have the words The Brethren on them or the club logo. That would be too close to allowing the ultimate offence in The Brethren's world of a non-member wearing an image of the club's patch, about as guaranteed a way of getting yourself, as Wibble had put, 'filled in' as I could think of. Instead The Brethren's support gear was always based around their nick name of the Menaces and themed in black and red.

But this was different. It bore the club logo. It was official. It was club flash.

'So, are you going to put it on?' Bob asked 'You know what it means don't you? That you are under his personal protection, that no one else in The Brethren can touch you.'

He paused, and then added.

'Or at least they can, but then they'd have to answer to Wibble for it afterwards, not that it'll do you much good I suppose by that stage.'

I put the phone down. Well at least the editor would be happy with today's work. I had my next piece.

The Guardian

Tuesday 4 August 2009

Police Fear Patch War

Iain Parke, Crime Correspondent

There is a new patch on the UK outlaw biker scene and its presence means the police fear significant further violence may ensue after last Sunday's attack on The Brethren MC's Annual Toy Run, which may even lead to the eruption of a full scale biker war.

The new club's patch depicts a skull, wearing a headband with a single broken feather, between top and bottom rockers in the old Harley Davidson brand colours of orange and black bearing the name of the club above, The Mohawks MC, and their charter territory below.

And for the first time ever this rocker now gives a mainland Britain location following the 'patching over' of two existing independent UK outlaw motorcycle clubs, Capricorn MC based in East Anglia and Dead Men Riding MC based in Yorkshire, to become The Mohawks MC in the UK. As a result, the new club has a territory stretching up the east coast of England from Suffolk to North Yorkshire.

Unusually for one of the international outlaw motorcycle clubs, The Mohawks originated in Canada rather than in the US. Its 'founding' or 'mother' charter formed in the late sixties in British Columbia where it quickly became heavily involved in commercial marijuana cultivation. Subsequent charters were created in other countries, notably Australia, where the club is believed to have become major producers and distributors of amphetamines.

Despite this spread, The Mohawks remain outside what are known as the Big Six of the internationally organised outlaw motorcycle clubs, but the police fear that they are gunning, sometimes literally, to move up the ladder. And in the UK this would automatically bring them into conflict with one or other of The Rebels MC or The Brethren MC.

This prospect is unlikely to deter The Mohawks' new member club in the UK as The Mohawks have a reputation for violence. They have fought wars with several of the Big Six clubs in each territory they have entered as they have looked to carve out a niche for themselves, and the new UK charter may feel pressure to move aggressively against one of the other clubs to demonstrate its worthiness to wear The Mohawks colours.

Sources within both the police and outlaw bikers therefore believe this is what lay behind Sunday's attack during which six people were killed.

The president and senior officers of both The Brethren and The Rebels were present at Sunday's event, and sources at SOCA speculate that it may have been an attempt to decapitate the two clubs.

'It would certainly have given the new club time to make their move and consolidate their position if it had worked,' said a police source.

One outlaw biker source meanwhile described it succinctly as 'their [The Mohawks] coming out party.'

Given the ferocity of Sunday's attack and SOCA's belief that the existing UK outlaw clubs may have substantial stocks of weapons at their disposal, the police are therefore worried about the potential for the situation to deteriorate into further serious violence. They point out that similar biker wars in other countries have led to numerous deaths, both within the biker community and of innocent bystanders caught up in bombings or shootings.

The police are therefore remaining on alert for any signs of further clashes between the clubs and are also continuing to appeal for witnesses to Sunday's events to come forward.

5 Rules of engagement

Thursday 6 August 2009

Wibble had called, inviting me to meet up with him again. But there was to be no cloak and dagger crap this time. I was to come over to their London club house and he'd see me there. The house would be a fortress, I assumed. Wibble and the other Brethren would feel safe from attack by The Mohawks there inside their Wembley castle, while they waited for the Cambridge charter to sort things out to everyone's satisfaction.

When I got to the end of the little side road a mile or so from the stadium, the atmosphere was very different from the last time I had visited. I found a spot way down the other end of the road, parked my car and made sure it was locked, and then hiked back along the street the way I had come. The kerb outside the clubhouse was deserted between its battered police parking cones which were still out and obviously none of the neighbours had decided to try and move, except for an empty, marked, cop car which was parked smack outside the front door. I assumed the occupants had to be inside as I pressed the intercom buzzer beside the steel shuttered door and felt the CCTV cameras boring into me. Whoever was inside took their sweet time thinking about it.

'Who's there?' rasped the intercom.

'It's Iain Parke. Here to see Wibble. He asked me to come over,' I replied to the grille. They didn't even bother to tell me to wait, they just left me standing there feeling increasingly like a target on a range in front of the silent brick frontage for another few minutes.

Then without warning a buzz and a click announced the door had been released and I turned the handle and walked inside.

'How's it going?' Wibble asked, as Bung showed me into an upstairs room where he was waiting, before commenting, 'Good, I see you've got the patch on OK.'

I had thought it over a lot, but eventually I'd ransacked my kitchen for where I'd stashed away a sewing kit I'd stolen from some hotel and then, sat down with a bottle of beer and a barrow load of curses at the thickness of the leather, I had painstakingly stitched the patch onto the flank of my jacket.

'Well I'm surprised to be asked over to see you to tell you the truth. Given what's going on I'd have thought talking to a journalist is the last thing you would want to do right now.'

He seemed to think it was a fair enough point. 'Well, I need to try to stop this thing getting out of hand. And I still have the project that I wanted you to do.'

'PR?' I asked him, 'You can't be serious mate? In the middle of a bloody war?'

He took me up short with his reply.

'Yeah well, we need to win the peace as well as the war now don't we?'

Wibble was a media savvy operator. Still it was true he was thinking of PR and perception rather than anything else. His interest was bluntly in Brethren propaganda and not much else so it just seemed another case of what they always said about war and the first casualty.

'They want you downstairs,' Bung said to him.

'OK,' said Wibble, 'Tell them I'll be down in a minute.'

Bung shut the door behind him as he left.

'You saw the cops are here?' It was more a statement than a question, 'They're with the guys in the pool room out the back.'

'Well I saw the car outside, yes. What are they doing here?'

'Oh, they want to talk to us,' he told me.

'I didn't know you were talking to the cops,' I said, momentarily surprised. Keeping shtum whenever the old bill were around was the inviolable rule number one of outlaw biker life. He didn't like that.

'We aren't, and don't you ever fucking suggest that we are or I'll have your guts for garters,' he snapped.

'So what are you saying to them then?' I asked, 'I can't believe that they're just all sitting round in silence down there.'

He shrugged, 'The usual. That we don't know what they want to talk to us for. That we didn't see anything. All the normal shit.

'I just don't know why they bother,' he continued, 'they must know by now that it's all they're ever going to get out of us.'

'Going through the motions?' I suggested, and he grunted something dismissive and unintelligible. 'Or is it tea and sympathy? Victim support perhaps? Are they here to offer you counselling?'

'Yeah, right,' he said standing up and walking to the door, 'cos we're all just so fucking traumatised, but it's our fucking tea they're drinking. It's OK though, they'll get bored and fuck off soon enough.

'Hang around, get a drink in the bar downstairs if you want,' he instructed as he left, 'while I go and find out what they're up to. I'll be free soon, then we can talk.'

*

So there I was, hanging around at a loose end in The Brethren's London clubhouse, while I supposed they were all preparing to go to the mattress, helping the police with their enquiries, or not more likely, and potentially expecting another attack at any moment.

Was it just me, I wondered, or were there times when other people just asked themselves, how did I come to be here? What weird set of choices over the years had led me to be here, now, doing this?

Well, whatever, I thought, I'm here now so I'd better just deal with it.

From the hallway I had come straight up the stairs to see Wibble, but through the other open doorway off the hall I had seen that on this side of the pair of joined-up terraces the house had been knocked through so what had been the front and back rooms were now a bar with a full sized snooker table, leading through to the lean-to kitchen which was out at the back.

Taking a drink from The Brethren bar while no one was around seemed a bit too much like trying my luck I thought, but a cup of coffee wouldn't hurt. I guessed they would have a kettle about the place, so I wandered downstairs after him, being very conscious of the support patch peeping out, I hoped visibly enough, from under my arm as I walked down the stairs.

Walking into the bar area I found that actually it wasn't empty.

Danny the boy was there. He had all the chairs stacked up against a wall and had a broom out which he was pushing inexpertly around the floor.

'Hey,' I said as I walked in, 'you still here then?'

'Oh, hi there,' he said looking up and greeting me with a slightly uncertain smile, 'yeah they're still letting me hang around. Isn't that great?'

Hmm, I thought, that's not exactly what I would call it, but hey, who was I to judge? He was a skinny kid, and his fresh face looked a little lost against the backdrop of The Brethren's bar with its members' wall of photos of fallen brothers, and adornment of Brethren patch themed plaques on the wall commemorating visits to or from charters around the world. But like before, he also looked determined to hold his end up. Even if, at the moment, his end involved nothing more than sweeping the floor for the guys.

'Whoa,' he exclaimed, straightening up, the broom in one hand, and peering closely at my jacket, 'is that one of Wibble's support badges?'

There was a tone of awe and respect in his voice as I walked past him and into the kitchen in search of mugs and instant. 'Wow, that's seriously cool.'

While I waited for the kettle to boil I found an assortment of mugs in a cupboard over the sink. Even in an office like mine back at the rag, I knew people could get pretty touchy about someone else using their mug. Getting filled in by one of The Brethren for using his favourite mug really didn't appeal so I called over my shoulder to where Danny was back on with his desultory cleaning to ask if he knew which ones were safe.

'Sorry, I don't know,' he confessed, appearing at the door.

'Probably not this one then?' I said holding up a mug for him to see which was emblazoned with the slogan *If you value your life as much as I value this mug, don't fuck with it!*

He laughed, 'Probably not.'

Stuck at the back of the cupboard there were half a dozen or so mugs printed with The Brethren logo. I guessed they wouldn't be anyone in particular's so decided that one of these would be the safest choice.

But he was wrong about my badge I thought, as I poured the boiling water in and stirred. It wasn't cool. It was dangerous. And I decided, as I walked back into the bar area, I wanted him to see that.

But whatever I said as I lounged around talking with him as I sipped my coffee and looked around the bar, checking out the selection of tunes on the jukebox which were much as I expected, *Lynyrd Skynyrd, Motörhead, Blue Oyster Cult, Pistols,* it was no good. There was simply no getting through to him.

What's said in here, stays in here proclaimed a sign above the bar.

And in here, I thought, I would have to be pretty careful about what I said. Support patch or not, I would need to watch my mouth for fear of who might be around, who might overhear, and what they might do about anything I said which they didn't like.

I picked up on where I'd left off speaking to him before. I tried to get him to tell me why he was here, not just because I wanted to hear it, but somehow,

I felt, that if I coaxed him into articulating it, it might help him think it through. To think about what he was getting involved with and where it might all lead.

And I cringed inwardly whenever he came back to my book. Every time he spoke about it, he just made me feel more and more guilty that I had been a part of glamorising this life, that I was partly responsible for this kid being here. If he ever sat down later and looked back at how and why he had got involved, I knew that I would have had a bit part to play, and it wasn't a feeling I was comfortable with.

I tried, as circumspectly as I could in the circumstances to warn him off, to talk him out of it. I kept bringing him back to the events of the last weekend, the serious nature of what he might be getting himself hooked up in.

But it was no good. Too late I realised that the kid saw it as some kind of test of manhood, that knowing The Brethren was a lucky, once in a lifetime chance to join something special and to potentially be an insider, and that a biker war would be a chance to prove himself.

There was no helping him. All I did was get to know him better.

In the end I just gave him my card.

'Listen kid, if you ever want to talk, give me a call.'

I never thought he would.

*

Wibble appeared in the bar after about half an hour as I heard the security door being buzzed open to let the cops out and a somewhat sarcastic 'Do call again officer,' floating in from behind him in the hallway.

'So, how did it go then?' I asked cheerfully.

'A complete waste of fucking time,' he said disgustedly.

'Yours or theirs?'

He laughed, 'Both I reckon. Come on.'

He pushed at the back door which opened out onto the yard by the side of the old terraced house. There were three Brethren bikes parked up, probably because they were safer there than in the street outside I guessed, and the inevitable striker lounging around looking bored on sentry duty.

'Walk with me,' Wibble instructed as he pulled a packet of cigarettes out of the breast pocket of his padded work shirt.

He wanted to smoke so he was going outside. It seemed strange that after all they did and stood for, the smoking ban would have that sort of an effect on The Brethren in their own clubhouse, but there you go.

'Fag?' he offered, as we stepped round the corner and onto a scrappy piece of lawn that had once been the two houses' gardens, at the end of which The Brethren had built a quite impressive brick barbeque area.

'No thanks,' I replied as we sat down opposite each other at one of the old wooden trestle tables, the sort of thing you see in pub beer gardens, which dotted the lawn.

'No, of course I forget,' he said casually, sticking one into his mouth and thrusting the rest of the pack back into his pocket to swap them for a Zippo lighter, 'you gave them up didn't you, about 20 years or so ago wasn't it?'

That stopped me in my tracks cold. I'd never spoken to Wibble, or anyone else in The Brethren about my smoking habits as far as I could remember. I'd never told him or any of them anything much about me really, but here, as we sat outside, he casually reeled off my complete unauthorised biography and CV as I sat in stunned silence. He gave me names, addresses, friends, relatives, schools, qualifications and jobs, as he smoked. He had the lot, and covered just about everything bar my bloody bank balance and inside leg measurement, although it wouldn't have surprised me if he had known those too.

When he reached my sister's name and address I had had enough.

'What's this about Wibble?' I demanded. 'Are you threatening me?'

He didn't move a muscle, he just sat there opposite me and exhaled a long stream of smoke. Then he slowly and deliberately stubbed out his cigarette, crushing it firmly against the scarred surface of the plastic ashtray on the table top.

'Me threaten?' he said with a grin, 'No, you don't get it do you? I just always like to know a bit about people I'm dealing with.

'You ask people a load of questions in your job right? You told me that. Well sometimes we ask questions as well, so we know where we stand with people. Like whether they were the best man at a copper's wedding…'

Ouch, that one hurt, I winced. They had been digging, seriously digging, into my past to find that out. How many people would know that about me, I wondered?

'So we can know how far we can trust them.'

'That was what, twenty odd years ago?' I protested, 'I haven't seen the guy in what ten, and what's it got to do with anything anyway?'

'Yeah we know,' he nodded slowly, 'Like we know when you go to see your little mate over at SOCA.'

By now I was seriously pissed off.

'I'm a fucking journalist Wibble. I write about crime. You know that. So of course I speak to coppers from time to time. Who the hell else am I going to speak to? What the fuck else did you think I did when you asked me along on your little trip?' I demanded.

'Hey,' he said reaching over and pinning one of my wrists to the table as he stared at me, 'calm down. It's no problem. It's just that I know. And now you know I know.'

But whatever he was saying, the subtext was obvious. He simply wanted me to know how much he knew about both me and mine.

'So what's the deal here then, Wibble?' I demanded. 'I'm a journalist, doing my job, like you seemed to want me to.

'To do that I talk to people, people on both sides of the law. You've been happy to talk to me, you've seen what I've written. If you don't like it, or you don't like me knowing some shit then it's in your hands isn't it? Either don't talk to me at all or don't tell me what you don't want to.'

'OK...' he began but for once I rode over him.

'But I'll tell you this for free, if I find stuff out, from talking to you, or your guys, or some other gang or even God help me the cops or uncle Tom Cobbly, then if it's a story I'm going to print it, and if that's what you're worried about, then be worried.

'But if you think I'm here to go running back to the cops as some kind of spy then you can...'

'Oh?' he raised a warning eyebrow at me.

I'd been about to tell him he could fuck off, but then some semblance of sense finally caught up with my mouth and shut it down before I said something that I would regret. Mainly due to the broken bones it would lead to.

I was quite keen on carrying on using my own teeth for a while yet.

'No,' he said casually, as if ignoring my outburst, 'you're not a cop or working for them. I knew that when we started and everything we've got,' and what would that be I wondered, 'says you're still clean.

'But even if you're not a snitch, you still need to realise the risk that we are taking just by letting you be around, particularly at a time like this. It's just a fact of life.

'You're speaking to people, you're making notes, you're writing stuff. It builds a picture you know? It can't help but broadcast some shit that we've never been used to being out there for Joe Public to see.'

'And,' I joined in; I could follow his train of argument clearly for him so that he could be sure I understood what he was saying, 'some of the guys will be worried about some specifics that I might come across, even if I'm not looking for them? Already or in the future. Is that it?'

It was an old problem, and one that I'd often touched on before when speaking to guys in the clubs or on other parts of my crime beat for the paper. The photo or the interview which shows someone was somewhere just before an unfortunate incident, something innocent at the time that could be a serious problem for them later. It was a risk they were conscious that they were running in letting someone like me hang around.

And I was also acutely aware it was a risk I ran in being around them, although for slightly different reasons. *Three can keep a secret,* was an old outlaw biker saying, *if two of them are dead,* which seemed to about wrap it up for both victims and any inconvenient witnesses who might be around.

'Well that's the way it is,' he agreed.

'So I'm embedded now am I?'

He smiled at the reference and pulled out his packet of cigarettes again, this time he plonked the packet on the table once he'd taken one out, 'Well, you could see it that way.'

'The quid pro quo is that I get to see, and write, what's safe. Your sanction in essence is that you know where I, and my family and friends live if I stray too far or you think I'm grassing you up. Is that it?'

'That's about the size of it,' he agreed as the Zippo flame flared in front of his face and he snapped the cover shut.

'Fucking fantastic!' I muttered.

'Great, isn't it?' he said in a perfectly friendly way.

'So then,' he continued, 'Let's do it. I've got some time.'

'Do what?' I asked in confusion.

He shrugged. 'You tell me. You're the one with all the questions Mr Hot Shot Hold-The-Frontpage Journalist. So what do you want to know?'

And so began what I have to say looking back was one of the strangest interviews of my entire professional life.

*

I was unprepared, so I improvised.

'Well,' I floundered, wondering where to start, 'So I was talking to the young lad in there. He was one of the tagalongs on Saturday, him and a striker. They seemed very young to be running with your crew, is that unusual?'

'Who, Danny and Charlie?' he asked.

'Yes, but they seem very different,' I ventured.

He considered this for a moment. 'Well Danny's an outsider,' he concluded as if it explained everything, 'Charlie's an insider so I guess that's a part of it.'

'An insider?'

'He's Damage's kid,' Wibble said offhandedly, as if it was the most obvious thing in the world.

'What?' I squawked in surprise.

'Yeah,' he shrugged, 'naming him Charlie was one of Damage's little jokes. So he's like family. It's like natural for him to be on his way in.'

So that was what he had meant by it being in the kid's blood I realised.

'But Sharon...' I started to say. I have to say I was just shocked at this revelation. I had known Damage, I had interviewed him many, many times, I'd written his bloody life story for Christ's sake, based on what he'd told me in hour after hour of taped sessions sitting there time after time in a visiting room at Long Lartin gaol. And he'd never, not once, breathed a word about anything like this.

'Yeah, sure she was his old lady,' said Wibble wreathed in smoke, 'but it's not like he didn't screw around occasionally when he felt like it.'

'Does she know?' I asked.

'I don't think so,' he shrugged, 'why should she? It was never a big deal.'

But by then I was feeling like an idiot. So Damage hadn't told me all about it, so what? Would I really have expected him to? Why the hell should I have expected that he would tell me about it of all people; a journalist who he knew was going to be writing a book about him? If he'd cared anything for Sharon, and I was still convinced that he had, then I wouldn't expect him to have mentioned anything about having had another kid. Or even kids, I now wondered to myself.

And who was I fooling? How well had I really known Damage? I'd just seen the face that he'd wanted me to see, and in this at least I'd fallen for it hook line and sinker.

We talked for probably about an hour, as Wibble gradually filled the ashtray.

But there was one thing that was still bothering me, niggling away at the back of my mind. Irritatingly it was the one thing that I realised from our previous conversation Wibble did not want to discuss, perhaps I guess because of the implications it might have for his club. So I kept pushing it to the back of my mind. But even as I thought desperately of other things to ask, it kept on shoving its way back to the front again, like a sore tooth which you just can't leave alone.

How had The Mohawks known about the event, I wanted to know? If you assumed that the attack had deliberately targeted both clubs, and that was my gut feel, as otherwise it was just way too much of a coincidence, then someone had to have tipped them off. There was no other way round it as far as I could see, so the question simply came down to who had done it and why.

And the answer there seemed to clearly point towards some kind of dissidents having set up, or even to have actively co-operated with The Mohawks in setting up the attack in order to sabotage the deal between The Brethren and The Rebels.

It made sense in some ways. There was clearly an anti-rapprochement faction in The Brethren, which from what I'd seen so far looked as though it sat under Thommo, although whether his beef was with the principle as such, or just with Wibble as its public face, I couldn't tell. And I guessed there would be an equally strong anti-Brethren section of The Rebels' members.

So the question as I saw it simply boiled down to which club's ultras were responsible and how they had arranged things.

And of course, what, if anything, Wibble and Stu could or would do about it?

And so, inevitably, our discussions kept on circling around and coming back to the events of Sunday, the spinning black hole which had formed itself at the centre of this particular universe.

'All that hostility at the run on Saturday, I asked, 'what was that all about? Was it connected to the guy they'd lost?'

'What, Thommo you mean?' Wibble just looked amused at the thought, 'No, it was nothing to do with Chugger. He was a new patch, he'd only had his vote a month or so ago and he was working his way in. Story I heard was that he was up there to collect in a debt...'

'A drug debt?' I asked, thinking well that wouldn't be such great PR so no wonder Wibble wasn't pushing it.

He shrugged, 'Could be, I didn't ask and I don't know.

'Anyway, he heads up to Leeds which is way off turf with a striker in tow, but whoever it was he'd gone to lean on had organised themselves some local back up, so he has a stand up run in with a local mob. There's nothing doing about getting his cash then and there so they go back to their car with a plan to come back with reinforcements. But someone has followed them to it and that's when they get popped.

'No, with Thommo it's about letting off steam. There's some big egos, and even bigger eyes, sometimes in this outfit. Not everyone voted for me you know.'

No I thought, I didn't know that.

'You mean someone wants your job?' I asked.

'Hey, no surprise in that is there? There's always someone who's ambitious in any outfit. It's just the law of the jungle.'

'And you're not worried?' I asked.

He just shook his head.

'But why did you let him diss you like that at the run? Wasn't that a challenge to your authority? I was surprised the way you seemed to let it go.'

'Nah, sticks and stones mate. I just let him rant on and it winds him up all the more that I don't let it get to me.'

'But doesn't it build him up in the eyes of anyone who's against you, and diminish your authority with the others?' I pressed, genuinely surprised.

'Don't worry about it. It's all under control.'

I was still unconvinced, I had to say. As an outsider, being anywhere around The Brethren felt like a bit swimming with sharks. There was a feeling that you were seeing a fascinating and almost elemental power, mixed up with a constant lurking terror that at any moment explosive bloody hell would be unleashed for no apparent reason. So the idea of Wibble being relaxed about what seemed tantamount to insubordination from a local charter member seemed incredible. I would have thought he would have lost face, whatever his reasons for doing so, but I left it at that, as it seemed something that he didn't want to discuss.

Besides which, despite the fact I couldn't fathom why, Wibble seemed supremely relaxed about it.

'Naw, better to know who it is and keep an eye on them than not know who's plotting. Besides which, we've all got bigger fish to fry now.'

But even as we were speaking, there was now another separate train of thought that was running in parallel, and no matter how much I tried to concentrated on what Wibble was saying, it refused to go away. It kept on bothering me. What else had I fallen for in the story Damage had told me? What else had he or hadn't he told me, that I might need to know.

I was startled back to the present again by something Wibble said.

'Greedy? Well yeah I suppose so, but it's like the banker said, greedy in a long term way, that's the smart way.'

'Do you want to be top dog, be independent of everyone else, is that it?' I asked trying to gather back my end of the conversation.

'Shit no, who would want the grief that comes with that?' He seemed surprised I'd even suggested it.

'No, make yourself too independent at the top of the tree and all you do is make an enemy of everyone else below you and paint a big target on your arse for everyone who wants to take a pot shot at knocking you out of the tree.

'No, Damage understood that mutual dependence was best, if everyone is indispensable to everyone else then he could maintain stability…'

'…and the status quo that was then maintained was that Damage was in charge?' I suggested.

'You got it. Just like he told you,' Wibble smiled.

*

As I left the clubhouse and headed up the road towards where I'd abandoned my car earlier, I was thinking about Wibble's agenda here.

He had told me he was looking to improve the club's public image, but there was more to it than that, there just had to be.

Was it personal, I wondered? Was Wibble looking to boost his own image, did Wibble want to become some kind of celeb? Now I smiled to myself, that was an interesting thought. It even made some kind of weird sense. If Wibble became more of a public face for the club, might that make it more dangerous or difficult for someone to unseat him?

Possibly, I thought, although I guess there was also a danger of pissing off that tendency in the club which didn't like the idea of publicity, that was suspicious of infiltration by poseurs and show offs. I toyed with the idea of Wibble a 'New Brethren' moderniser for a moment. It had a bit of a ring to it I had to say.

And of course, he had big shoes to fill, I could see that. Damage had to be a difficult act to follow, no question about it, when you looked at what he had achieved.

Even if it was just building on the foundations Dazza had laid, there was no denying Damage's achievement in establishing The Brethren as a powerhouse in bringing in gear and creating a working relationship with their main rivals The Rebels on the distribution side. With a modus operandi operating between the clubs and a protocol for handling disputes, business had been good all round under what Bob described as the *pax Damage* it seemed.

So was that why Wibble was interested in PR? To help consolidate his own position? Possibly, I conceded, but it still didn't seem enough, not for the grief he would be getting from the traditionalists within the club, and the risks he was running if anything was seen to go wrong with our little arrangement.

There had to be more to it than that.

I wondered again about one of the central mysteries in my relationship with Wibble, and the club itself for that matter. One to which I guessed I'd never now get a clear answer: whether Wibble was Damage's killer or not?

It was clear at least that, whatever he said, with a potential war like this, Wibble had some other agenda than PR in wanting me to hang around. My problem was that I couldn't work out what it was.

And then it suddenly hit me as I thought back to that meeting last week, Christ, was it really only a week ago? The one in the motorway services. Of Wibble sitting there and asking me the question.

If I said I hadn't, killed him, I mean. Well, would it make a difference? Would you really believe me?

Of us discussing it.

Well if you didn't, who did?

Now that is a very good question.

And do you know the answer to it?

So, I was forced to ask myself. What if Wibble wasn't, as I had assumed all along, Damage's executioner? What if it had actually been someone else? And what if Wibble, genuinely, didn't know who it had been? What would that mean for what I was getting myself involved with here?

I was lost in thought, trying to work out where this chain of speculation might lead me.

If Damage as Wibble's predecessor had been murdered, and Wibble didn't know who by, then surely Wibble would be very interested in trying to work out who had done it and why? Of course he would, because whoever had taken care of Damage might have similar reasons for wanting to take out Wibble mightn't they?

Was that why he wanted to get me involved. Did he think I might know something? That there might be something in what Damage had told me that would give him a clue? Or that he thought he might use me to dig and find out?

Is that what he was after, I wondered, did he want to use my contacts in other clubs and even SOCA to try and work out who the real killer was?

I got back to my car to find a clear plastic envelope stuck to the windscreen.

Fuck it, the peril had been about. I'd got a parking ticket. Over two hours in a one hour waiting zone.

Monday 10 August 2009

'Hi, it's me,' said the voice.

The weekend had been quiet as far as I could gather, so it was a surprise when I picked up to find him on the line at lunchtime. But it clearly showed I was now on the network.

It was Wibble calling with the funeral details.

'The cops have released the bodies,' he announced without preamble.

'Oh yes?'

'So the funerals are on for Saturday. The ride out starts here at ten.

'Here being?'

'The London clubhouse of course,' he sounded surprised at the question. 'Don't be late.'

'I won't. Hey,' I said quickly before he could get off the line.

'Yeah?'

'How's it going?'

'How's what going?'

'You know, the thing.'

'And I don't know what you're talking about,' he said sharply. It was obvious he wasn't going to talk, even in the most general terms, on the phone. His working assumption was that any club phone line would be tapped and should be treated as such.

'OK.'

'OK.'

There was evidently going to be no update on the war from Wibble, at least without trying door stepping him at the clubhouse, and with the Brethren in their current mood I really didn't much fancy my chances at that.

So I thought I would try my luck elsewhere.

I called Bob.

'I assume you've heard?' I asked.

He knew what I was talking about of course. He would have known the bodies were going to be released so he wouldn't have needed a bug to work it out but it did make me think. Were they really tapping The Brethren's phones, I wondered? It wouldn't surprise me. The club was a SOCA target and with what was going down at the moment with The Mohawks if I was a copper I'd have been tripping down the courts for a warrant for sure.

89

'Yes, it should be a big show we hear. All the jungle drums are working overtime on getting a good crowd of scum organised. Speaking of which, are you going?' he asked.

'Yeah well. It's not like I've got much of a choice it seems.'

'Well that's the price you pay isn't it?'

'Price I pay for what?' I asked.

'Getting onside with them of course.'

'Who, The Brethren?'

'Yes.'

'Hey, you just wait a minute,' I protested angrily, 'I'm not onside with them, I'm independent. You know that. I'm just a journalist doing my job.'

'Yeah sure you are. It's just you're a journalist wearing Wibble's personal support patch,' he fired back. So how independent does that look?'

'I don't really care how it looks,' I retorted angrily. And just how the hell did you know that I wondered? I'd only sewn it on yesterday.

'It's just something I've got so I can get in and do my job. It doesn't mean anything more than that.'

'Oh yes? Do you think Wibble sees it like that? I'd guess in his world, support means exactly what it says.'

He had a point.

'Yeah, well, maybe you're right,' I conceded. I would have to be a bit careful about that, 'but it's like, once he'd offered it to me it was a bit difficult to refuse, you know?'

'Yes, I guess it would be,' he said, 'not unless you never wanted to see them again.'

'Which given my job isn't really an option is it?'

'No I suppose not.'

Which brought me round to why I had called him. I was after an update.

'So how's the war going from your side?' I asked.

'Well it's much what you would expect really at this stage,' he said, and filled me in on what the cops were seeing.

According to Bob, it was simple. The two sides were out hunting for each other.

'They're all in lockdown. All the full patches have gone underground, club houses, safe houses, you name it. They've got tagalongs and prospects patrolling the streets around each club house on the look out for raiding parties and each one is even more of a fortress than they were before, if you can believe it.

'No one gets into a car without looking underneath it with a mirror on a stick to check for booby traps and they're wearing Kevlar under their colours in case someone takes a pot shot.

'They all know that stepping out with a patch on at the moment is just like going out with a target painted on your back.

'At the same time they all feel they have to keep up a presence, fly the clubs' colours, demonstrate that they're not taking any shit. So they're each determined to make a show of going on runs, like these funerals. But it means that if they do go out, they do it in strength and anytime they do, you can be pretty sure there's some bloody serious back-up close by. They're having cars go ahead to sweep the route and there'll be a van or two lurking in the background with God knows what inside.

'Meanwhile though, they're each out looking to see who they can pick off from the other side, so they'll set out in small groups, twos, threes or fours, probably including a striker or a tagalong to act as a spotter since there's more of a chance that they won't be recognised if they're seen. They're checking out known bars and hang-outs, just trying to see if they can find someone on their own that they can take out.

'I'm telling you, it's fucking dangerous for them out there at the moment.'

'Christ!' I said, 'can't you stop it?'

'Stop it? How?' he asked, 'and why? If they're all barricaded inside their club houses as far as some of our lads are concerned it just saves us the bother of locking them up ourselves.'

'You can't be serious!' I said.

'Can't I? OK then,' he said as we wound up, 'I'll see you at the bash on Saturday.'

'Yes, see you there,' I replied.

'Oh I doubt that sunshine,' he laughed.

'Why?'

'I'm running the surveillance operation,' he said offhandedly, 'So be sure you give a nice big smile for the piccies when you're on candid camera. I do like a nice happy snap for the album.'

'What about my human rights?' I asked. I wasn't sure I really fancied being in SOCA's catalogue of snapshots.

'What rights?' he asked, 'You'll be with the bikers won't you? And worse, you're a journalist. What right do you think you lot would have not to be snapped as and when we feel like it?'

'You're a right twat sometimes, you know that?' I said.

'Careful sunshine. Bit of respect for Her Majesty's Constabulary now.'

Tapping the Brethren? I thought as I put the phone down. Screw it, knowing Bob he's probably had my phone tapped.

*

I just did a filler piece for the rag.

The Guardian

Tuesday 11 August 2009

Four Funerals And A War

Iain Parke, Crime Correspondent

As outlaw motorcycle clubs The Brethren and The Rebels prepare to bury their dead at what are expected to be highly charged funerals on Saturday, police sources confirm that they believe a full blown biker war has now broken out between the two clubs and the newly formed Mohawks MC.

Police are making preparations for the funerals which will be going ahead in an atmosphere of tight security, both from the authorities and by the bikers themselves. The events are expected to attract large attendances from outlaw bikers and their supporters and police are not ruling out the possibility that any of the events which will be taking place in London, Birmingham and Liverpool may act as a catalyst for further violence.

'The clubs are in lockdown,' said a police spokesman, 'while each side has raiding parties out looking to pick off anyone they can find on the other side.

'At the moment we are seeing relatively little violence, but mainly because we believe other than at large events such as these funerals, most members of the clubs have gone underground for their own protection, however this may not continue and it's unclear how this situation will unfold. We don't yet know how it will end and we would appeal to all parties involved to co-operate with the ongoing police enquiry.'

Speaking on behalf of The Brethren, a spokesman denied there was any such war:

'This is all just crap that people say about us to sell newspapers. We're just going to bury our brothers and then have a wake to remember them by.'

6   No flowers

Saturday 15 August 2009

It was to be a full dress funeral.

I had heard about a patch funeral from Damage.

I had read about them in my research.

I had even written about them before now.

The one thing I'd never done was actually participate in one. But Wibble had made it perfectly clear that whatever my personal agenda or preferences might be, I had no choice but to go to this one. And I had to admit to myself, Bob had been right in his taunts, at least to a degree. It was part of the ongoing web of obligations to The Brethren I had let myself in for in accepting and then flying a Brethren support patch from Wibble.

You wear The Brethren's flash, in whatever capacity, you represent the Brethren was the rule. I knew that, I'd heard it from Damage, sitting across the chipped Formica prison table long before the idea of actually doing so had ever crossed my mind.

And if you represent The Brethren, it isn't any part time thing. You turned out when The Brethren turned out.

And clearly there was no more important turn out than to the funeral of a dead brother or brothers, and particularly murdered ones.

*

It was a mark of how times had changed over only the past fortnight that there was a small Rebel contingent, flashes of blue and white amongst the red and black gathered at the head of the milling crowd of bikers assembling as I rode up.

As I joined them, Wibble and the lead Rebel rep, the club VP no less, were in a quiet discussion about what position the Rebels wanted to ride in. In an unprecedented move Wibble had offered that they could ride up front, in parallel with the lead Brethren riders, an offer that the Rebel's VP, whose name was Tank I discovered, politely declined.

'Thanks but no,' he said, shaking Wibble's hand, 'we appreciate the invitation but we shouldn't. It's your show, they're your brothers, it wouldn't be right. We'll ride behind you.' Then they embraced, diplomatic niceties observed.

Stu wasn't there of course. The Rebels had their own funeral to hold today up on Merseyside to which Wibble had despatched Bung as his personal representative, together with a selection of Brethren chosen to stand for all of the UK charters. I didn't see Danny anywhere about so I guessed as Bung's tagalong he was probably making his way up to Liverpool behind his sponsor.

With the size of the event and number of bikes present, it was difficult to tell numbers. I guessed at a couple of hundred full patch Brethren including representatives of European charters, as well as some from further afield, I saw South African, Australian and American state bottom rockers amongst the crowd, who had obviously flown in to be there.

Then there were the strikers, the formal tag alongs which I guess had to include me now, which added to the purely Brethren contingent.

As Bob had indicated when we spoke, The Brethren had obviously also put the word out widely. This was going to be a high profile event and they were determined that it would be a good show. They wanted to send out a strong message. And they wanted a demonstration of loyalty from all those who were onside.

So, in addition to The Rebels, there were packs who had ridden in to represent other UK MCs, independents like The Hangmen come to pay their respects, and support clubs like The Reapers come to pay their dues. There was a sizable contingent from The Chopper Riders Club of Great Britain and a multitude of groups from smaller side patch and rallying clubs.

And there was a sizeable overseas contingent as well from friendly and Brethren affiliates and support clubs across Europe. Across the car park I saw a gamut of foreign patches, some of which I recognised like Saturnalia MC and Ragnarök MC, as well as some that I didn't, such as Loki MC.

All told, we ended up with a funeral column of probably about a thousand bikes or so together with a nervous, heavy and very visible police presence.

I found out that the plan was to hold two funerals today. First we would be riding over to a crematorium at Mortlake for Shady Aidie. Then once we were done there, we would form up and ride to Birmingham for Nugget's send off in the afternoon.

Greasy Fingers' family had requested a private event and after some negotiations the club had given its permission but it had been agreed that the North East Charter members would go along on a low key basis to represent the club.

I watched the TV coverage of the convoy later the next day. It was like the beginning of *Stone*, the Aussie biker movie. One of the networks had filmed it from a bridge above a bit of dual carriageway, and for minute after minute the camera just ran as below it swept a slowly travelling twin line of outlaw and associated bikes that seemed to stretch out as far as the camera could see in rigid formation and dead silence apart from the continuous rumble of the passing exhausts. And then finally, once the last of the outlaws had passed, there came a mass of other bikes, a knot of individuals with no particular order, trailing after the convoy like a shoal of pilot fish around a great white shark.

It's a weird thing to look at that piece of film and to realise that I was actually in it, part of one of those crawling lines of threat.

And outside of the convoy, riding in formation with it, a screen of police bikes and marked patrol cars, their high vis jackets, full on headlights and circling blue lights providing a strange strobing unreality to the scene and the darkness of the body of bikers.

Many of the outlaws were riding bare headed. If asked they would say it was a sign of respect to their fallen brothers. Perhaps it was, but it was also a huge two fingers to the escorting cops, a provocation, but one the police wisely ignored. The bikers weren't in a mood to be fucked around with and the cops knew it.

All the same the substantial size of the police presence was a deliberate statement on the part of the authorities. What were they afraid of, I wondered? Hundreds of bikers turning east after the body was in the ground and riding across to lay waste East Anglia's biker haunts, killing any Mohawks that they could find on the way in some two-wheeled bloody pogrom?

Probably.

And given the grim mood the guys were in, I couldn't blame them if they were.

Monday 17 August 2009

Bob was being his usual acerbic self on the phone.

I thought about asking him if he could sort out my traffic tickets as part of our deal but decided against it. I might just piss him off more than he already seemed to be.

'Well, the way I'm hearing it from my sources,' said Bob, 'it was your boys that started it.'

'My boys?' I said, 'What do you mean, my boys?'

'Your mob, The Menaces, that's who you're riding with now isn't it?'

'Oh do me a favour, give over will you?' I said in exasperation, 'you know that's crap,' but I couldn't help glancing over from where I was sat talking on the phone and through to where my jacket and its half hidden support patch was thrown over the back of the chair in the kitchen where I had left it.

'But anyway, I don't understand what you mean,' I said, turning back to the desk to focus on my notes which were spread out in front of me, 'The Mohawks had a go at the Toy Run with heavy artillery. In what possible way is that The Brethren starting it?'

'Because they were provoked, that's why,' he said firmly, 'as far as The Mohawks were concerned it was just a matter of defending themselves.'

I snorted. 'By carrying out a pre-emptive strike? Getting their retaliation in first you mean?'

'Have you asked yourself why Capricorn and Dead Men Riding patched over to join The Mohawks in the first place? Have you?'

'No,' I admitted, mentally kicking myself. For a moment I was glad I hadn't gone in to see him and that we were just on the phone. That way he wouldn't see the expression on my face. How could I have been so stupid, I wanted to ask myself, it was such an obvious question, but it was one which I had completely overlooked.

'When they would have known it could only mean one thing, and that was trouble?' he continued.

He had a major point there, and I knew it.

'Like I said, based on our crap Intel as you put it, as far as we knew up until two weeks ago, all was peaceful out there in the big bad outlaw biker world.'

'Apart from the odd murder in Lincoln and nightclub bombings you mean?'

'But it was quiet in the top clubs' world,' he insisted, 'they were getting along, they each had their territories. Sure there was the odd bit of friction but everyone was making money. And right up until Boom-Boom got his, that included the bigger regionals like Capricorn and Dead Men Riding. And if there was one thing that the existing senior big clubs could agree on, it would be that they wouldn't want a new hustling crew like The Mohawks setting up on UK turf.'

'So if they were taking each other out why did Capricorn and Dead Men Riding bury the hatchet and join up to rock the boat?' I asked out loud.

'So, indeed, why rock the boat?' he repeated. I could just hear the sound of smugness in his voice now that he knew he had one over on me.

'Even without that weekend, just the patch over itself would guarantee trouble. Capricorn and Dead Men Riding knew that, knew that they would be attacked just for changing the scene, so why do it?' he continued, dragging it out.

'Alright then clever dick, you obviously seem to know, so why did they do it?'

'Well, we've been doing some fast digging since then, playing catch up on these shits, and now, like I said, we think it was because they were provoked.'

'How?'

'Seems like The Brethren's charter up in Cambridge were getting greedy. Believe it or not there's a clubbing scene even up in Lincolnshire...'

'Is there?' I interrupted, 'Where for God's sake?'

'Peterborough, Grantham, Lincoln; anywhere there's a town big enough to support a club or two, and both Capricorn and Dead Men Riding had interests in it.'

'Interests?' I asked out loud.

'Security, doors, clubs, raves, all the usual crap.'

It made sense. Controlling the doors was one of the key ways to move gear anywhere in the country. If you had the bouncers, then you were in charge of who came in, which if you were dirty would naturally include your dealers, and who stayed out which would mean anyone else. With Capricorn being into E and acid, the dance scene was a natural fit for them.

'Any problems between them? The two clubs I mean, before this?' I asked.

'No, not really. The two clubs have rubbed along together alright generally. Sure there's been a bit of grief between them occasionally, but for the most part they had it divvied up nicely between them and we reckon that in any event Capricorn were Dead Men Riding's main wholesalers.'

'So Dead Men Riding wouldn't want to tackle Capricorn because they would lose their main source of stuff...' I said.

'And Capricorn were happy to leave Dead Men Riding be as it gave them a route over into Leeds for their gear,' he replied.

'A marriage made in Heaven.'

'Whatever.'

'So then,' I asked, 'if they were both so chummy then who...'

'Stuck Boom-Boom?'

'Yes.'

'I'm coming to that.'

'And the nightclub bomb?'

'That too.'

I waited. He was enjoying his little triumph so I guess I just had to let him get on with it.

'Anyway, so all was cosy until earlier this year, when The Brethren decided that they wanted a slice of the action and tried to muscle in.'

Cambridge, I thought, so that would have been Thommo and his boys. Had Thommo decided to make a bid to expand his territory, his influence, and his income? That could make sense from what I had seen of him. I guessed that the triumphant conquest of a new producing territory, for the club, and everything which would come with it, was a prize that he would be keen on, one that would help him raise his profile and his standing within the club.

To the victor the spoils, I thought.

'So what happened?'

'It was just low level stuff to start with. Punch ups, beatings. The Brethren told them how it was going to be from then on, after which they just tried to enforce it and anyone who didn't toe the line, didn't want to fit in with the new arrangements, well they were fair game as far as The Brethren were concerned.'

'And the other clubs? What did they do?'

'Well, what do you expect they did? It was their local livelihood that was at stake so to start with they fought back to defend it.'

'And then?'

'Well, you can work out for yourself how it went from there. Things escalated.'

'Boom-boom?'

'Boom-boom and then bang.'

So it hadn't been a beef between the clubs, Bob was saying. Instead it had been The Brethren putting the squeeze on both clubs with the hit and the arson. And if you put enough pressure on something, occasionally what you got was fusion, and a bloody great bang.

Suddenly something made sense. Something, what with everything else going on I'd been meaning to speak to Bob about anyway.

'I'll tell you something I have found out that your lot haven't picked up.'

'Oh, what's that then?' he asked.

'You know that shooting in Leeds, the one a couple of days before the run?'

'Yes.'

'It's connected.'

'Connected? How?'

'The bloke that was killed, Jeremy Arnold…'

'What about him?'

'He was a new Cambridge patch, went by the name of Chugger. He'd only just been made up which I guess is the reason no one's made the link so far at your end.'

'Christ, so that was the answer then!'

I was confused by that.

'Answer? Answer to what?' I demanded.

'DMR and Capricorn were putting out feelers after the squeeze started. They were trying to speak to the powers that be in The Brethren, they sent at least one, maybe more messages asking The Brethren to call the dogs off, and get Cambridge back in check before it got too late…'

'Before it came to war you mean?'

'Yes. And that last week they were waiting for a response.'

'But the Brethren didn't make it? And then Chugger from Cambridge pitches up in Leeds looking to put the squeeze on someone over a drug debt and Dead Men Riding and Capricorn take that as their answer?'

'Looks like it doesn't it?' he agreed.

'Jesus! So then what?'

'Well Capricorn and Dead Men Riding are regional clubs, big in their areas but they would have known they would be no match for The Brethren with their national and international network and resources if it came to all out war.'

'So they had decided they needed allies if that was the way it was going?' I guessed.

'Got it in one. If you find yourself getting into a fight with The Brethren and you haven't got the numbers or the access to the hardware they have, what are you going to do? You're going to look to team up with some big hitters yourselves aren't you, someone who you know wants an in to the country and someone who has access to the heavy gear that you don't have, but are going to need to take on The Brethren.'

'So they patched over to The Mohawks since they were the ones who could provide them with the weaponry they would need?'

'Absolutely.'

'Christ.'

The Guardian

Tuesday 18 August 2009

Takeover Attempt Backfires

Iain Parke, Crime Correspondent

Police sources believe a dispute over territory lies behind Sunday the 2nd's attack during which six people were killed as well as a fatal shooting in Leeds the week before.

Senior officials within SOCA point to an apparent attempt over the last few months by The Brethren charter in Cambridge to muscle in on the security and door trade in Lincolnshire and Yorkshire as being the spark which lit the fuse leading directly to the violence at the Brethren's event.

'This region was regarded as belonging to local independent clubs: Capricorn MC of East Anglia and The Dead Men Riding MC of Yorkshire,' said a spokesman. 'Initially it was feared that the recent upsurge in trouble, which started with the murder in May of Archie 'Boom-Boom' Norman, vice president of the Lincoln charter of the Dead Men Riding, outside the Aurora nightclub in Lincoln where he was in charge of security, followed by the firebombing of a Capricorn MC linked nightclub in King's Lynn, was the result of a local power struggle between the two clubs.'

However according to police sources, it now seems that the attacks were actually conducted by members of The Brethren who had decided to move in and take over and there is speculation that the fatal shooting in Leeds on 28 July of Jeremy 'Chugger' Arnold, a recently made up member of the Cambridge charter of The Brethren may also be linked to the dispute.

'But the local clubs chose to stand and fight rather than give up their ground,' said a police spokesman, who believe that it is this action which then led local clubs to merge, and to form a UK charter of The Mohawks so as to gain access to the support of a rival internationally organised club in their struggle with The Brethren.

'We think that's where the weaponry used came from,' said the spokesman, although as yet the police do not seem to have been able to identify any individual suspects in the assault, while a spokesman for The Mohawks MC charter denied the club had any involvement.

'People talk about bikers like us having a war with other clubs but it's not like that at all. Sure there's rivalry and we are proud of our colours and occasionally there's a bit of aggro or a punch up, but it's nothing like it says in the papers. The people who write this crap, they do it to sell newspapers, they like to make out we're some kind of mafia but it's just not true. We're just ordinary guys who like riding our bikes and our club, but people don't write that since it doesn't sell papers.'

Meanwhile, following the massive turnouts for the dead bikers' funerals at the weekend, behind their steel shuttered clubhouse doors, the outlaw biker scene has returned to being eerily quiet.

7   Causus belli

Wednesday 19 August 2009

I was on the phone to Bob again.

'So how's the war going then?' I asked.

'Still low level,' he confirmed, 'just tit for tat stuff at the moment. The Cambridge crew versus their local targets.'

Then I heard the blare of the horn outside. I peered out to see what the noise was.

'Oh shit!'

'What's up?' he asked.

'It's Bung,' I told him, almost whispering as I continued to watch out the window to where Bung was sitting, one spider's web tattooed elbow hanging out of the car's open window in the sunshine, one burly hand in a fingerless black leather glove flat on the roof of the car, his black shades trained on my front door, 'he's turned up outside my house.'

The Brethren dropping by with no notice was not a development I was very comfortable with, particularly given what was happening at the moment. I didn't want to become a casualty in their war.

'What's he doing?'

'He's parked up and is just sitting there at the moment.' There was another blast of the horn.

'What does he want?'

'How the hell do I know? Wibble hasn't been in touch about getting together.'

'Well go and see then.'

'OK, but hang on will you?'

'I'll be here.'

*

Cautiously I stepped outside, darting looks either way along the street, just in case there was something wrong, and leaving the front door open behind me for a fast retreat.

Bung waiting in the car watching me expressionlessly as I came down the path and leaned down to talk to him through the open window.

'You're wanted,' he said without preamble.

'What for?' I asked.

Behind the caveman beard he almost cracked a smile.

'Witness for the prosecution,' he said sardonically, 'get in.'

*

I went, but on conditions – no blindfold, I wanted to see where the hell I was going this time.

'Fair enough.'

And I went back inside to get my shit together first. Lock up and stuff.

'OK, but don't take long.'

Hurriedly I picked the phone back up where to my relief Bob was still holding.

'He wants me to go with him,' I said, 'he says Wibble wants to see me.'

'Well that's hardly a surprise now is it?' he commented. 'Not after your last little piece.'

And then for the lack of anything else, I gave him as much detail as I could about the car.

*

'Called the cops?' Bung asked conversationally as we pulled away from the kerb.

I glanced across at him, but he seemed perfectly relaxed. 'Didn't need to,' I said, 'I was on the phone to SOCA when you turned up.'

Bung just laughed at that. 'Well, that'll have saved you the cost of a call then won't it?'

'You could put it that way,' I said glancing away again as we headed out into the ordinary traffic, 'So where are we going Bung? Is this another mystery tour?'

'Nope,' he said, 'clubhouse.'

'To see Wibble?'

'All the guys. Wibble, Scroat, Toad.'

105

'Toad?' I'd heard of him but never met him.

'From up north.'

'Oh, OK.'

But then to my surprise twenty minutes or so later, instead of ducking off the North Circular towards Wembley, Bung kept going. I had a sudden sinking feeling in the pit of my stomach about where we were heading, it didn't take a genius to work it out.

'M11?' I asked with a sinking heart.

'Yep,' he said.

So that was it, I might as well settle back for the ride. We were off out towards Cambridge.

*

I hate the M11. It's one of the most boring bits of road in the country.

One of the weirder moments of my riding career was coming down it one weekend on my own back when I had a seven-fifty in the days before the Guzzi, travelling mile after straight mile of seemingly endless and deserted road. I don't know whether it was just the boredom or whether I was still a bit stoned after the night before's party but it seemed as though I was going nowhere. All sense of progress was just falling away and it felt as though I was going slower and slower, crawling almost to a halt, the tarmac unmoving beneath me until eventually I put my feet down off the pegs and flat onto the road so convinced was I that I was still.

Only to be jerked awake by the near tank-slapper that ensued as my boots got kicked from underneath me at nearly ninety miles an hour knocking the bike sideways with a shock as for a moment my balance was thrown all over the place. The bike was fishtailing wildly and with an instinctive and desperate twist of the throttle and a stamp down on the gearshift I gunned the already screaming engine, the tacho zooming into the red zone at nine, ten thousand rpm and threw myself down, zits to the tank and elbows tucked in, pushing my weight forward as I wrestled the bars back under control. With my heart in my mouth, the bike hung on the edge for a moment that felt like forever, and then the torque snapped in, lifting the bike's head and trying to fling it to either side as the back hunched down and then shuddered back into line as I accelerated wildly, touching the ton before I wound it back down again and retired my shattered nerves to turn off at the next exit and go looking for the first lay-by burger van for a coffee, fag and bacon sarni.

I'd never been back on it since, in or on any form of transport.

So meanwhile, I had plenty of time to chat to Bung as he drove, if I could get him to give me anything more than monosyllabic answers.

Much to my surprise, he seemed happy to talk, even after some careful probing and working around towards the subject, about the taboo area of The Brethren's internal politics.

'So what's Wibble's standing like?' I asked him eventually, mentioning some of the points that had come out of my last interview with him, 'Is this situation damaging it?'

Bung shrugged. 'Wibble sort of inherited the club when Damage died, he didn't seize it in an open contest...'

'So do some question or challenge his right to be in charge?

He just grunted dismissively at that.

I thought about our destination and what I'd seen to date of the Cambridge crew, as well as what Wibble had said, and hazarded a guess.

'Was Thommo one of those?'

'Why d'you ask?'

'Oh I don't know. It's just Thommo seemed to be arsey, you know, before the thing.'

Bung smiled grimly, 'Yeah, Thommo fancies himself.'

'Is that a problem?'

'No. It's nothing Wibble can't handle,' he said with an air of finality that discouraged further questioning so we fell silent for a while. Outside the flat fields beside the motorway sped past in boring monotony under the open blue sky.

*

From the road signs I could see we were getting close now, so I stirred myself to break the rumbling silence.

'Can I ask you a question?'

'If you like.'

'Well,' I started, unsure as to how to phrase what I wanted to say, 'Look, normally you guys don't talk to anyone outside the club about what you do, do you? I had it from Damage a lot, *club business is club business.*'

He shrugged without even glancing towards me as if this was all just obvious. 'Yeah, so what?'

'So why are you guys talking to me now? Why are you telling me all this stuff?'

'Beats me.'

'Sorry?' I asked in surprise.

'I've no idea,' he replied, 'It's Wibble's idea, not mine.'

'*Wibble* told you to tell me all this stuff?' I repeated in amazement.

'Yeah. He said that he wanted you to be fully briefed.'

He glanced across at me and added in a perfectly friendly tone of nothing personal, that's just the way it is chum, 'If it was up to me I'd tell you jack shit, but that's the way Wibble wants to play it.'

'Christ,' I said.

Really, I needed to digest that. Apart from anything else I wasn't too sure about how I felt about being 'fully briefed' about what The Brethren were up to. That sounded like very dangerous knowledge to be carrying around.

'And Wibble's the boss, what he says goes, is that it?'

'Sorta.'

Bung had gone back to ignoring me and watching the road as he spoke.

'Sorta?' That sounded odd to me, 'The way Damage told it, when he was in charge he was pretty much top dog and everyone did what he said.'

'Yeah well, that was back when he was around. Things aren't quite the same these days.'

'Aren't they?'

'No.'

'In what way?'

'Well,' Bung shrugged, 'when Damage went, we had to rally round to replace him. There was no one obvious to fully step into his shoes and we didn't want any instability at the top after what had happened, so the three main guys got together to work it out, how to handle it I mean.'

'The leadership?'

'Yeah, we didn't want any trouble over it that could give us grief. After all we'd just lost Damage which was a big shock. He'd been central to the club's business, so it needed to be looked after.'

'So what happened?'

'Well, there's not a lot to say really.' He shrugged. 'Wibble and a couple of other key guys from across the country got together. They agreed it was in everyone's interests that there was a quick succession that could be announced after Damage's funeral because the priority was to keep the business going.'

'Was that it?' I asked.

'Yeah.'

'As it was in everybody's interests?'

'That's right.'

'And Thommo? Was he involved in this?'

Bung glanced across at me and gave me a look as if to wonder whether I was a bit thick.

'Yeah, of course Thommo was involved. He represented the southern charters and Toad represented the northern ones. But someone had to have the title so Wibble took it.'

'Why Wibble?'

'Wibble's Freemen, Thommo isn't.'

Now I realised the real situation at last. It wasn't a dictatorship at all, it was really a triumvirate.

'So there were three of them running it to keep the peace?' I wanted to check my understanding, 'a southern rep, a northern rep and Wibble as P? So Wibble was in office, but not fully in power the way Damage had been?'

'Something like that,' Bung nodded distractedly as he negotiated a roundabout on the outskirts of town and I digested this news and its implications.

'And the Rebels? Where do they fit into this?'

Bung shrugged as if it were of no account. 'It's just good business. If we're in competition then all we're doing is cutting each other's...'

'Throats?' I suggested.

He laughed, 'Yeah well, sometimes I guess, but actually 'margins' is what I was gonna say.'

We took another left turn, passing through what looked like a rundown housing estate.

'But if we co-operate,' he continued, 'we can keep prices high and make more money with less hassle. It's a no brainer.'

Wibble didn't, as Bung put it, seize the post of President, I realised. That was the key. From what Bung was telling me, Wibble was seen to have almost inherited the title. Alright, formally he had been voted in, but I now understood that some of The Brethren undoubtedly saw him as piggybacking on Damage's achievements. So Wibble's problem in essence was that he hadn't yet proved himself, he hadn't won the position outright and in his own right. And until he did so, he would be vulnerable to the barons with their own powerbases below him, who would be continually manoeuvring against him, jockeying for power and looking for their opening.

And proving himself was going to be bloody difficult, especially after the reign of someone with Damage's stature. It was one of those basic rules of life I suppose, never succeed a successful bloke.

I thought about what Bung was saying and what it could mean. It made some kind of sense of what Wibble was up to I supposed. If Wibble hadn't clearly taken the presidency on his own, hadn't built his position on his own reputation, and was having to deal with powerful and rebellious barons beneath him, then would that be a reason for wanting to build his own PR reputation?

But it only made sense so far, I decided. No matter what anyone outside the club thought about him, that surely wouldn't do him much good internally with the guys.

Plus I kicked myself that I'd been missing something so obvious here that I should surely have seen before! The most obvious beneficiary after an event isn't the only beneficiary, or even the only one who expects to benefit.

It was the old *cui bono* issue. Just because he had succeeded to the top title of president didn't mean that Wibble had been the only one to have had, or even just hoped for, a bump up in power as a result of Damage's death.

Of course, Wibble was not the only Brethren who would have had an interest in Damage's death. On the basis of what Bung had just said, there was at least Thommo and this other bloke Toad.

Thommo, obviously, I'd met already. And Toad, while I'd not yet come across him in person in my dealings with any of The Brethren, was a name I recognised. He was a man with quite a reputation within the club.

Of course I remembered then, he'd not been at the Toy Run. Toad had been The Rebel's guest for the day, enjoying their hospitality, as Stu had put it.

Which in reality meant that Toad had been The Rebel's hostage, to be held as their guarantee that they weren't simply riding into an ambush by their old enemies The Brethren. And it was a role for which Toad would have had to volunteer.

So Christ, he had to be someone with balls to step into that one I decided.

Both of them had been promoted to key roles in running the club after it had happened. And who knows, perhaps one of them might even have been expecting to be in with a shout at the top job?

And that, I decided, might shed a whole new light on Thommo's attitude problem with Wibble.

After all, whatever else they were known for, triumvirates weren't famed in history for their great longevity.

Which, I thought, as we passed high hedgerows along a leafy street back out of town, raised another interesting question which I'd been puzzling about on and off over the past year or so, and which had assumed even more relevancy since Wibble and The Brethren had barged their way back into my life at the end of last month.

And that was, why had Damage talked about Wibble in the material he had given me in those prison interviews that went on to become his biography *Heavy Duty People*? In general, as I had realised when I was reviewing and editing the tapes as I prepared the material for writing, Damage had been scrupulous to only name members of The Brethren who were dead as being involved in any crimes.

With one exception. And that was Wibble.

Damage knew his words were going to be published. Hell, that was the reason he had wanted to speak to me in the first place, to get his story out. So why, I asked myself, did he run the risk of implicating Wibble in crimes in what he told me? Wibble hadn't been central to what was going on at the time Damage wanted to talk about, in fact he'd been The Legion's junior patch at the time of the patch over. It would have been easy for Damage to have left his name out altogether, he could have quite easily told his story without it, so why hadn't he?

111

Could it be that far from being his chosen successor as so many assumed, Damage had actually been trying to damage Wibble with what he said?

Certainly that explanation had seemed to make sense if you assumed that it was Wibble who had had Damage killed, and that Damage's speaking to me was intended as his posthumous revenge on the people he realised were moving against him.

This explanation also tied in and answered another question I had asked myself, which was why, in talking to me, had Damage blown the very smuggling route that had been the basis of his power within The Brethren?

The only answer I had been able to think of at the time was that it had been some form of a scorched earth policy. That Damage felt he had already lost control of it and therefore he just wanted to take it down so no one else could benefit from it.

But this all rested on an assumption that Wibble and Damage had fallen out, that Damage believed Wibble was organising some form of coup and had been using me as a tool, for, if not fighting back, then at least taking his revenge.

But what if it wasn't like that, I now wondered.

Did it also work the other way round?

Because even though Wibble was the only living Brethren that Damage had come anywhere close to dropping in it with what he'd told me about Wibble's links to business, he hadn't actually given anything definitive that the cops could use to nail him, had he? Undoubtedly he could have done so if he had wanted to. Damage must have had enough real dirt on Wibble to have the cops bury him if that's what he had wanted, but he hadn't dished that dirt.

But what if, instead of thinking that Wibble was the one moving against him in the club and that Wibble was going to be the one that was going to have him killed so he could take the top slot, Damage was actually supporting Wibble as his chosen successor?

Seen in this light, suddenly what Damage had let slip about Wibble, the hard man who'd become intimately involved with The Brethren's drug business, looked very different.

What, I asked myself, if Damage had been looking to send out a different message about Wibble? A message that Wibble was the one who he wanted as his successor, that he knew the gang's business and that Damage trusted him. What if all that stuff about Wibble had actually been Damage giving him a public character reference for the guys?

And how did this then fit with the way Damage had blown the drug route to me?

Was it, I wondered, because he had come up with something else? Something new that would be under his control or that of someone he trusted? If that was the case, then blowing the old route might simply have been a way to stop other officers in the club from trying to take the operation over and run the business independently of Damage or his chosen proxy.

Christ, it was a long old road I thought to myself, trying to second guess what was going on here.

Bung was slowing down as we approached a small parade of boarded up shops on an out of town estate. He pulled over and parked up in the lay-by in front of the middle one. It had The Brethren's colours painted across the shuttered windows.

'We're here,' he said somewhat unnecessarily as he tugged up the handbrake.

But I was still thinking furiously.

If all this was the case. If Wibble really was Damage's groomed successor, then just because Damage wanted him to get the job didn't mean everyone else would accept him, did it? Particularly once Damage was out of the way. And anyway, what would be in it for Damage once he was gone?

But I could answer that for myself as soon as I asked it. Lots of reasons.

The club for one.

Sharon for a second.

His kid, no – kids, I reminded myself, for a third, as we climbed out of the car.

Was that it, I wondered, thinking about the way Wibble had the attitude-filled young Charlie riding with the club. Was that the deal? Damage would back Wibble so Wibble would look after Damage's kid as the quid pro quo? Was Wibble his guardian, or did it go further, was Wibble really no more than regent for Damage's kid?

I shook my head as I stood back while Bung pressed the clubhouse intercom. It was all just speculation I told myself, all ifs and buts and

113

maybes. I could read everything either way with as much conviction. If I was trying to just theorise I would be building a house on sand.

*

Other than the strikers who were mounting security at the front door under the watchful supervision of a full patch, the place seemed empty, deserted, and silent as we stepped inside and the steel reinforced door was quickly secured behind us.

'Hi Mikey,' said Bung giving him a one-handed clenched arm shake and backslap and completely ignoring the strikers on station by the CCTV monitors, 'how's it going?'

'All quiet,' he replied giving me the evil-eyed once over.

'They out back?'

'Yeah,' he said, 'they're expecting you though. Go on through.'

'That's unusual isn't it?' I asked, 'Having patch on security duty? I thought that was a striker's job?'

'It's a lockdown,' Bung said simply, 'and he's the junior patch, so he's in charge under the sergeant at arms.'

Which, he seemed to think, explained everything I needed to know.

Inside, the old shop was gloomy after the bright sunshine of the drive up since only the light at the back of unit was on, and it took my eyes a few seconds to adjust. The space went a surprising way back. What would once have been the shop at the front of the building was now a bar and poolroom and I followed Bung as he walked through it towards a door outside of which lurked, or tried to in Danny's case, two familiar young figures.

They fell aside without a word to let us pass and as we did so I glanced at Danny to give him a smile and a nod of greeting. He nodded back but I noticed with surprise how changed he seemed. Instead of his usual cheerful demeanour he looked drawn and pale, scared even.

But I didn't have a chance to talk to him as Bung pushed open the door into a room at the rear of the building and led me through. In the dim and distant past I guess it must have been some kind of stockroom, stacked high with tins of beans and racks of canned meat, but now was serving as some kind of a meeting room.

Inside, two chipped metal-legged Formica tables had been pushed together board room style, around which were gathered a set of mostly familiar faces in varying degrees of unwelcoming scowl that checked me at the doorway.

What the hell had I walked into here, I wondered. And more to the point, was I going to walk out of it again?

Wibble nodded Bung and me towards two spare plastic stacking chairs that were empty at the far end of the table. It felt as if everyone's eyes were following me as I reluctantly followed Bung round to the spaces left for us, which I noticed were at just about the furthest point from the door. Although, as I pulled my seat out from under the table and sat down, I tried to console myself with the thought that any idea of escape from the room was pretty academic anyway, as I would still need to get past a security crew on a war footing to exit the clubhouse.

No, I was here for good or ill I decided, as I looked around the room and met the intent states of the silent faces and took stock of my situation.

It looked and felt like we had interrupted a council of war.

Wibble broke the silence after the scrape of our chairs on the lino flooring, asking Bung, 'Did he speak to the cops?'

'I think so,' said Bung matter of factly, without bothering to look at me.

Wibble just shrugged, 'OK, well, it'd be the sensible precaution to take so let's just assume that he did shall we? I guess you're a sensible man in that regard aren't you?' he said, his gaze switching to nail me in my chair.

'I try to be as careful as I can,' I said warily, not knowing where this was going, but not caring for it either.

'Well then, let's all be careful men too shall we?' said Wibble, turning to address the meeting in general.

I thought the plate of biscuits on the table was a nice touch.

8   Business planning

To my left as I faced down the table was Wibble.

Beside him, the blue and white colours of the Rebels' cuts were in stark contrast to those of the Menaces surrounding them, sat Stu and Gibbo, the Rebels' national sergeant at arms. It had to be the first time any members of The Rebels had ever sat on a chair at a Brethren clubhouse I guessed, at least without being tied to it that was.

To my right, facing them on the opposite side of the table, were Thommo and beyond him, one of his Cambridge crew sidekicks whom I'd seen backing him up at the Toy Run confrontation. From where I was sitting I couldn't see his tabs but I guessed he would be the Cambridge VP.

Opposite Bung and me at the far end of the table, and with their backs to the safely closed door was Scroat – there I guessed in his capacity as The Brethren's sergeant at arms. That also explained Charlie's presence outside the door. Since Scroat was Charlie's sponsor as a first tagalong and now striker, in the way that Bung was Danny's, wherever Scroat went, Charlie was expected to follow.

Beside him sat another Brethren whom I'd not seen before, this one with a head shaved bald that had somehow made the rolls of fat that were showing around the back of his neck above a thick gold chain all the more noticeable when I'd come in. So this had to be Toad, the third member of the triumvirate, here to represent the interests of the northern charters.

Toad was a man to be careful of. While I'd never seen him before I still knew about his fearsome, even by Brethren standards, reputation.

Ordinarily I would have assumed that he would therefore be something of a natural ally for Wibble. After all, as northern Brethren they would have a shared history, but I reminded myself, that was probably a dangerous assumption to make, given their current respective positions.

Toad, like Thommo, was one of the barons that Wibble would be having to deal with.

*

I was wrong about the meeting though.

Wibble was obviously in the chair and as he called it to order I quickly realised it wasn't so much a council of war, it was more like some kind of a kangaroo court.

And despite it being on his home turf, equally obviously, it was Thommo who was in the dock.

Bung hadn't been joking with his witness for the prosecution crack. He had been entirely serious.

'Right then,' announced Wibble looking down the table and directly at me with an expression that made me want to crap myself, 'now that you're here, we can begin.'

Begin what? I wondered for a moment, before Wibble pulled a rolled up newspaper from where it had been stuffed into the pocket of the jacket slung over the back of his chair and threw it across to land in front of me.

'Recognise it?'

I hardly needed to glance at it to know what he was talking about, but just to make sure he had it folded to the page of my report. So as I suspected, that was what the silent eye treatment had been about when I walked in.

I decided I had no choice but to try to front out anything that came.

'Of course I do,' I said, looking him straight in the eyes. 'I wrote it, you know that. So what?'

'So what we want to know is, where the fuck did you get it?' he demanded.

'The police, like it says,' I answered.

'Yeah, but who?'

'I can't tell you that.'

There was a growl from the general direction of Scroat which Wibble quelled with a swift flick of his eyes. I never let my gaze switch for a moment. Wibble was my ticket out of here, I knew that. He was my only hope, but equally I knew, only so long as I helped myself by doing whatever it was that he wanted me to. The only trouble with that was, that I didn't know what role he wanted me to play.

The only things I did know for sure were that none of the outlaws were used to anyone saying no to them. But equally, none of the outlaws would have anything but contempt for a grass.

'What the fuck do you mean you can't tell us that?' Wibble demanded, his voice level and cool, but undeniably threatening.

For an eternal moment I didn't say anything. He waited, unblinking, as I made up my mind. I had a choice to make, which way I was going to play it.

I would have one go at this. And if I got it wrong, the chances were that life was about to get seriously unpleasant.

I risked a shrug and a shake of my head. 'I'm sorry Wibble but I just can't. I'm a journalist. We don't do that. I can't reveal my sources.'

Pins dropping would have been noisy. I had just said no to a room full of senior outlaws. This could be about to become extremely ugly extremely quickly.

I couldn't take my eyes off Wibble's face as I desperately searched for some sign as to whether I'd picked the right option.

'You what?' he asked quietly.

I swallowed. Was he giving me a chance to change my mind? A last chance to put a murderous djinn back in the bottle? There was no clue in his voice either way.

There was no sense in backtracking now I thought. That would be a show of weakness, it would just add the abject cowardice which I was certainly feeling to the crime of being a grass in their eyes.

So I answered him back in what I hoped would come out in as level and strong a voice as I could manage.

'Look, it's simple Wibble. We don't snitch. Not to you. Not to anyone. Sorry, but that's the way it is.'

'OK?' Wibble asked the room without looking around.

Out of the periphery of my vision there were nods. I guess I probably remembered to start breathing again about then.

*

Wibble let his gaze drop and I slumped back in my chair feeling lucky to be alive and not pissing blood as Wibble's glare turned to focus on Thommo.

'So is this right?' he demanded jerking his thumb in the direction of the paper.

Thommo just shrugged in response.

'I don't know what he's on about. We were doing some business up that way sure but so what?'

'You were muscling in on the goatfuckers and zombies turf like it says?'

Thommo just shrugged again. 'I don't know where he got that,' he said, darting me a look of pure venom.

'I don't give a flying fuck where he got it, that wasn't the question. Is it right?'

It looked as though Thommo had decided that offence was the best form of defence.

It was just normal business, he told them. Sure they had some business up that way but since when were the zombies' and goatfuckers' patches sacrosanct? And since when did The Brethren need to get anyone's permission to work a patch anywhere?'

'And bring all this crap down on everyone?' Wibble demanded grimly.

'How were we to know it would end up like this?'

'But you know the policy,' Wibble overrode him, 'never to give any excuse that might let those squaw bastards in.'

'How the fuck were we meant to know they'd go running to the squaws?'

It seemed a reasonable point to me but I wasn't going to interrupt. What the hell, it wasn't my party and God knows I didn't owe Thommo and his bunch any favours.

Thommo was still defending himself.

'You want us to push the stuff, so that's what we were doing. That's how you do business, you know that.'

But it looked as though Wibble and the others had heard enough.

'So you started this. So you need to finish this,' he told Thommo, 'and soon.'

Then he added, 'Or if you can't handle it we'll come in and do it for you. Is that what needs to happen here?'

'You?' Thommo snorted, 'You couldn't handle shit.'

'You watch your fucking mouth,' snarled Toad from the far side of the room in a warning tone.

'So what are you going to do?' demanded Wibble.

'Now you want me to talk business is that it? In front of him?' asked Thommo, nodding at me.

Wibble ignored him.

'What are you going to do?' he repeated.

'Well, we know where the squaws' P lives.'

Wibble looked relieved.

'Well at least that's something,' he said, 'Don't tell us anymore, we don't want to know, but make sure it gets done, and soon.'

'And gets done right,' added Toad for emphasis.

The meeting broke up with Thommo and his VP effectively dismissed from the office at his own clubhouse. Scroat and Stu wandered out together, I had the impression that they had separate business that they wanted to discuss.

I stayed sitting at first, waiting for my cue from Bung or Wibble. After the look Thommo had given me I wasn't planning on going anywhere in this clubhouse on my own. Then Bung started to get up and I went to follow him. He was my lift after all and it would be a long walk back to town without him.

But as it happened, it turned out Wibble wanted a word or two anyway once the room had cleared to just us and Toad.

'Where the hell do you think you're going? We've not finished with you, not by a long way. You sit down and shut the fuck up,' he snarled as he saw me move.

I sat back in surprise. I thought he had got what he wanted out of me so I hadn't been expecting an assault like this.

He let me know he was angry at me for having written the story, although it wasn't clear at first which aspects he was particularly concerned about. Certainly the way that it suggested that The Brethren had some responsibility for starting the war seemed to be a major part of the problem. It didn't help with the PR image he was interested in I guessed, but then, I just reported the news, I didn't make it.

'Why not check this shit with us first?' he demanded. 'You've got a Brethren support patch on,' he pointed at the LLH&R tab on my side, 'more than that, you've got my fucking support patch on, so you'd better start thinking seriously about what that means.'

'You spent enough time with Damage,' Toad interjected for the first time. 'We know that and we can see it in your book. You ought to know how it works.'

I'd heard Toad's nickname amongst The Brethren was 'The Terminator.' While Scroat as sergeant at arms was in overall charge of club security, like any serious club The Brethren had some members who were more up for the wet jobs and war than others. In fact there were some who positively liked it and whenever needed would go out of their way to get involved in seeking out and taking down the club's enemies.

And at the top of that list in The Brethren as I understood it, sat Toad's name.

The unspoken implication in Toad's nickname was that he was the club's key hit man whenever there was serious trouble with another club. Even other members of the club could sound slightly nervous when they spoke about him.

'Why do you think we make guys take so long to go through being a striker?' asked Wibble suddenly from out of left field.

I threw my mind back to those long afternoons sitting in Long Lartin listening to Damage and gradually starting to understand how he saw the world. And I knew it wasn't just being about being a striker. The testing never really stopped in The Brethren, there was the formal vote at the end of your first year to catch those who might kick back and slacken off after getting in, and in truth, the club could pull your patch at anytime, busting you back down to striker or even out altogether, *pour encourager les autres.*

'So they can prove themselves? So you know you can trust them?' I ventured.

'So they can handle themselves and won't rat us out you mean?'

I nodded.

'Yeah well sure, it's partly that,' said Toad, 'we can't have no wimps in the club. But it ain't just that. It's also a whole lot more. It's to make sure they're sure. That they've tested themselves and made sure they want to commit...'

'And also,' Wibble continued, 'to see that they are prepared to work hard enough at it to make it. This is something where you only get out of it if you put everything, and I mean everything, into it.'

'Heart and soul,' confirmed Toad seriously.

'It's about LLH&R,' he said, holding up his clenched fist so I could see the ancient green stain of the letters jail tattooed across his broad knuckles, 'If you don't get that about us you don't get shit.'

121

'That's right,' agreed Wibble, 'and you're now wearing a tab that says you support that, so like I said, you'd better start thinking seriously about what that means.'

'LLH&R,' growled Toad with emphasis.

Screw Bob and his *my boys* I thought, the patronising shit.

Meanwhile, Wibble was still preaching the word according to The Brethren.

'You've gotta keep working, you can never stop showing your loyalty to the club; no one's safe from being busted back down to prospect, or even booted out of the club altogether.

'Nobody has a God-given right to the colours, no one, not him,' he said nodding at Toad, 'not me, nobody. Anyone who can't cut it can lose them at anytime.'

'No one?'

'No one, not even me.'

'Well, maybe not Bubba,' joked Toad who seemed to think that their point had been made and was now sitting back to watch Wibble's show.

Bubba was the club's international P back at the mother charter in Detroit, legendary founder of the club back in the late sixties as a roughhouse bunch of bar room brawlers and all round biking bad asses, and still going strong and still firmly in position as P almost half a century later.

'Maybe so,' conceded Wibble reluctantly, 'but it'd be a brave man who tried to take Bubba's patch off him.'

'I'd like to see someone try that stunt.'

'It'd be worth watching.'

'And you're not printing any of this shit here today. You understand that right don'tcha?' said Toad levelly, turning back to me.

The underlying threat was unmistakable.

I nodded. Oh yes. I got the picture.

As I walked out, the two kids were still on slouched sentry duty outside the door. I caught Danny's reluctant eye as I went past but he didn't speak.

I stood by the bar waiting for Bung to finish chatting to Scroat about something so we could go, and to kill time I looked around.

There was definitely something wrong with Danny I decided. I stared at him carefully again and I was sure I hadn't been wrong about what I'd noticed before. The kid was definitely looking shaken.

Ah well, I thought to myself, perhaps he's seeing sense at last and getting out.

Still, I couldn't let him be my problem now, not with what was going down here. Sorry kid I thought, but you're on your own from here on in. I could see all of this going badly wrong if I wasn't careful, and even if I was, who was to say it couldn't still get ugly?

From now on I just needed to make sure I was looking after number one if I was to make sure I was going to get out of this OK.

Other than its somewhat open plan nature due to the type of building, the clubhouse followed much the same interior decor approach as the London one and the North East one I'd visited when I first met Damage. There was a memorial wall where photographs of fallen Brethren took pride of place at the far end of the bar, while the walls elsewhere were covered in plaques and framed souvenirs of runs, parties and shows, and the ceiling was shrouded in a huge Confederate flag.

The bar was brick built with the words Brethren MC worked in relief under an inset cast stone plaque of the patch. There were the usual 'what you see and hear in here, stays in here' notices hanging from the optics and at the far end of the bar a display of support materials for sale, from *Support Your Local Brethren* T-shirts and caps, to a selection of *ACAB* and *Fuck the rules!* style stickers with which to adorn your lid, bike or whatever.

But most striking and affecting of all as I waited was a framed handwritten poem about membership, comparing and contrasting, which hung at the side of the memorial wall. I didn't have my notebook with me at the time so I didn't get a chance to write it down, even if I'd thought it was an appropriate moment to do so, but the sentiments have stayed with me ever since; as it demanded that the reader ask themselves to think if they were someone who just belonged to the club; or someone who contributed to the club.

It made me ask questions about myself.

Was I the type of person who would just be pleased to be identified as something for my own sake? Or would it only mean something to me if it meant being part of a community, a family, with tight bonds, where brother would help brother without question or hesitation?

123

LLH&R, as they said.

Where would I stand if I was put to the test I wondered?

Friday 21 August 2009

The text gave me the address of a phone box in Feltham and a time to be there which was just as darkness was falling. I didn't recognise the sender's number but then that wasn't too surprising if it was from someone paranoid enough to want to play spy crap in West London. Disguising the source of a call from being traced was easy these days if you wanted to, it was just the cost of a fresh pay as you go that could then easily be dumped once you had used it. But why did he want to ring me at a call box I wondered? That was odd.

It did occur to me that it might be a ruse, a call designed to lure me into some kind of an ambush. But then the people I was most scared of just at the moment all knew where I lived anyway so why would they bother? Briefly the plot of that thriller about someone trapped in a phone box by a sniper reared its head. Now who's being paranoid, I thought.

I considered calling Bob to ask his advice about it but the memory of our last conversation still rankled, particularly in view of my most recent dealings with Wibble and The Brethren and besides which, it was too small a thing. Why the hell should I tell Bob everything or worse still, go running to him for advice about every move in my life?

No, deciding whether to go and answer the phone or not was something I felt I ought to be able to handle on my own these days.

The call box stood on its own at a street corner to the side of an Indian owned late night Spar shop. It was an old fashioned red one, stinking of old fashioned piss. I got there ten minutes early. It gave me time to check out the area a bit. There didn't seem to be anyone around. No cars parked with a couple of goons casually sitting waiting, no battered white transits waiting to disgorge a hammer wielding horde.

It was just a quiet street in a rundown suburb.

The phone rang a minute or two after I'd ensconced myself inside and extracted a small reporter's notepad and pen from my backpack.

'Hello?' I said.

'Is that Iain?'

It was the nervousness in the voice that got me. Oh shit, I thought as I recognised it.

'Hi Danny, yes it's me.'

'Are you alone?'

That rankled, but mainly because of my irritation with myself that I had felt as though I might want my hand holding by Bob in order to go to a phone box.

'Danny, I'm in a fucking phone box. How many people do you think are going to be in here with me? Of course I'm on my own.'

'But you came alone?' he insisted, 'No guys, no cops?'

'No,' I sighed, 'No guys, no cops. It's just me here Danny. So what's up? What do you want to talk about, and why all this cloak and dagger.'

'You know you said to give you a call if I wanted to talk.'

'Yes I did, Danny. But funnily enough I've got a perfectly good telephone at home and a working mobile so what I'm a bit puzzled about is what I'm doing in a phone box? What are we doing here?'

'I couldn't call you on those.'

'Why, you think they're bugged?' I joked.

'Yes,' he said with a disarming simplicity.

'Who by Danny? The cops?'

'Them, or the others.'

'What others?' I asked before I worked out who he was talking about. 'Do you mean The Brethren? Come off it, these are bikers for fuck's sake. I know they're tough but they're not the CIA.'

'No, I'm serious, you don't know what it's like. They use detectives to check things out...'

Well I knew that was true from my little chat with Wibble about my long dead smoking history.

'...guys who can find things out. They can hack mobile phones, all sorts, so you just can't be sure what's secure.'

'Like the News of the Screws thing?' I asked since it was back in the papers again.

'Yeah.'

Well I could be in exalted company then if my mobile had been hacked by the same sorts of guys who had gone after the phones of the Royals, MPs and god knew how many celebs for tabloid fodder.

'But now you want to talk?'

'Yes, sorta…'

There was a time when I would have welcomed a conversation with Danny. A time, not so long ago when I would have seen him as a strong potential personal interest story, a source of information, a different viewpoint on the phenomenon of The Brethren from my own; and I think being charitable to myself about my motives for a moment, as someone that I wanted to talk to, to warn off if possible, to help him avoid some of the life choices Damage had made while it wasn't too late.

But that was then. This was now.

And now I knew I probably didn't sound too sympathetic at this stage. My last meeting with Wibble, put together with my last conversation with Bob, had shaken me more than I'd thought. From being independent and above the fray, it now felt like I had slipped through a crack and was rapidly becoming trapped between two large rocks that were beginning to grind together. And it wasn't a pleasant feeling.

But I still didn't really know what it was that Danny wanted to talk about. If it was just how he was feeling, well, I was sorry, but that time had passed and he was on his own on that one. But it could be something more I know. I realised that Danny had gone from being star struck to shit scared between the last two times I'd seen him. Which meant what, I wondered?

But almost immediately I answered my own question. He had to have seen something, heard something, learnt something that had changed him almost overnight. And that something had to have been serious to have had such an effect on him.

And if it was something that serious, then given the sort of shit that was going down at the moment and the potential this situation had for spiralling way out of control, then I guessed it was something that I was going to want to know about.

So it was with a slightly more positive tone that I said, 'Well come on now Danny, make up your mind. Either you do want to or you don't. And if we've got this far I'm guessing you want to, am I right?'

There was silence at the other end of the line.

Make an assumptive close I decided. 'So how do you want to do this Danny? Do you want to talk on the phone or do you want to meet up?'

He wanted to meet up. Well that was good.

And once he had decided it was as though he had screwed up his nerves and just wanted to get on with it before he changed his mind. He was instant, it had to be now, must be this evening. I had to come, he could show me, well tell me, what was going on. But it had to be tonight, now in fact. He named a café out towards the airport by Staines, well away from Wembley and the clubhouse, I noted. I was to be there in half an hour. And I was to come alone.

The café was empty when I got there. I ordered a mug of coffee from the woman in the frayed white apron lounging behind the counter. It's not often you get asked if you want Nescafé these days.

Other than a pair of shell suited youngsters who came in a couple of minutes later and made a beeline for the fruit machine in the corner, there was no one else around. Danny arrived after a few minutes just as I was sweeping up the gritty mess I'd spilled onto the tacky surface of the table whist trying to fill a teaspoon from one of those glass jars with a metal spout on top that was sitting on the table inside which until the vital moment the sugar had seemed to have set into one solid lump.

He had obviously been waiting for me to pitch up to make sure I had come on my own, and then had kept an eye out for a while to see if anyone came in after me.

Danny was crapping himself about being here. I could see that. His eyes swept the room, checking out the woman behind the counter and the swaggering oiks hitting the hold keys on the flashing bandit in the corner as he slipped quickly in through the door and parked himself across the table from me. He was wearing a hoodie, which he kept up so that as he sat facing me, no one looking in from outside would be able to see his head or face.

Paranoid was the word, I decided. Was he on the edge of a nervous breakdown?

I left him there as I organised and paid for another mug of coffee and brought it back to the table.

'Watch the sugar jar,' I warned as he reached for it and indicated the table in front of me, 'it can be a bit of a mess...'

'Unhuh,' he grunted, upending the dispenser over his mug to dump a slew of crystals directly into the swirling brown and white scum of his mug.

'So,' I said, after I'd left him to take the first slurp from his steaming mug as I used my teaspoon to scoop out a few dark spots of undissolved granules, 'what is it that you can show me?'

He lifted his head and his eyes peered out at me from under his hood. 'Like I said on the phone, I can't show you. It's too dangerous.'

'So what are we doing here then?' I cajoled.

'I can tell you about it,' he said in a low voice. Despite the frantic beeping of the fruit machine that seemed to be absorbing the pair in the corner's combined IQ he evidently didn't want to run the risk of being overheard.

'Tell me? About what?'

I sat back in my chair and picked up my coffee. 'Alright then, I'm here, I'm all ears, so what do you want to tell me?'

'Do you know what's going on?' he asked.

'That's not telling me Danny, is it?' I pointed out.

'No, I guess not,' he shrugged, 'but it's just something big is going down and I don't know how much you might already know about it.'

'So what is it that you know?' I pressed.

'You don't tell anyone where you get your stuff from do you?' he asked, 'I heard Bung saying something about it.'

'No, I don't, not without their permission.'

'Not to the cops?'

I shook my head, 'No.'

'Or even the guys?'

I shook my head again, 'No, that's probably what Bung was talking about.'

'Yeah, he was saying that you'd refused to tell them something. He thought it was funny but Scroat thought they should have filled you in for it.'

Jesus, I thought.

'Yes, they wanted to know where I'd got a story from.'

'And what did you say?'

'I said I couldn't tell them.'

'And that's it?'

'Yes, sorry, but that's it. And that's why you've come to me? Because you think I won't tell anyone where I've heard it, whatever it is, from?'

'Yes,' he nodded, 'I guess that's about it.'

'But what is it you want to tell me? And why is it so important that you stay a secret?'

He hesitated, and looked down at the coffee mug he was now grasping in both hands on the table as though trying to order his thoughts before he spoke.

'What is it Danny?' I asked gently eventually, afraid that his nerve might fail at the last moment and he would bolt without now talking about whatever it was that he knew. 'Come on then, tell me about it.'

'Well…,' he sighed at last, putting one hand up to rub first his eyes, and then the stubble of his shaven head, 'I don't know anything for sure.'

'OK then, tell me what you do know, and we'll just take it from there,' I said, and he began to speak.

9   The mixing desk

Danny hadn't been on the funeral run he told me.

I explained to him that I knew that, as I had been there as part of The Brethren contingent.

Instead, as Bung's tagalong, he had followed his sponsor and headed his bike on up to Liverpool that day at the back of the pack as part of The Brethren's delegation attending The Rebel's own grim faced run as a mark of respect.

It had been a heavy day. Danny had been acutely conscious of the need to keep his end up. He was representing The Brethren, even as a tagalong, in what had only the month before, been sworn enemy territory where being caught wearing a Menace flash would have resulted in a ferocious kicking at best. And now here they were, here he was, mingling with The Rebels as they buried one of their own, killed at a Brethren event.

His job as he saw it was to maintain a tight-faced dignity. He was relieved that there was little outward sign of hostility from The Rebels towards The Brethren contingent on their arrival. They had been welcomed by Stu who had assigned Badger, the local charter's sergeant at arms to act as liaison and the rest of the crew treated The Brethren patches with respect.

But then as a tagalong, Danny's lowly status meant that he hardly counted anyway in dealings between patches of the two clubs. He was used to the way a patch holder would order him around and the same sorts of ranks seemed to apply within The Rebel's hierarchy so he just slipped in behind Bung and acted as normal and that seemed to work.

The Brethren had formed up as an element of the convoy that cruised slowly along behind the hearse, lids off in a silent show of respect that the escorting cops wisely decided to turn a blind eye to.

They had stood as part of the crowd around the graveside throughout the service and had listened as Stu said some words.

Then they had formed up again and ridden back with The Rebels to their clubhouse where the boozing would start.

Bung had kept The Brethren on a tight leash that night. They were there to party, to show their respects and to uphold the honour of the Brethren. But they were also there as part of an only recently concluded peace deal with some of their most bitter rivals and neither Bung nor Stu, with Badger's help, wanted to let any incident occur that might threaten the new entente. Stu and Badger wanted to make sure there was no needle about the death happening at The Brethren's run and Bung wanted to ensure no Brethren overstepped the mark on The Rebel's hospitality whatever any previous beefs might have been.

And again, Danny had kept close to Bung as his sponsor, so as to be useful and keep out of trouble.

And that's what had done it.

'That's when I heard them,' he said.

'Heard who?'

'Bung and Stu. They were talking.'

'About what?'

'About what's going on. And what's going to happen next.'

It was a wake for their guy Ric, so it was a party. The beer was flowing over the bar and the jukebox was going in the corner with an eclectic mixture of the usual fare, rock and metal *Quo, The Damned, Guns 'n 'Roses, Metallica*. A shit-kicking party style selection of white trash pride southern boogie from the likes of *.38 Special* and *Molly Hatchet* was stomping out at full volume, so when Bung and Stu had wanted to talk about what was happening, they had needed to just about shout in each other's ears to be heard. Which was fine, and reasonably secure until Danny had wandered up from behind them with their next round of beers.

'They didn't notice I was there at first, they were sort of huddled together over a table so I had to edge round them to put the glasses down. I only caught the end of what they were saying really. Bung shut up once he realised I was there.'

'Yes. And what had he been saying before then?' I asked.

'Well that's it really. I wasn't too sure. But it made me start thinking.'

So he repeated what he had heard for me.

'Bung was saying something about *Not to worry, they were meeting up to organise it. As arranged.*'

'It? What's it?' I asked.

'Then he said something about *taking both of them out as one operation.*'

'I don't like the sound of taking them out.'

'Well, no shit Sherlock!' Danny hissed, 'why the fuck do you think I'm talking to you now?'

I had wondered about that myself.

'So why are you talking to me then Danny?' I challenged, 'Why not just keep your head down and get on with doing your time to get in to the club?'

'But that's it, don't you see? I wasn't joining up to take part in some kind of fucking war. Killing people, that's not what it was about for me.'

Well welcome to the real world son, I thought as I listened. Better late than never.

'And Bung knows that I must have heard something.'

'*Three can keep…*' I started but he waved me quiet before I could finish and buried his head in his hands again.

'Was there anything else?' I asked. 'OK, so what you heard wasn't pretty but it doesn't sound like the end of the world either does it?'

He didn't move.

'Well it's hardly worth knocking you off for is it, if that's what you're worried about?' I said, hopefully with more conviction in my voice than I actually felt.

He lifted his head slowly and looked back up at me, his hands still covering the bottom of his face.

'Then he said that *Scroat was organising the necessary and if Stu's guys wanted in they should send someone down.*'

'And when was this to happen?' I asked.

'When? Tomorrow night.'

'Did they say where?'

'No.'

'That's a pity,' I said.

'Not exactly,' he added

'What do you mean not exactly?'

'Well Bung didn't give him an address as such, that was just when he noticed I was there. But he said enough that I recognised where he meant.'

I wanted him to go with me to show me, but that was a step too far for Danny.

He told me about it, the old factory unit that Scroat used for his operation respraying ringed cars before he shipped them on.

'That's where it's going to happen. That's where they're organising it. Bung didn't say so but he let slip enough that I realised it's where he had to be talking about.'

'Organising what?' I wanted to know.

'I told you, I don't know!' he protested, 'Other than that it's obviously something big and it's not just the squaws they're after.'

'Woah there! Now wait a minute,' I said taken aback in surprise. I had missed something here. 'What do you mean it's not just the squaws? I thought you said Bung told Stu they were going to take out both of them?'

'Well exactly. That's just what I said. *Both of them.*'

'You mean…?'

'I mean it's not just the goatfuckers and the zombies they are after is it? It can't be. They're all now one club aren't they? The squaws?'

'Yes, I suppose they are. But then…'

'So then if they're one, and Bung's talking about taking out two, you have to ask the question don't you? Who's the other one?'

'Christ!' I said. Who indeed, I wondered to myself as I realised that this was what had really freaked Danny out. He could have handled a plot to get The Mohawks I decided. He would have seen that as fair. They had committed an act of war, they had to be answered back in kind and in extremis. That was how war worked and he was signed up for it.

'So who do you think it is?' I asked. 'You must have some suspicions surely?'

'I don't know and I don't want to know.'

He was lying. I was sure of that. Either Bung had let slip more that Danny was telling me even now, or he had worked it out for himself. But Danny had realised that this was going to be a war with casualties in unexpected places. Places he was not comfortable with. Places too close to home. And that was his real problem with the whole thing.

'And I don't want to know either. But I do know I don't want to have anything to do with it. I don't want to spend the rest of my life inside for what an arsehole like Scroat gets up to, Bung or no Bung.'

Yeah, but Bung won't protect you if you become an issue with his brothers, I thought. He'd probably see it as his job to do you himself.

No, in Danny's shoes I decided that I'd probably be more scared of Bung at this stage than Scroat, whatever he was up to. However cuddly a Wookie impression Bung could give, he was a full patch Brethren who acted as Wibble's bodyguard and personal rep. If there was some serious club business that Bung ever came to realise he had let slip to Danny, then making sure no one else knew he had done so would undoubtedly be high up on Bung's personal agenda.

*

As he had requested, I waited in the café for a quarter of an hour after he had left, a hunched figure that immediately disappeared under his hoodie into the darkness.

Was this some kind of set up I asked myself?

Was it a trap?

Was this some kind of test?

Had Wibble had Bung put him up to it? Had the kid come to see me with this story to see what I did?

I didn't think so, not unless the kid was a great actor, and frankly I didn't think he was. Danny was too stressed for it not to be real.

He might not have heard what he thought he did, or it might not mean what it sounded like, but I was convinced that Danny believed what he had heard.

It didn't rule out that Bung might have deliberately set him up, that it might be a test of Danny and his ability to keep club business quiet, but you could go down a whole rabbit hole of what ifs and how do you knows about anything if you weren't careful.

But one thing was for sure. I had had all I was going to get from Danny on this. He was going to keep hanging around with Bung and act like nothing had happened in the hope that this would all blow over with no more comeback.

So he wasn't going to contact me, or tell me anything more.

And he certainly wasn't going anywhere near Scroat's factory unit tomorrow night to see what was actually going on. If I wanted to take that trip, then I was firmly on my own as far as he was concerned.

I think he had wanted to talk to me since I was the only one he thought he could talk to, whether it was to get his side of the story told to an outsider in case trouble came later, whether it was to unburden himself, whether it was to help him think it through, or a mixture of all of these and other reasons, he didn't say and I didn't ask.

I think it was only when I started to press for details of the address he was talking about that he starting to realise what the implications of speaking to me might be. I don't think he had ever expected that I might actually want to go and investigate. I think he just thought I would be a safe pair of ears and nothing more.

Towards the end and before he walked out, he became quite agitated. Luckily the teenagers had left just before, no doubt in search of a corner shop which would sell them some no questions or proof of age asked cans of Special Brew.

'You don't go and get yourself fucking caught you hear me?' he hissed. 'And whatever the fuck you say to anyone, you didn't hear nothing from me? Get it?'

'I get it,' I tried to reassure him. Don't worry.

'Don't worry? Don't fucking worry?' he scoffed as he stood up, 'you've got no fucking idea what you're dealing with here mate.'

'So just don't pull me down with you when you go that's all,' was his parting shot.

I was on my own then.

Well there was nothing for it but to check out his story I supposed.

Carefully.

And there was no time like the present.

*

The place wasn't too hard to find from Danny's description and directions. It was an old yard at the far end of a nondescript industrial estate's concrete slabbed cul-de-sac.

The whole estate was just across a dual carriageway from a bright new modern white and shiny plastic looking 24 hour Tesco's Extra so I had

135

dumped my car in the car park and had walked out of the car park and into the night. The estate was sporadically lit by blue-white security lighting on some units and yellow sodium lamps from high up windows in units that were obviously running some kind of night shift. As I turned the corner and headed down towards the end where Scroat's yard was, I left even these and the glow of the one working concrete streetlamp behind, which suited me just fine.

The site when I got there was surrounded by a tall chain link fence on concrete posts, overhung with a roll of barbed wire. Inside, most of it seemed filled with high piled door-less and wheel-less sagging car wrecks waiting their rusty turn for the crusher. The building itself covered the front left hand corner of the plot beside the double gates with their banner announcing the business's dedication to reclamation and motor salvage, all bought for cash and best prices paid; and was an old, steel-framed shed, clad in grey corrugated boards tastefully decorated by the local kids with an assortment of spray-painted tags and pictures of dicks.

Being careful to watch out for the dog shit, I edged my way down a track that ran through beside the unit from the concrete apron out front and onto some wasteland behind that looked an ideal spot for a bit of shagging and glue sniffing for the yobs from the estate on the other side. Here a thick bank of brambles and stinging nettles separated the narrow tarmaced path from the yard's fencing which had an added facing of rusty and corrugated iron sheeting, again decorated in various sized tags mainly by someone called something that looked like *Tozer1*, and gave an added deterrent to the barbed wire above.

At the end of the plot the path went over a small ditch of black glutinous looking mud sprinkled with old drink cans on a thick planked bridge and opened out into the blackness of shadowing trees. Turning across the grass I walked on, along the back of the site until I saw what looked like about as good a place as any for what I had in mind.

There was a bit of a gap in the brambles and reeds on either side of the ditch so I jumped across easily. The fence ahead of me was about ten foot high and immediately behind it were looming black ranks of piled dead cars between me and the shed inside. I'd seen no sign of an alarm and I doubted that they had one since the local kids would set it off too regularly, so I was prepared to take the chance.

I had thought about bringing bolt cutters to make a hole in the fence but had decided against it as it would leave behind evidence that someone had been visiting. Instead I had decided to climb the fence. I had brought my bike gloves with me anyway to wear since I didn't want to be leaving any fingerprints behind and there was nothing for it but to take my chances with the three strands of barbed wire at the top.

It was a bit of a scrabble, and for a moment I thought I was going to do the striker's trick or worse on the spikes, but I managed to get my legs over without ripping my nuts off and was quickly down the other side.

I stood stock still for a moment, waiting for any noise of an alarm or shouts or hurrying feet that might have meant I had been heard, or spotted on CCTV or set off some alarm that I hadn't noticed. Shit what did I know about it? I was a journalist not a cat burglar for Christ's sake.

But over and above my pounding heart and gasping for air after the unaccustomed exercise there was nothing I could hear. So after a minute or two to get my nerves and my breathing back under some kind of control, I began to worm my way cautiously into the yard.

The one thing I had been able to get out of Danny was that there weren't any guard dogs here, which was something I had been afraid of. Danny said Scroat had tried them but found they were too much hassle with the numbers of people he had coming and going; while when they bit the general punters it just brought the cops sniffing round, so reluctantly he'd got rid of them.

'Got rid?' I had asked.

Danny had cocked his fingers and fired silently.

Great, I thought.

I didn't have much of a plan. It was really just to get in, see what I could see, and then get the hell out again. Keep it short and simple.

Now I was there and in, the only way to see something looked like it meant getting close to the building, so that was the way I headed through the yard.

The serried stacks of cars stopped a dozen or so yards short of the building. Beside it lay an open apron, on the other side of which was the huge shape of a car crusher and the parked skeleton of a mobile crane which I guess was there to feed it.

From this angle though I was now looking at the back of the building, which had a couple of roller shuttered entrances and I could see that unlike at the front, here there were vehicles parked outside and glimmers of lights showing from inside.

There didn't seem to be anyone on watch. Was whatever they were up to too hush hush even for strikers I wondered? So I decided to take the chance and get closer.

As quietly as I could I crept along the line of the stacked body shells until I could scurry across the open space to the shelter of the shadow of a parked up transit van. Scanning the building behind it I saw that a row of windows ran along the wall beside the shutters. So crouched over, I slunk across the gap and peered in through the glass.

No joy. It was just some kind of office. There were desks covered in papers and phones, with a girlie calendar from some tool suppliers hung on the wall above battered looking filing cabinets, next to a whiteboard with scribbled notes of jobs to be done in overlapping smudged blue marker.

It was at about this point that I asked myself the question that I should really have asked sometime before. What the fuck did I think I was doing here?

But then I didn't listen to myself. Quietly I ducked down and crabbed sideways to the next opening.

More offices. But this time with an open door and a glazed internal wall that gave a restricted view into the shed's interior where there were lights on and figures working.

I shuffled sideways a bit more, still keeping my head just at the level of the windowsill to prevent any chance of being seen from the inside although in reality there was little chance of that, and I settled down to watch.

At first, I couldn't work out what it was that I was seeing going on.

*

Inside there were three guys working, no, four, I corrected myself, as another figure emerged from a blind spot behind the wall of the first office. I recognised Scroat immediately of course, as well as Toad. He seemed to be in charge and was peering into the maw of some kind of a machine that looked a bit like a cement mixer painted yellow on a blue stand, and then, as if having made some kind of judgement, pointing at two pallets of sacks stacked in a corner. The other guys walked over and began picking them up and bringing them over to where the machine was rotating. The sacks looked heavy from the way they were being carried. I guessed at around twenty-five kilos each.

Scroat had a knife opened and he began to slit the top of each bag as it was brought over so that the other Brethren could pour the contents, which were some kind of off-white granules, into the mouth of the machine discarding the sacks into a bin bag, of which I noticed there were a couple already stacked and tied beyond the machine. The guys were working quietly and efficiently, as if it was something they had had plenty of practice at.

They put six bags of whatever it was into the machine, leaving a whole stack more on the pallet, and left it to rumble on for a while. Whatever it was they were doing, they were doing it in batches, presumably based on the capacity of whatever the machine was.

After a few minutes, Scroat and Toad checked the machine again and seemed satisfied.

Scroat stopped the machine. There was a logo on the side and some kind of name, a SKIOLD KB160, whatever the hell that meant.

As Toad disappeared out of view, the others slowly tipped the maw of the machine sideways and then poured out the machine's contents onto a blue tarpaulin they had spread in front of it at which point I understood what it was.

It wasn't a mixer, it was a crusher. A farmyard barley crusher.

They had used the machine to grind the granules down into a fine powder and from the careful way they were handling it, they evidently didn't want to make any mistakes with whatever it was. Then they dragged the tarpaulin away from below the mouth of the crusher so the next batch of granules could go in.

Then I really got confused.

Toad reappeared from behind the other office bearing catering sacks of what I could clearly see from the labels was icing sugar. What the hell does he want that for I wondered? Only to see him take out his knife again and slitting the first of the bags, he dumped the contents onto the pile of powder already there.

Then as the other two recharged the crusher with fresh supplies of granules, Toad and Scroat each took one of those big plastic shovels, they sort they sell for clearing snow, and began to carefully and thoroughly mix the heap of powder on the tarpaulin.

When they had finished to Toad's satisfaction, one of the other guys was instructed to fetch something else, disappearing somewhere inside the workshop and reappearing a moment later carrying an oil drum that he set down on a wooden pallet beside the tarpaulin.

They packed it carefully. First in went about a quarter of the powder to fill the bottom of the can, then as the other guys kept shovelling, Toad bent down and picked up a length of steel piping which was about three quarters of the depth of the drum in length and perforated along its length with lines of drilled holes. As he held it in place, the other Brethren continued to fill the drum, packing powder in around the pipe with the plastic shovel until at last it was full to the brim and Scroat could gently ease the top back on with just the wires from the end of the pipe sticking out through the holes that had been drilled in the lid for them.

Then calling the others over to join them, the men between them cautiously manhandled the full drum up and into the back of a white transit van parked in the shed. From the angle I was looking at I could see that the bed of the van was covered with a thick layer of corrugated cardboard to act as packing. I watched while the outlaws carefully slid the drum along it until it butted up against the two others that were already in place, and cushioned it against them by yet more packing materials.

Then they jumped down from the bed of the transit and went back to the barley crusher to work on the next batch. From the stores of sacks and drums it looked as though it was going to be a long night for them if they were going to process all of it.

Shit. I gasped as I realised at long last what I was looking at.

The bags of grey-white granules had to be fertiliser, ammonium nitrate granules, which ground down to a powder and mixed with icing sugar made pretty effective explosives, after all the Provos had used the same recipe to make the docklands bomb back in 1996.

As a crime reporter I'd had to look into it at the time and had learnt more about bomb making that I'd ever really wanted to.

The fertiliser mix was used to provide the main body of the bomb, but the Provos always used a thing called a gaine to set it off, a booster made from a length of old scaffolding pole, stuffed with about five kilos of a mix of PETN and RDX, the major components of most plastic explosives. That had to be what Toad had been sticking down the centre of each drum. The drilled holes were there to help ensure the booster set off all of the bulk explosives packed around it as efficiently as possible.

I'd had a long talk with a techie from the army's bomb disposal squad, the Royal Engineers, and he'd given me all the detail I had wanted for my piece, right down to the fact that the gaine materials were reasonably sensitive, so the Provos used a number six detonator, equivalent to a gramme of an eighty percent mercury fulminate and twenty percent potassium chlorate mix just to be sure to set it off, which in turn would detonate the surrounding drum of homemade powder. I'd thought he was about to give me the recipe for each to try at home.

Toad, Scroat and these other guys were building a truck bomb.

Hence the use of a tarpaulin and the plastic shovels for mixing. That's why the drum was stood on a wooden pallet to be filled and not the concrete floor of the shed. That was the reason for all the packing on the bed of the truck and between the drums.

Of course! They wouldn't want to run the risk of striking any sparks at this stage or they could all go up.

Jesus Christ. I needed to get the fuck out of here.

Outside in the dark I started as I heard a movement behind me, but I was a fraction too late.

I froze as I felt the arm around my neck and the cold steel of a hunting knife at my throat, just as a cold voice whispered in my ear, 'Gotcha! They said you might be here. Now don't you move a fucking muscle until I say so.'

'Hello Charlie,' I croaked.

10 Executive action

The pain exploded.

I got a kicking of course. Down on the ground, heavy boots stomping into ribs, kidneys and groin, arms wrapped over my head, my body scrabbling around on the floor, desperately trying to avoid the next kick as waves of blinding pain and gut sucking nausea swept over me.

*

Charlie had dragged me inside, the knife still at my throat and announced to Scroat that he'd caught me sneaking around outside and spying in through the window.

I had been stupid anyway to think that The Brethren would do anything like this without having some security outside. It was just that instead of a few lounging strikers having a smoke, this time Scroat had had the likes of Charlie patrolling the yard.

And all the while I was acutely aware that it was more than that. Charlie hadn't just found me; he'd come looking for me. I'd been damn lucky not to have run straight into him and his knife out there in the dark as I made my way through the yard. He, they, whoever they were, had known that I might have been going to be there. And I very much wanted to know how.

The only other person who might have known was Danny.

But that didn't make any sense, there was no way Danny would have told anyone, he was just too scared, I was sure of that. Unless he'd been caught and they'd forced it out of him of course.

*

I think if he'd had the choice, Charlie would have slit my throat then and there and then just dropped me into the car crusher, but Scroat was more thoughtful and through my haze of body wracking pain, to my utter astonishment I realised he was responsible for probably saving my life.

Although whether that was just because he had other plans for me I didn't know. So, he had a couple of the guys reached down to drag me up from off the vomit covered floor where I was lying, moaning and keening in a foetal ball, my hands thrust down helplessly at the agonising pain in my crotch, and outside where they threw me into the back of another smaller van that was parked in the yard.

Powerless to resist, they quickly trussed me up in gaffa tape, securing my wrists and ankles and then ignoring my sobbing attempts to breathe, more went across my mouth and eyes.

I don't know how long they left me there. I couldn't keep track of time and anyway I think I must have passed out for a while.

Eventually I heard voices and felt the rocking of the suspension as people climbed into the van. Someone got into the back and the door was slammed behind them from the outside as the engine started.

I stiffened as I felt a pricking at my neck and prayed that the van didn't jolt over a kerb or anything as I heard Scroat's voice.

'You're to keep quiet while we take a little ride. One wrong move out of you before we get to where we're going and I'll stick you. You understand?'

I grunted my acknowledgement and nodded as far as I was able with the point of his knife pressed against my jugular.

Then to my intense and blessed relief the knife disappeared again as the van lurched forward.

The kicking had been just as a matter of principle I guess as much as anything else, but given what I'd just witnessed I thought I was relatively lucky to be alive.

We drove for what seemed like forever before I felt a familiar lurching sensation as suddenly we swung off the road and headed down a ramp.

I felt Scroat's hand grab my leg as he used his knife to hack apart the tape binding my ankles, then the bang of the van door echoed around the underground car park and arms reached in to pull me roughly to my feet and shove me forward out onto the ground and into a stinking lift.

We were back at the same place. It had to be, I thought with a sudden unexpected surge of hope, as the lift began to whine and clatter upwards.

I might, just might, get out of this alive after all.

They frogmarched me down a corridor and then I heard them knocking at a door which opened with a fusillade of rattling bolts.

A hand in the small of my back gave me a sudden shove through, which sent me sprawling helplessly onto the floor, my arms still pinioned behind me as I tripped over the bar of the inner cage doorframe.

As I lay there braced for another kicking I heard Wibble's voice.

'You complete twat,' he spat in exasperation, 'You just couldn't stay away could you?'

*

Someone ripped the gaffa tape from across my mouth, but then with a tearing noise more gaffa tape went on. They had grabbed one of the wooden chairs from out of the kitchen and I was quickly strapped to it. It meant my kidneys weren't as easy to get at but still gave them plenty of scope from the front.

'So what did Danny tell you?' Wibble demanded.

Fuck it! That was a shock. Where the hell had they got that from.

'What? I don't know what you mean.'

'Don't piss me about,' he said, 'Danny, the kid, he called you earlier this evening. He rang you and you arranged to meet him at a café. Ring any bells?'

There wasn't much I could do but nod.

'Good, now we're getting somewhere. You see,' he said, 'we know, so let me ask you again, what did he tell you?'

They only wanted to know one thing really as Wibble's reasonable voice pointed out from off to one side as Scroat and one of his guys went to work.

And that was how I had found out what was going on and where.

I'm no hero.

I soon told them all about Danny and everything he'd said.

And then it stopped.

'So what are you gonna do now?' I mumbled as I got my breath back but I didn't get an answer.

'I'd keep your mouth shut if I was you,' said Wibble's voice from somewhere behind me.

Mentally I shut my eyes and gave thanks that I had actually sat down and sewn the support flash on. If it wasn't for that, and the way it said I was under Wibble's protection, I knew that chances were I would be dead by now. Anyone else caught spying on The Brethren like that, Charlie would just have knifed them there and then in the yard. Without Wibble's patch I would simply have disappeared, with cans of old oil spilt over any blood on the ground and the rest of me probably crushed into a compacted car and sent off on its way to be smelted down in a furnace.

*

'Did you get his phone?' Wibble asked.

'His phone?'

'Yeah, his mobile. Did he have it on him? Did you get it?'

Toad shrugged. 'Dunno, I didn't look.'

This seemed to exasperate Wibble, 'Well look now willya?'

From behind, Scroat hauled me suddenly to my feet, the chair coming with me, and tipping me forwards, my arms screaming in their sockets as he forced me up bodily and then held me bent double while Toad gave me the once over, slapping at my pockets before thrusting his hand inside my jacket to pull out what he'd found, discarding whatever else came out with it on the floor. No one seemed to mind him littering.

'Bingo!' he announced.

'Great,' said Wibble, 'give it to me.'

*

Holding my phone, Wibble turned to interview me.

'Is anyone expecting to hear from you?' he asked looking up from where he was turning it on. 'Is there any time you've set up to check in or make a call?'

I shook my head, 'No, nothing like that.'

'Who's going to miss you if they don't hear from you for a few days?'

'A few days?' I started, 'What's going on here? How long is this going to take?'

'I don't know,' he said calmly as my phone bing bonged cheerfully into life. 'It's not all up to me. But less than a week I'd guess now.'

Deftly he called up my contacts list and scrolled down it checking the names until he found the one he wanted.

'You're going to call your office,' he instructed, 'Tell them you're not going to be in for a while. And don't fuck us about. You know what'll happen if you do, don't you?'

I nodded weakly.

145

'Because we'll know you know. Not immediately perhaps, but we'll know, soon enough if you've shit on us, and I can promise you one thing if you do...'

'What's that?'

'That you'll fucking regret it for the rest of your life...'

'However long that is,' laughed Scroat.

'OK?' he said.

'OK,' I confirmed.

'Right then,' he said. 'Editor? That the one?'

'Yes.'

'His direct line?' he asked.

I nodded.

'It's a Friday night, is he going to be there?'

'Yes of course he will, they'll still be putting the Saturday paper to bed so he'll be there for a while yet.'

'OK then. Quiet you lot,' he shushed the other bikers.

'Now then,' he said turning back to me and bringing the phone up between us, 'after I've pressed dial you're going to tell him that you're going to be away from the office for a while, a few days, maybe a week. You've got a big new lead on a big new story. Serious shit, linked to the current biker thing. You're going to follow it up but it means you're going to have to disappear for a while. Will he buy that?'

'Buy it?'

'Will he believe it? Is it something that you've done before?'

'Well it's not usual but...'

'But..?'

'Well it's not completely out of the question, I mean it's... I have done it once or twice before...'

'Good...'

'But he won't like it,' Wibble started to say but I overrode him.

'... And he will be worried.'

'How worried?'

'He'll want to know I'm alright, that I know what I'm doing, that I'm going to be OK.'

'Fair enough, but will he believe you?' he insisted.

'Yeah, in the end, if I'm convincing enough.'

Wibble grinned at me.

'Well then mate, let's just hope you're a good actor, for your sake.'

And reaching over so the phone was upturned in front of my face, Wibble pushed the green call button, and then switched to speaker as we stood in the tension of the room listening to the far away brrr brrr buzz of the ring tone.

The call went much the way I'd expected it to. I tried to control the nerves in my voice. Not easy when your arms are gaffa-taped to your sides, a certifiable psycho like Scroat's arm is around your head and his knife at your throat, and Wibble's face is staring silently and warningly into your own as you try to argue convincingly with your sceptical editor that yes, I do know what I'm doing, and no, I can't tell you what all this is about just yet, or when I would actually be back; although at least those last parts weren't the lies the rest were.

'So make sure you keep in touch,' my editor instructed.

My eyes locked with Wibble's. His face was expressionless.

'Yeah, OK,' I said.

'I want a call every day,' he continued.

'Well...' I started.

'Don't shit with me Iain, you know the rules. You want to go off piste on this? Well, OK, I can authorise that, but you do it my way or not at all. Is that clear? I want to hear from you every day, you understand? No exceptions or I'm pulling you out, story or no sodding story, you understand?'

Wibble nodded.

'OK boss,' I said, 'you've got it. Every day, like clockwork.'

'Right then. You've got a week, and then I want you back in the office; and Iain...'

'Yes?'

'You'd better have a fucking good story when you do; otherwise you will be in the deepest shit you'll ever have seen in your life.'

If only he fucking knew. Even Wibble smiled at that one.

'Yes boss, see you in a week,' I said and shut my eyes.

'Righto,' he said, signing off, and with a click, Wibble snapped shut the phone, killing the line.

I held my breath. This was it I thought, I could feel the edge of Scroat's blade chafing against my jugular and I had just bought them a week's head start on the cops on getting rid of my body and sorting out their alibis. I swallowed hard, imagining the burning hot sensation of the hunting knife slitting my throat.

But there was nothing.

Then there was a sardonic clap from Toad and almost like a physical sensation I could feel the tension ease in the room. 'Give that man a fucking Oscar.'

I opened my eyes again. Wibble was still standing across from me, calmly pocketing my phone in his cut's breast pocket.

'So then,' he asked in a business like way, 'will he call the cops?'

I shook my head as much as I dared with what felt like a short sword pressed against it, 'No, why should he?'

'Well I don't know do I?' he said, 'There wasn't any shit in there was there now? No secret codewords or crap? Nothing that you should have said to confirm to him that you were OK?'

It would have been a good idea I thought regretfully, but it wasn't something that I'd ever arranged with my editor.

'No, I'm a reporter for fuck's sake, not Jason Bourne.'

'Ain't that the fucking truth?' snorted Toad.

'Is there anyone else you need to call to make sure no one reports you missing?' Wibble continued, 'Girlfriend? Mum, Dad? Mates?'

'Boyfriend?' suggested Scroat from behind me.

'Oh shut up,' said Wibble matter of factly, 'he ain't got one of those.'

He seemed very sure. But then I knew he would be. He'd been having me tailed and investigated long enough so I guess he knew most things about me.

'No, no one.'

'Well right then,' Wibble said, nodding his head as if to acknowledge that he was as satisfied as he could be about the point for the moment and stepping back away from me.

I froze and instinctively screwed my eyes shut as time slowed to a standstill. Scroat's grip was tight around my head. Pinioned as I was I couldn't really move but even so I bucked in the chair, trying desperately to twist myself, my body, my head, and most of all, my achingly exposed neck away from the razor sharp hunting steel burning against my skin. There was a mewling noise in the room which it took me a while to realise was coming from me. I was convinced as I strained against the binding tapes, half wrenching the chair off the floor in my struggle to break free from the vice like grip from behind me.

This.

Was.

It.

'Oh for fuck's sake shut up will you?' Wibble's voice cut through the madness, 'And you, let him go, we don't need that yet.'

And as if by a miracle, all of a sudden the pressure was released and my head fell forwards. There was no arm twisting it off the top of my neck and there was no knife pressed against my flesh. At Wibble's command, Scroat had just let go of me and let me and the chair drop to the floor again. For a moment all I could do was throw back my head and gasp for sweet, sweet breath again. Even in this flat that stank of damp, dead fags and old beer spills on the carpets.

'So what now?' asked Toad.

Wibble looked thoughtful for a moment, as though he was mentally calculating the odds and implications of a few courses of action, working through the scenarios to see which would work out best.

'I think I need to make another call first,' he concluded, reaching back into his cut's pocket, 'so make sure he stays quiet will you?'

He flipped open my phone again and once more rapidly flicked his way through my contact list as Toad tore another strip off the roll of gaffa tape they'd used and with Scroat crunching my jaw shut from behind with his forearm, he expertly stuck it across my mouth.

Then with a couple of stabs of his thumb Wibble selected and dialled, turning to face me as he held my phone to his ear and waited for an answer.

'Hi.'

I couldn't hear who it was he was talking to or what they were saying.

'Yeah it's me.

'Yeah, of course it's his phone. Surprised?

'Well it was bound to happen sometime wasn't it?

'I'm looking at him right now.

'Yeah, that's the place.

'No. Bit worse for wear but he's OK.

'Scroat and young Charlie did a number on him. But he'll live.

'Yeah well, for a while anyway. That's one of the things I wanted to ask, you've not heard anything about him have you?

'No?

'No alerts, none of that sort of shit? No notices he's missing?

'OK then, check it out, but do it discreetly. Don't want to set alarm bells off unnecessarily. And keep an ear out. If anything comes up I want to know about it sharpish.

'Yeah, call me on this phone, but only once you've done it. Yeah it needs to come off now.

'Right. But that's not what I called up to talk about. Not the main thing anyway…

'No.

'That other thing we talked about? You remember?

'Yeah?

'Well, I'm just calling to let you know that we're on.

'Just sit back and watch your TV. It's all you fucking ever do anyway. You'll find out.

'Yeah right.

'OK, I'll wait for your call.

'Like I said, this number, right?

'Yes of course I'm sure. I wouldn't have said it if I wasn't would I? Just make sure it's clean from now on OK?

'No it ain't going anywhere either.

'OK then. See you.

'What a dickhead!' he added, after he'd hung up, as he stuck my phone away again in his pocket.

And while they weren't the questions at the absolute top of my list, not in comparison with how the fuck I was going to get myself out of this and what the hell Wibble was doing keeping me around while whatever was about to go down happened, even then I did have to wonder.

Who was he calling?

And why was he using my phone to do it?

*

'So what about him?' Toad asked again, nodding at me.

'Oh just stick him in the hole for now,' Wibble instructed, his mind obviously elsewhere.

Oh shit, I thought, I really was dead already.

He must have seen the expression on my face since he smiled and said, 'Don't worry mate, I need to think about what to do about you, so it's not that sort of hole. At least not yet.'

Toad and Scroat tipped the chair backwards and dragged it and me bodily across the room, through a doorway into an inner hallway and then into the first room off it where unceremoniously they just let go of the chair, letting me and it fall heavily to the floor. There, rather than the further kicking I had instinctively started to try as far as I could whilst still strapped to a chair, to roll myself into a ball for, squirming in anticipation of trying to keep my kidneys on the ground, they just dumped me.

But it was a sixties built thin walled flat, one of those where you could hear next door's every fart, and so from where I lay I could still hear what was going on in the living room through the thin partition and open doorways.

They had left me there with instructions to keep quiet and stay still although there really wasn't a lot else I could do.

Back inside the other room there was a knock and the clank of the door being opened to admit someone.

Then as they moved between the lounge and the kitchen to make some drinks there was a discussion, some of which I could overhear and some of which was obviously about me.

'...well he can't stay here.'

'But there's nowhere else to put him.'

'For the moment...'

'Yeah well...'

'Do we need him?' said a new voice that with a chill I recognised as Bung's.

Wibble's voice cut through above them.

'Well he's here now. Might not have been the smartest thing in the world to do...'

There were some unintelligible objections, then Wibble's voice again. 'Yeah yeah, I know, you had to do something, I get that...'

More rumbles.

'Well, whatever,' he said, sounding dismissive, 'it doesn't matter now. The fact remains he's here now and we can work with it. Now, does everybody know what they're doing?'

There was the sound of a round of affirmative grunts.

'You finished?' asked Wibble.

'The first bit yes,' said Toad. 'I still need to do the wiring but we had to stop to bring matey boy over here and see what to do.'

'Can you get the rest done tonight d'you think?'

'Yeah, should be able to if we get back over.'

'OK then, let's get organised. It would be good to get it all ready tonight,' Wibble instructed, before adding 'and Bung, can you sort your lad out?'

'Sure, no problem,' said Bung smoothly, 'I'll catch him first thing.'

Oh God, I thought to myself. That had to be Danny they were talking about Bung sorting. What the fuck had I done?

Just then there was the sound of a mobile phone ringing. Not mine this time, It was Wibble's.

'It's him,' he announced and the others all fell silent as Wibble answered it with a cold 'Hello?'

'Yes?...

'How did?...

'You're fucking joking?...

'No, not on this, we need to speak...

'Yes now!...

'Here, the usual place...

'How long?...

'OK, well hurry it up then. I'll be waiting.'

I heard the click as he snapped the phone shut.

'Right then,' he announced to the silently waiting group, 'Bung, make the calls, I need everybody together for a meet tomorrow morning.'

'We're on?'

'It's on. Surprise, surprise, they completely fucked it up and the tosser is on his way here now.'

There was the sound of a general exodus from the flat to do whatever it was they were supposed to be doing; until as far as I could tell the only people left were Wibble, Bung and me. But since no one came in to see how I was doing it was difficult to tell.

*

I think it was just about midnight before Bung appeared in the cell doorway.

Bung slipped out a knife and wrenching my arms up from where they were taped to the arms of the chair so that he could get at them, slashed through the tape at my wrists and elbows before letting them fall again.

'You might as well make yourself comfortable,' he grinned, 'you're going to be here for a while.'

I slumped down and with an effort and a thump rolled the chair over onto its side. My hands were an agony of pins and needles as the blood began to flow again while I fumbled with what felt like swollen and cartoon sized fingers and thumbs to pick an edge of the gaffa tape from off my face, and then once I had a fuzzy hold of it, with a rip and a grimace, to tear it from across my mouth and gasp for some precious fetid air again.

From my restricted vantage point on the floor as I lay wheezing to get my breath back again and tried to make what sense I could of my situation, I peered around me. Once upon a time it had obviously been one of the bedrooms. Now as I lay there still curled up against the chair, my ankles still trussed with duct tape that I hadn't even started to struggle with yet, I could dimly make out a bed, and in the corner what looked like one of those chemical toilets you have in caravans and that sort of thing. Beyond the bed I could see the windows which had been boarded over with the perforated steel sheeting that councils use to seal off condemned and empty buildings.

'What's this all about?' I asked.

'You'll see soon enough.'

'Have you had other people here?'

'What do you think? You reckon we set all this up just for you?' he shook his head in disgust, 'Jesus, you don't think you're the first we've had to take care of do you?'

Take care of in the keep sense I hoped. Not in the get rid of sense.

'All the same, you're staying here for a while, and piece of advice?'

'Yes?'

'You keep your mouth shut while you're here unless we want to talk to you. You understand?'

Oh I got it alright…

There was a clang as a steel barred grille shut across the doorway and the rattle and click of a bolt being shut and padlocked and that was it, I was to all intents and purposes locked inside a cell. I was a prisoner and they were right. I wasn't going anywhere.

So it looked as though they had thought this through. It was a prison alright, and not one where anyone outside could see, or I thought, hear me.

Saturday 22 August 2009

I guess it was about two or so in the morning before there was a knock at the outer door.

'It's him,' I heard Bung say.

'Alone?'

'Yes, looks like it.'

'Alright then, let him in,' Wibble instructed.

And from where I sat and listened it was immediately apparent who *they* were and what they had *completely fucked up*, although really it should have been obvious already.

The visitor was Thommo, and he'd come to report what had gone down, which was nothing good. In fact it was, as advertised, a complete fuck up.

Cambridge had gone after Noddy.

Thommo had personally led the attack on the home of The Mohawks' president in the new regime which was out on a farm Ely way.

Noddy as the ex-Capricorn P and representative of the larger club had taken the top slot with Leeds Kev of the zombies taking the VP position on the ticket so that both predecessor clubs were represented in the merger. Being the more local and senior officer he was the most obvious target, something that the Cambridge crew should really have taken into account in their planning I guess.

In any event, Thommo, his crew and their strikers and various tagalongs eager to be seen to be on board had tooled up with axes, petrol bombs, pistols and shotguns, before riding over in a couple of old transits. The plan had been to park the vans up in the woods along the lane that led down to Noddy's place and then split up to creep down either side of the track to surround the place from both sides. The petrol bombs would go in the windows to set the place on fire and The Brethren crew would be waiting outside the doors to take out whoever the fire flushed out from inside.

The only problem was that The Mohawks had been waiting for them.

'It was a complete fucking ambush!' Thommo was complaining. 'The squaws must have known we were coming. They were camped outside in the woods, and just as soon as we pulled up they opened fire. The guys didn't stand a chance. They just fucking riddled the first van before we could get a fucking door open. I reckon one of them must have had one of the AKs that they used the first time. The others had shotguns and stuff. We got some off ourselves but we just had to hightail it out of there.'

'Jesus Christ!'

'Our guys?'

We had to dump Timbo outside A&E. Santa's got a bad one in the arm and Kenny caught a load of shot in the leg but Oddball's wife's a nurse so she's cleaned and sewn both of them up OK. Otherwise it's minor stuff, cuts and bruises.

'And them?'

'Fuck knows. Like I said, we rode straight into an ambush. We popped off what we could but fuck it, after that it was just about getting the fuck out of there.'

'So you never got near the house?'

'Shit no. Have you been listening to what I've been saying? They were waiting for us I tell you.'

'Christ. What a fuck up.'

*

'Well that proves it,' I heard Wibble say.

'Proves what?' Thommo sounded puzzled.

'You've got a snitch in your crew haven't you? You said it yourself, they must have known you were coming. So someone's feeding stuff to the squaws. Stuff from the inside. How else did they know what was going to go down?'

'Well...'

'And it's not just now is it? What about the Toy Run? Someone snitched then as well...

Thommo started to protest but Wibble wasn't having any of it.

'Oh come on Thommo for fuck's sake, we all know it even if no one's saying it. How else would the squaws have known what we were going to announce?'

Thommo tried again, 'Well other people knew...'

'Not fucking many, that's for sure,' snarled Wibble, 'and how many people knew about your little trip tonight?'

'Well…'

'No you've got a snitch, and this needs sorting pronto.'

'So I'll…'

'So you'll just shut the fuck up and I'll tell you what to do,' Wibble ordered and Thommo fell silent at last.

'You'll get all your guys together,' Wibble continued authoratively as he issued his instructions, 'it's full high church. You're calling a crash meeting tomorrow night at your clubhouse, and once everyone's there, you keep 'em there. D'you get it?'

'Yes but…'

'But nothing. You just do what I've told you to do. In the meantime I'll get our crew together as a nutting squad and we'll head up to meet you. Once you've got everyone there, send someone over to fetch us. Someone I know. Who's your junior patch at the moment? The one who was on the door last time we were down?'

'Mikey?'

'Yeah, that's the one. Send him. We'll arrange to wait somewhere local, at the Little Thief or whatever, for him to come and fetch us. Then me and my guys'll come over and you and me, well mate, we're going to sort out your little snitch problem once and for all.'

'What if anyone can't make it?'

'Well if anyone no shows, they're your snitch for sure aren't they? Still, whatever. You get the guys together, you send Mikey and then you keep everybody else with you at the clubhouse till we get there, is that understood?'

It was understood.

Thommo left with his orders.

*

It was difficult to tell for sure but I guessed it was about midday.

There were more voices next door. People had been arriving over the last half hour or so and sorting themselves out with drinks in the kitchen.

Sorting out their own drinks just confirmed what Wibble and Bung had already said. It meant that there weren't any strikers around; if there had been no full patch would have lifted a finger in the kitchen, expecting without question to be waited on.

'OK then,' I heard Wibble's voice rise above the other to call them to order as I guessed they must have perched themselves around the assortment of battered sofas and chairs in the flat's living room.

'Let's get started.'

*

'So what happened?' someone asked in a Geordie accent. So Toad was back then I realised, but then I'd assumed he would be, to represent the North.

'Well according to Thommo it was a straight out ambush, and the twats walked right into it.'

It wasn't a meeting I realised. It was a council of war.

There was a chorus of groans and 'Oh shits' which Wibble had to shut down a couple of times as he gave the assembled group a flat report of what Thommo had said last night, about how The Brethren had been beaten back, together with his interpretation of the implications.

'The squaws were waiting and ready for 'em. That's clear enough. So to me that means they had to have been tipped off by someone.'

There was a general murmur of agreement.

'And that someone, whoever the fucking rat is, has to be on the inside.'

The growl of agreement from inside the room made my hair stand on end. Christ if there was one thing that all outlaw bikers hated with a vengeance, it was someone who betrayed a club's secrets. In their lives, someone who ratted them out, whether to the cops or a rival gang was the lowest of the low, the absolute scum of the earth.

Informers are a dying breed wasn't just a joke as far as these guys were concerned. It was the law they all lived by.

'So it's not just the squaws anymore,' he continued, 'We need to sort out Cambridge once and for all as well.'

Again there was a noise of agreement, although more subdued, more circumspect this time, as if the men in the room were waiting for him to make himself and his intentions plain, or as plain as they would ever be expressed in words.

'They brought the whole of this shit down on all of us and now they can't handle it. So somebody needs to arrange to take care of business, agreed?'

This was a language and an issue they all understood.

One of the first duties of a charter was to hold their turf for the club and if they couldn't control their local patch, then they didn't deserve to wear their patches anyway. Worse still I knew from my conversation with Bob, Wibble would be concerned how this might reflect on the national charter as a whole.

Like he'd said, no one had a God given right to the colours. If the whole club over here got tarred by Bubba and the boys back in the States with the Cambridge brush of not having been tough enough to hold onto their territory, then it might not just be Thommo and his boys who would have to worry about having their patches pulled.

'Agreed.'

'And is that something you are going to do?' came a voice that sounded like Stu's, 'on your own I mean?'

'Yes.'

'Is it in hand?'

'Yes.'

'Well, good, because if you need any…'

'Thanks,' said Wibble firmly, 'but like I said, it's in hand. It'll be taken care of to everyone's satisfaction.'

'Well, like I said,' Stu replied, 'that's great.'

The what was in hand was never stated. Even here, they were still too careful for that. The consciousness that anywhere you went could be bugged by the cops was just a part of their life now. But like the minutes from *Wansee*, the underlying meaning was crystal clear.

Wibble had just proposed adopting a final solution to the Cambridge and Mohawk questions; and it had passed nem com.

'Oh yeah before you all go, I've got something for you.'

'The new flash?'

'Here,' he said.

There were murmurs of appreciation and approval and the backslapping sounds of mutual bearhugs.

'Hey, not bad,' I heard Bung say.

'Bubba's going to hate it!'

'Well, Bubba's not here is he? So I just guess we're going to have to live with that aren't we?'

'We'll be getting a visit from evil.'

'Oh he'll be coming alright; we just have to be ready.'

'Everybody up for this?'

'With pride mate, with pride.'

*

As they left I heard two of the bikers joking.

'Three can keep a secret...'

'You bet...'

I didn't have to hear them finish it as the steel security door clanged behind them, I knew how it went.

Again it was a famous maxim amongst the outlaw clubs. *Three can keep a secret, if two of them are dead.*

The Victim.

The Witness.

The Brethren.

One survivor.

11   Freedom's not free

Wibble leant against the door jamb, the other side of the grille secured across the entrance to the room where I was perched on the bed, my back against the wall.

I think he must just have been bored waiting around for whatever was expected to happen next, so he'd come to pass the time.

'What about me?' I asked.

He seemed to find that amusing.

'So what about you?'

'What happens now?'

'Are you slow or something? We're hanging on to you for a while, that's what.'

'But what the hell are you doing?' I insisted, 'Letting me hear this stuff?'

'I thought you'd be interested.'

'Bollocks!'

He pretended to be shocked and dismayed, 'And you a scribbler and all!'

*

There was something different I noticed. He was wearing a new tab on the front of his colours. It was a variation on the classic outlaw biker's diamond 1% badge. But instead of being the traditional white on black, this one had a white 1% embroidered over a background Union Jack. It must have been what he'd been handing out earlier so what was it all about I wondered?

He was still hanging around outside the cell door when there was the ring of his mobile again sometime early in the evening. I guessed it was Bung on station somewhere up by the Cambridge clubhouse.

'Yeah,' said Wibble, 'you there?

'Good. How far is it?

'Five minutes or so? Yeah that should be fine. No cameras? You sure?

'Yeah well, I'm just being careful.

'Good.

'OK, so now you call Thommo. He knows all this already, but tell him again from me. Just to be sure.

'Tell him I'm on my way. You can say I'm rounding up some more guys or something.

'Anyway, that's not his problem. His job is to get everyone into the meeting room at the back. This has to be a fucking secure meeting and I want him to have every patch there. Make sure he understands, this isn't just High Church, it's the fucking Vatican as far as their guys are concerned.

'Once they're all in, Thommo's to send Mikey over to you. Mikey's job is to let you know if anyone hasn't made it. If anyone's skipped out then they're a snitch and we'll need to arrange to deal with them direct.'

A snitch, I wondered. Surely the snitch? Was Wibble worried there was more than one in the Cambridge crew?

'You tell Thommo we're going to send a van round the back of the clubhouse. It'll have our guys in it, they'll be there to block off the back door, stop the snitch from legging it if he makes a break for it. Thommo's to start the meeting once he sees it's arrived.'

'How will he know it's ours? Oh Christ, how many other fucking vans are going to park across the back of his clubhouse? Simple. You get your tagalong kid to drive it, Danny. He's seen him before.'

So Danny was still around I noted. So was he playing some kind of game? Had he set me up? I still couldn't believe it. The kid had been really shit scared when I'd seen him I could tell. If he'd been putting that on to set me up for The Brethren he deserved an Oscar not colours.

'Then you give Mikey the number and tell him to take it to where Danny's waiting in the van round the back. You tell him that once he's there, he and Danny are to call it to let you know they're both in position as you and your lads will be heading round to the front. In the meantime you just get the fuck out of there.

'Got that?

'No, don't dump the phone. Make sure it's turned off so it can't be traced and then bring it back here and we'll get it dabbed up again.'

So Bung was using my phone for some reason I gathered, before I heard Wibble's next chilling words.

'For insurance.

'No it's OK, they can't trace this call back here, the VOIP thing bounces it all over the web first.

162

'OK, see you then.

'What?

'Yeah, you'll need to fetch the cleaning gear. We'll need it but it can wait awhile.'

Wibble clicked the phone off.

I didn't like the sound of cleaning gear.

'The call?' I asked.

'Yeah. Danny thinks he's back-up and that Bung'll be hightailing it round to the front. He's got a number to call, we've told him it's Thommo's to let him know to open the front door to let us in.'

'But Bung's not going to be there is he…'

'No of course he isn't.'

I couldn't believe how stupid I had been about what was about to happen. But suddenly I was as sure as I could be that I knew what was going on.

I'd seen the van and what was being loaded into it.

I knew without ever having seen it what it was that Toad would have been wiring up back at Scroat's yard.

I knew what it was that Danny would be calling, even if he didn't.

And it wasn't Bung and his outlaw cavalry.

'You bastard!'

The other side of the bars Wibble just smiled and shrugged. 'Maybe.'

*

Wibble brought a little colour portable in from the kitchen and perched it on a chair in the hallway where I could see it. And after a bit of fiddling with the old wire loop aerial off the back of it we got a reasonable if slightly snowy picture.

Then we watched TV. Just like he'd told whoever it was on the phone to do.

It was on the news of course. The Beeb had sent their young local stringer, all blond ambition wrapped up against the night and staring into the harsh camera lights saying the inevitable words.

Reports of an explosion…

Building destroyed…

163

Police cordon…

The reporter standing beyond the taped barriers, strobing blue lights and fluorescing hi-vis jackets in the background, with nothing to say at this stage beyond the barely obvious.

Massive explosion…

The scene behind me, as you can see, ripped through…

Police sources saying substantial casualties…

It was all *local-sources-local-rumours-lack-of-confirmation-filler-rolling-24-hour more-guesswork-and-platitude-than-news-fodder-Thank-you-Sarah-that-we'll-be going-back-to-as-soon-as-there's-any-more-news-meanwhile-back-in-the-studio-we don't-want-to-speculate-but-on-the-line-we-have…*

And that was when I knew for sure.

There was no way I was walking away from this alive.

Three could keep a secret. Me, Danny and Wibble.

And one of them was gone already.

'OK?' said Wibble.

'OK?' OK? No! Of course I wasn't fucking OK.

'Fancy a coffee?'

*

In my calmer moments over the next few hours, I reflected on the fact that it was a very odd situation. Wibble had obviously moved in here for the duration and set the flat up as his wartime HQ with Bung, who had arrived back later, as his number two.

It made sense. It was obviously a safe house for them and would be easy to defend if it ever were attacked.

'We like these blocks,' he said, gazing out of the window.

'The whole floor's ours,' he added conversationally, 'Not directly of course. It's through a couple of our holding companies. It's been a good investment over the years, for business I mean. It's good to have somewhere away from the clubhouse for stuff, a bit out of the limelight. We've got the next floor down as well. It's empty at the moment but gives us a little privacy, know what I mean?'

164

I understood. Anyone who wasn't with the club or coming up on club business would stick out like a sore thumb. There was no other reason or excuse for being up here.

It also meant that as I had suspected, there really was no point yelling for help. There was no one who was going to hear.

'So is the rest empty?' I asked.

'Pretty much. There's a couple of the lower floors that're squatted, but that's fine by us. Otherwise it's just here and the shunting yard.'

'Squatters?'

'Punks, dealers and stuff. Kids and crusties, but there's some fun chicks as well so we party sometimes. Always has an eye for the ladeeez has Bung.'

'The shunting yard?'

'The boys've got some beds set up in the flat down the hall. It's always good to have a place to take some patch snatch.'

'Yeah,' Bung gestured as though he was Casey Jones pulling a whistle, 'specially if you want'em to pull the train.'

But with me there as well and time to kill there was just no way that we weren't going to talk about something.

And what was there to talk about other than what was going down and why?

'You aren't using this as an excuse to settle some business are you?' I asked, 'That's what this has all been about for you hasn't it? Getting to here?'

'Hey, never waste a good crisis.'

From what Bung had let slip on the way up to Cambridge, Thommo was already a threat to Wibble and I realised that Wibble had obviously known it when we went on that run. After all, everyone knew that a triumvirate wasn't the usual way to run any kind of outlaw club, it had only come about as an interim solution to solve the immediate problems caused by Damage's assassination, and in reality, behind the appearances, from the moment it was formed, no one in the club actually expected it to last.

Rubbing Thommo's nose in it to make him mad the way he'd done at the run hadn't been creating an enemy for Wibble the way I had feared, it just made an existing enemy mad. And if you made an enemy mad while you remained calm, you put yourself at an advantage.

'What about Danny?'

'Who, the kid?'

'Yes.'

'He was expendable.'

'How about Mikey then? He was a patch. He was your spy in the Cambridge charter, wasn't he? Was he expendable too?'

'That was good, how did you work that out?'

In truth it was a lucky guess as to who, but the fact that Wibble would want to have a source inside Thommo's crew seemed obvious. As Damage had given me one of his bastardised quotes once, something about how a guy in charge uses spies to see, the way ordinary guys use their eyes.

'Well,' Wibble shrugged, 'never trust a grass. He's turned once, what's to say he won't turn again for someone else?'

*

In truth I was still struggling to grasp the scale and implications of what had just happened.

'Christ you've taken out an entire chapter of your own. You'll never get away with that will you? What will the rest of the club think?'

'What will they think? I can tell you what they'll think. They'll say Thommo and Cambridge fucked up. Thommo got too ambitious, too greedy and as a result they brought a whole shitstorm down on all of us just as things were going well and everyone was earning, that's what they'll think. That they were given a chance to make it right and they fucked that up as well.

'They'll think that I'm a patient man, that I gave them a second chance. Some of them'll think I've been too patient, but all of them'll think that enough is enough and they didn't get or deserve a third.

'They'll think that someone had to step in to clear up the mess in the interests of the club before it got completely out of control, to do what had to be done.

'And they'll think, that's what Wibble did, he stepped in and cleaned up the mess once and for all.'

'That you cleaned house?'

'Fuck yes, I cleaned house.

'And now,' he said breaking off and glancing at his watch, 'nice as it is to chat, I've got some stuff to organise so I'm going to leave you in the capable hands of Bung here.'

*

Bung was happy to keep on chatting, happier than I was considering what I knew he'd just done.

'There's one thing I don't get,' he asked.

'What's that?'

'You keep asking about Damage. Why? What is it to you? Is it just another story for your rag?'

It was a good question. It was a bit of a mystery I suppose. Not just Damage's death, now that was a mystery, who had organised it and how.

But my reasons for needing to know, they were a bit of a mystery to me as well. It could make a good story, sure, but it was more than that. Lots more than that. It was more personal. I'd spent quite a lot of time with him by the end, he'd spoken to me about his life and what he'd done, the good the bad and the pretty bloody ugly, in a way that I doubted he'd spoken to almost anyone, even his club brothers. Not because he wanted to confide in me per se, I knew that, it wasn't that he wanted me to know, I wasn't some late found bosom buddy, I realised that. I was just a means to an end, I was just a convenient channel for his to get out what he wanted. Our discussions had always been about Damage's agenda and on his terms.

But all the same, we had spoken. I'd met his wife and kid. Or kids now, I corrected myself.

I felt I knew him, had known him about as well as anyone ever had, he had opened up to me, even if for his own reasons and hardly the truth, the whole truth and nothing but the truth. And he'd got under my skin.

So no, it wasn't about just another story for the rag. It was for me. It was something that I wanted to know.

If I thought about it, I didn't really know why, or even what I would do with the knowledge as and when I ever found it. But it wasn't for the rag. It was personal. It was between us. Me and Damage's leering ghost that I couldn't seem to shake off and who's baleful influence seemed to have taken over my whole damn life and brought me to the straits I was in now.

'No, not for the paper. It's just for me. It's just I want to know.'

'Like I said, why? What's it to you?'

'Christ I don't know. Frankly I don't fucking know how and why I got myself mixed up in all this shit in the first place.'

He seemed to find that funny.

'So you want to find out who killed Damage?'

'Yeah. Much good it'll do me now. Why, are you going to tell me?'

He seemed to find that even funnier.

'Shit. I don't know what crap they taught you at journalism school but seems to me you're asking all the wrong questions.'

'Oh?'

'Well, you want to find out who killed Damage right?'

'Yeah.'

'So you keep asking who killed Damage. Well you're never going to find out asking that way; no one's going to tell you that are they?'

'Not so far,' I admitted.

'No, you need to ask why he was killed. Then you'll know who killed him.'

'Cui bono?'

'You what?'

'Cui bono, who benefited?'

'Maybe. Or who thought they would win out of it.'

Like I said before, it was something that I'd wondered from time to time. More than that, it was something I kept coming back to.

Whenever people looked to see who had done something, they always looked to see who had done well out of it. But that wasn't really the point as far as I could see. Life wasn't always that neat. No one was ever really in charge of all the variables, or really knew what everyone else was up to or how they would react to events, so no one could ever really guarantee that they would end up coming out on top from whatever it was they had started.

No, to see who was behind something you didn't need to look for who had actually benefited, as they may just have been the luckiest or best at reacting. Instead, you had to look at who thought they would be in the best position to benefit before the deed was done.

But since that meant understanding people's mindsets, how they read the political landscape, their relative powers, prospects, alliances, opportunities, trusts, supporters, enemies and threats, from the outside and a year on, I still didn't see how that would help me.

Unless. It was worth a try.

'So then Bung, you tell me then, why was he killed?'

'Well now…'

'I thought Wibble told you to tell me everything?'

'Yeah, well he did. But there's everything and everything, and anyway, I guess things may have changed a bit now, don't you?' he said nodding at the grille of the cell door.

'Maybe,' I conceded.

He grunted a snort at that one.

'God loves a tryer,' he said, 'anyway, I didn't come to talk about Damage.'

'No?'

'No, I came to ask you an important question.'

'Oh really? What's that then?' I said.

'I'm going to ring for an order. D'you fancy a pizza?'

Well at least whatever they were or weren't planning to do with me, letting me starve to death wasn't one of them I thought, as I asked for extra cheese.

Sunday 23 August 2009

It was after another takeaway when I heard a mobile phone ring again in the other room. It was a call on mine again, I was sure of it. He was getting good use out of it. I was just wondering who it was who would be calling on my phone that Wibble would want to speak to? And if it was for Wibble, why didn't they call Wibble direct on his?

'Hi. See the show?

'Well I told you it would be worth watching.

'Yes. Are they meeting?

'No? What d'you mean no?'

Wibble sounded genuinely disturbed, perhaps for the first time since I'd met him. Whatever was happening wasn't going to plan.

'Is that reliable? Why the fuck not?

'You sure? Your bloke has enough access doesn't he? We're paying enough for it remember?

'Christ almighty, why not?

'Laying fucking low! Fuck. Wankers.

'No, no I don't know. Hang on a minute, I need to think.'

From where I was sat, I could hear Wibble as he paced furiously across the room and back muttering 'Shit! Shit! Shit!' to himself.

Then the door into the hallway banged open as he strode through and stopped outside my cell, staring in at me. Like I was going to give him some inspiration for whatever the hell his little problem was. He stood, his glare fixed on me for a moment as if I was something he could attack just to vent his frustration. Then, as suddenly as he had come, he swung on his heel and marched off back into the main room.

'You still there?' I heard him say.

'OK then, we can still work this out. It's not the end of the world. In fact it might make it easier.

'If they aren't going to do it themselves, then we need to do it for them.

'We need to organise a joint meeting, the top guys, both packs.

'Yes you. You've done it before haven't you?'

Whoever it was on the other end didn't seem keen on this.

'We'll work something out. Perhaps you can tell them you know something about the bomb. We've got a while to think up a story.

'The usual.'

There was some urgent negotiation.

'OK twice the usual. Half up front, half afterwards. Yeah I can make a call and get it transferred.

'Will they trust you?

'No of course I fucking don't. I trust you to like the dosh that's all.

'OK then. You come to us and we'll get it planned.

'Yeah that's the place. Same as before.

'Right, see you in what, an hour?

170

'No, make it an hour.

'Yes, see you then.'

Wibble hung up with no goodbyes.

*

There was another call. Again it was on my phone. Wibble picked it up.

I had taken some comfort from the fact that Wibble had been using my phone and using it here. As I understood it, the cops could trace quite accurately where a phone had been used by triangulating the strength of the signals recorded at the three closest receiving stations. So if I did disappear, the cops would use this to trace back where calls had been made on my phone which would lead them straight here. And I had two assumptions about that. Firstly, I guessed Wibble and The Brethren, or at least the Freemen, wouldn't want this place investigated too much. Christ alone knew what had gone on up here over the years. And secondly I guessed that Wibble and The Brethren were savvy enough about mobiles and what they could do to know that.

So, on that slender chain of reasoning, I was starting to feel slightly safer as I listened to the one sided call taking place in the next room.

'OK.

'OK.

'Yeah, right.

'See you then.'

Wibble wasn't much of a conversationalist when he didn't want to be.

'Is it him?' I heard Bung ask.

'Yeah. He's coming round, wants to collect. Should be an hour or so.'

'OK,' Bung said, 'I'll be ready, I've got the stuff.'

'D'you want to get him back in here?'

'Yeah, might as well. He'll want to see this.'

'You sure about that?'

Wibble laughed. 'No, not really.'

'OK,' shrugged Bung, sounding unconvinced as I suddenly realised they were talking about me.

'Right,' Wibble said, appearing back at the grille to my cell bearing the roll of silver gaffa tape, 'now we've got a visitor coming so we need to get ready.'

*

I was taped tightly to the chair again which they had pulled into the centre of the room and plonked down.

'Not long to go now. Just the final act to play out,' said Wibble conversationally.

'See you at Philippi,' I muttered as I heard the rip of Bung unwinding another gaffa gag.

'What?'

'Doesn't matter,' I got out, before the tape went on.

And then it all went black as he slipped the balaclava over my head backwards again.

*

An age passed in the clinging claustrophobic blackness before there was a bang on the outer door when someone knocked.

'Is it him?'

'Should be, go see,' said Wibble.

I heard Bung's footsteps as he walked over to the door to check.

'Yeah it's him,' he said, as I heard the clang of the bolts being slammed back, before the buzz of the electronic door release and the click of the outer door lock opening.

The outer door clanged shut and then there was the clank of the inner dealer cage door opening as the visitor stepped through that as well.

They had let whoever it was inside.

'Hi there Wibble, Bung,' he said.

*

Jesus Christ! I started in shock, I recognised that voice.

'Hi there Iain, how are you doing mate?' it asked in a friendly fashion as I heard him walk towards where I sat.

And then I heard Bob say to Wibble, 'It's OK, I tried to recruit him once, to tout on your lot, but he turned me down. Journalistic ethics or something he said. Got very hoity toity about it, the little wanker.'

Then with a jerk Bob tugged the balaclava off my head and bent down to the level I was secured at to look me in the eyes. He was smiling broadly.

'And you did your bit too sunny Jim, didn't you? Printed what you were told to print like a good boy didn't you?'

He gave me a friendly cuff, patting me on the cheek a couple of times as I glared at him from above my silver gaffa tape gag.

'Don't look so surprised, mate,' he said as he set the briefcase he was carrying down on the floor in front of me, 'it's just business. We share an interest here, Wibble and me. Just keeping the Queen's peace here mate. And other things.'

*

He wasn't joking, they obviously did I realised as, standing up, he turned to Wibble and without any preamble went straight to it.

'So then, where do you want'em to go? Is it still the same plan?'

'Yeah,' said Wibble, 'we want to use the place you met them before. You brought the keys?'

'To the safe house? Yes, sure.'

'Good, hand'em over then.'

'I'll need to get them back...'

'Oh it's OK, you'll get them back alright. We need access so we just want to borrow them, we don't want to keep them.'

'Well I guess there wouldn't be much point afterwards would there?'

'No, not really.'

I heard a jingle as Bob pulled out a bunch of keys.

'No I don't need them, give 'em to Bung here,' Wibble said.

'Alarm code?' Bung asked.

'Four... Five... Seven...One...' he said slowly.

'OK Bung?' asked Wibble.

'Yeah,' he said, 'Four...Five...Seven... One... right?'

Bob nodded.

'No problems. I'll go get the guys and we'll head on over,' Bung said as he picked up his lid from one of the chairs and left the flat.

*

And then there were three of us. Two standing, and one sitting and shitting himself.

Christ if Bob was tied up in all of this, what the hell chance did I have of getting out of it?

But they were ignoring me for the moment.

'D'you want me to make the call now?' asked Bob.

'Might as well.'

'Right then, will do.'

*

It had been Bob all along I realised as they talked. He was the missing piece of the jigsaw. He had been the one that had set me up. It was obvious that he'd had my mobile tapped and texts intercepted.

How else could The Brethren have known that Danny had been in touch?

The answer was they couldn't, not unless either the whole thing was a trap from the get go, which from Danny's demeanour at our meeting I didn't believe for a moment; or they had caught and tortured it out of Danny, but then there was no way he would have been driving that van and obeying orders the way he had been. No, the only answer was they had been monitoring my phone, it wouldn't be easy but I wouldn't put it past them to have ways and means of doing it; or, last but most likely in my book, someone had listened in for them.

Someone like a copper doing undercover surveillance work on the club and it's known associates and tagalongs for example?

Christ, I'd even joked about it.

And of other clubs of course, I realised, following the logic as Bob made his call.

And if Bob was having all the clubs' phones tapped then how much information could he have on each of them to sell to the others?

174

Bob was calling the Mohawks I realised. It had to be.

'Hi.

'Yes, it's me.

'Yes we need to talk. What are you arseholes doing? This has got to stop. Yes I passed on your message. Yes, is the offer still open?

'What d'you mean it wasn't you? Who the fuck else was it going to be? Look, I need to see the both of you and I need to see you tonight.

'No!

'I need to see you. We need to meet. We need to get a grip on this before it gets completely out of control and nobody, not me, not you, not them want that. It's just bad business.

'Yeah I know you didn't want that, but that was then, this is now.'

There was some kind of angry protestation on the other end of the line that Bob just overrode.

'Yeah? And who was it who blew up the Toy Run with all those civilians around?

'Well whatever, whether you want to shut it down or take it all the way you need me right? I can either be your channel to talk or your feed of information you ain't going to get anywhere else, so whichever way you want to play it you still need to do a deal with me don't you?

'Meet me where we did before, you remember? But it needs to be both of you, understand? I'm not doing this with just one of you.

'No,' he growled angrily at an objection.

'It's my fucking rules or it's nothing. You want to meet me or not?

'Yes?

'Well then we meet where I want to meet.

'Don't give me that crap, we've all got too much riding on this.

'I don't care. Just do it. You're both going to be there? Right.

'Hey, no way! You wanted me to help didn't you? I passed your message on before, I can do it again, who else have you got that can do that for you? You need me.

'Oh and don't forget! It's one of the Firm's safe houses so it's bugged. So keep it quiet when you're inside and we'll talk out back when I get there.

'Time? Make it eight? OK?

'And you can guarantee Kev as well?'

There was a pause, before, 'Good. See you then.'

And he hung up.

'Will they be there?' asked Wibble.

'They'll be there,' Bob said confidently.

'Both?'

'Both of them? Yes, Noddy and Leeds Kev'll be there. Noddy's just told me not to worry about it, he'll make it happen.'

I had been right. Bob had been calling The Mohawks P and had arranged to see him and his ex Dead Men Riding VP.

'Sure? We need to make sure we get the top guys from both sides.'

'I'm certain. Noddy knows me and he knows not to fuck about with me.'

Wibble seemed to consider this for a moment, 'Well, you'd better be right.'

'I'm right. Just wait and see.'

*

'So how about matey boy here?' asked Wibble, as they both turned to look at me.

'What him?' grinned Bob, 'Oh yes, he's OK, I did it like you asked. I've planted stuff on the files. It shows he's tight with you guys. Photos of the support patch, everything.

'If he ever wants to write anything that's out of line or you just want to set him up to take the rap for something for the club, then the stuff on file will give it the right background.'

'You sure?'

'Yeah. It's all good stuff. I've even got bits in there showing he's been snitching on you to me, so it's covered from all angles. Photos, reports, tapes, transcripts, the works.'

Fuck it, transcripts! That confirmed it, the bastard had been bugging my phone.

'Good,' nodded Wibble approvingly.

'You want me to talk to him?' asked Bob.

'Yeah, you might as well.'

I yelled as Bob ripped the tape from across my mouth, taking it felt like a day's worth of stubble with it.

'Have you brought the pictures?' Wibble asked.

'Yeah, here, these are copies of some of what I've got on file. Have a look at the happy snaps,' he said reaching down into the briefcase on the floor and handing over a file fished out of it, 'the surveillance boys got some good ones.'

'Hmm…' said Wibble, as he started to flick through, '…nice.

'Hey, what did I tell you?' he said smiling as he flicked one of the 8 by 10s around so I could see it.

It was a bit of a grainy shot but it, and the next ones he flicked round in rapid succession were clear enough photographs of me arriving at his table at the services, shaking his hand, and sitting down to talk.

'Hey they've got you and Bung's good side haven't they?' Wibble joked as a glossy picture of the huge tattooed biker serving me my latte flashed past my eyes.

'Didn't know he had one,' said Bob.

'See?' Wibble said, ignoring him, 'I told you some fucker would be at it. The only thing you didn't know was that it would be these cunts.'

'So you knew there'd be cameras there?' I exclaimed.

'Don't be fucking stupid. Of course I knew the snappers would be there at the services. That was why we met there.'

'It was all part of you setting me up was it you bastard?' I spat at Bob.

'He's catching on isn't he?' mocked Bob looking over Wibble's shoulder at the file. 'There's some early ones, they got him talking to Scroat outside your place before the run. And then there's the funeral…'

'Ah sweet,' said Wibble stopping on a shot and then flicking it across for me to see myself standing side on beside a line of outlaw Harleys, 'they've got a good one of your support flash there haven't they?'

'Yeah, LLH&R,' Bob mocked.

'Why?' I asked.

Bob looked at me like I was some kind of an idiot and leant forward and down to speak straight into my face.

'The money of course, you twat. That's what it's all about these days, isn't it? You ought to know that.'

Behind him, over his shoulder, I saw Wibble casually raise his arm up. There was a sharp crack and a spray of blood and brains exploded into my face as the suddenly dead weight of Bob's lifeless body collapsed, slumping heavily down first against me where I was tied to the chair, and then flopped sickeningly sideways onto to the ground, the back of his head a mess of hair, blood and splintered bone.

As I sat open mouthed and dripping, Wibble stepped forward and prodded the body with his boot, the snub nosed revolver in his hand casually covering the lifeless form while he made sure Bob was dead.

There was no need for a second bullet. The first shot had been just into the back of his head behind his right ear and angled slightly upwards as he was bending down to talk to me. It had blown a hole in the top of his skull above the other ear on the way out.

From just six inches or so behind him when he had fired, there was no way that Wibble could have missed.

Despite that, deliberately and calmly he fired another bullet into the body where it lay with blood oozing out onto the pale carpet, and then another into the arm of the sofa on the other side of the room. It was as if he wanted to make a gift of ballistics evidence to whatever SOCO eventually got the shout here.

Christ, he's dropped him was all I could think, as I sat there stiff with shock.

And then I looked up at Wibble. The gun still casually in his hand.

And then I thought, Oh shit.

I was still having trouble processing what I had just seen, the way Wibble had just casually shot him execution style.

Shot him dead.

Killed.

In front of me.

Shock is a weird thing. In my experience, at least, you disassociate from the reality of the moment, you become a distanced observer, and you have almost an out of body experience as you see yourself and your situation, while at the same time, you fixate on the smallest things. It must be the brain's way of coping I guess.

And in my shock, all I could think about was to ask myself what Bob had meant by one of the first things he had said to me when he arrived.

It was a small nugget of a puzzle on which my brain focused.

And you did your bit too sunny Jim, didn't you? Printed what you were told to print like a good boy didn't you?

What was it that I had printed in one of my pieces that had come from him?

And the only thing I could really think of was the story that the Cambridge crew had been responsible for starting all this shit. Was that what he had meant?

But if Bob and Wibble had deliberately fed me with that, was everything that had happened since a set up?

*

Reaching down to me Wibble grabbed hold of my right hand where it was bound by my wrist to the arm of the chair. Before I could realise what he was doing he had forced the butt of the gun against my hand, using his other hand to press my fingers around it, wrapping it all in my fingerprints before placing it carefully in to a Tesco's carrier bag on the coffee table.

All the bikers I'd seen using this place had always been wearing gloves. Bob and I were the only people who'd ever been here without as far as I could tell. So when it came to dabs, mine would be the only ones around.

That's it I thought. There's no way I am walking away from this as a live witness now.

I knew too much.

And three can keep a secret.

12 Blood in, blood out

Wibble didn't seen too fussed about bothering to take me back to the cell so I just sat there while at my feet Bob's blood and brains slowly soaked into the filthy carpet.

Instead he wrote a number out on a scrap of piece of paper and once again forced my fingertips onto it before screwing it up and dropping it into a baggie which he slipped into his pocket.

*

The others arrived that evening. They came together as a group and I guessed they'd all travelled in one car which meant that they had to be very sure the flat was safe and not under surveillance by either the cops or The Mohawks. But then they could be sure of that sort of thing couldn't they, thanks to the late Bob's services.

Toad and Scoat I was expecting, it was the sight of the striker Charlie that was the surprise, Wibble had been so specific that this flat was for full patches only so I wondered what he was doing here with them.

No one seemed to be at all phased at the sight of the dead body of the copper on the floor, or of me taped to a chair as they automatically instructed Charlie as a striker to fix them drinks from the kitchen.

Either they really weren't bothered or they were expecting to see it.

Whichever way you read it, it didn't feel like good news.

*

But before they did anything else, Wibble had an announcement to make so he called the small group of bikers to order.

'Now, there's one important thing we need to talk about. As I think we all know, Charlie here's twenty-one tomorrow.'

There was a round of murmurs and jokes which Wibble waved down good naturedly.

'So we all know what that means don't we?'

There was another round of noise and then Wibble turned to focus directly on Scroat as the rest fell silent, whilst beside him Charlie stiffened in sudden anticipation.

'Scroat, you've been his sponsor,' asked Wibble quietly, 'so formally it's your shout, so I've gotta ask you the question. Is it time?'

Scroat glanced across at Charlie, who was now staring straight ahead. If he'd known how to stand to attention I guess he'd have been the pride of a sergeant major's parade ground, and then Scroat looked back straight into Wibble's eyes.

There was a hushed pause as everyone waited for him to speak. In their world, whoever the candidate might be, this was one of the key life changing moments for all involved, not just for the striker who was going to be put up, or their sponsor who was putting his reputation, and ultimately even his patch on the line for doing so; but for every member of the club who were potentially going to acquire a new brother to love, support and ultimately rely on.

LLH&R I thought suddenly.

LLH&R. This was what it was all about.

'For anyone else his age? No fucking way!' said Scroat eventually, and then his face cracked into an unaccustomed expression which I worked out had to equate to Scroat's nearest approximation to a smile.

'But for Charlie? Yeah, no question. He's got the stuff alright.'

At that there was an immediate outburst of cheering and backslapping for the now grinning and red-faced Charlie together with assurances that he'd make it and not to worry about the formal vote as it was a cert, while above the noise I heard Wibble asking somewhat superfluously, 'OK then, his sponsor is up for it. Any objections before it goes forward?'

And then he said something odd that I hadn't been expecting.

'How 'bout you Toad? After all, this affects you the most I guess?'

'No chance,' came an answering growl, 'it's cool by me. 'This was always the deal and I'm happy to stand by my part in it. Christ, man, I know it's an honour and all but as I always said, I never wanted the fucking aggro anyway. I'm happier being a soldier than an officer any day.'

'OK then, so that's it,' Wibble announced loudly to get everyone's attention back to proceedings, 'Charlie's up for a vote at full church on Monday.'

'Obviously,' he continued, talking directly to Charlie now with a serious expression on his face as the congratulatory huddle broke apart and rearranged itself into a meeting 'I can't promise what the guys are going to say…'

Then he smiled as well.

'But you've got my vote,' and with a throwing out of his arms he and Charlie bearhugged backslappingly.

The deal? What deal, I wondered?

'OK then lads,' Wibble announced as they broke apart, 'it shouldn't be long now so all we have to do is wait for the call.'

*

It came within about half an hour. Once again it was my phone, not Wibble's that rang.

'Are they there?' asked Wibble.

'OK? They've gone inside?

'Yes? You're sure it's both of them? Noddy and Leeds Kev?

Wibble gave the assembled silent room of bikers a quick thumbs up as he received the news he had been waiting to hear. And then the room went completely still as all eyes turned to Charlie.

'Great...

'Right, we'll handle it from here.

'You know what to do?

'OK,' he said, closing the call as the crowd gathered in a rough semicircle around him and Charlie who stood facing each other in front of where I sat.

Wibble stood there holding the phone and asked him quietly, 'Alright Charlie, you know what's happening here?'

Charlie nodded, 'Yeah, Scroat's filled me in.'

'Good, 'cos there's one last thing you can do, something that'll make it absolutely certain that you get voted in 'cos if anyone dares vote against you after this then they'll have all the guys in this room to answer to.'

There was a menacing supporting growl of anger and hackles raising in the room from all the bikers at the idea of anyone daring to gainsay Charlie's absolute right to a patch after what was about to happen.

'Are you ready for this?' Wibble continued, 'You know what they say, Blood in, Blood out.'

So that was why they had had so much fertiliser.

Charlie didn't bat an eyelid.

'Are you kidding? Give me the phone, I'm ready.'

They had been building two bombs.

Silently, Wibble held out the mobile and Charlie took it.

'Is it set...?'

Two bombs!

'The number's there, all you have to do is...'

'Dial,' Charlie finished it for him and without a flicker of hesitation he pressed the call button.

It was weird but you couldn't help but wait for the sound of a ring tone, or a noise of some kind.

As out on a quiet modern estate, somewhere on the outskirts of Luton and so handy for the M1, a circuit on the receiving phone closed...

I'd only seen one van in the yard. But there must have been another I now knew, there were certainly enough sacks of fertiliser for many more drums than I'd seen being filled. It would have been a smaller van this time I guessed, or something like an estate car. No, it would have been a small van I decided, something like an Astra or an Escort, an estate car was too risky, it would have been too easy to see into.

...the circuit sending a signal to the detonator...

It would be something that Bung could have driven to an anonymous modern detached house down some anonymous developer's cul-de-sac on an anonymous housing estate, and used the keys he'd taken from Bob to open up the doors to the integral garage and park it inside.

...and causing what, a couple of hundred pounds or so, of the tightly packed explosives packed into the bomb to erupt...

But here inside the room, for a second, there was nothing, before a roar of approval went up and suddenly the bikers were crowding round Charlie in a celebratory scrum as though he'd just scored a winning goal, rather than having cold bloodedly murdered at least two people, let alone whatever other casualties he'd caused on the estate.

...instantaneously blowing the small three bedroomed house, and everyone in it at the time, to smithereens...

Instead all around me there was an ongoing eruption of cheering and clapping from within the room as they fell on Charlie. I swear that if the ceiling hadn't been so low they'd have carried him on their shoulders on a victory lap round the flat.

...no burning debris falling to the ground, no car alarms wailing, no shattered glass scattered across the street...

Meanwhile, with one hand pressed against his free ear against the noise, Wibble was calling back his local observer for an immediate situation report and then his face broke into a broad grin of pure delight.

'Excellent...' I heard above the celebrations, 'now get the fuck out of there and I'll see you when you get back.'

Like Danny, Mikey and the Cambridge crew before them, Noddy and Leeds Kev had never stood a chance, never known what was about to hit them.

In one fell swoop The Brethren had just decapitated The Mohawks.

*

The guys had gone again, as quickly as they had arrived once the news was in.

It seemed from what he was saying that he and I had more time to kill as we waited for Bung to return to the flat with his cleaning gear, whatever that was.

If he had been the one with the keys to park the van inside the somewhat ironically named safe house, I guessed Bung had to have then stayed on to be Wibble's point man in Luton. The spotter, the observer on the ground checking the squaws into the house and passing word back for the hit. If I was right, I guessed he'd be a while. The road works on the M1 would be an absolute bastard.

It's a funny thing about knowing you are a dead man anyway. You end up being free to say whatever shit you want and eventually it was me that broke the silence this time.

'So Charlie's getting his colours I see,' I said, 'that's why you brought him up here tonight?'

'Yeah.'

'He's a bit young for it isn't he?'

'Well you know how it is, kids today...'

'But seriously...'

184

'No, seriously, have you seen some of the street gangs these days? DNS? OC? SMN?'

As a crime writer I knew of the likes of Don't Say Nothing, the Organised Criminals, Shine My Nine of course. The rise in street and young gang crime in London and elsewhere across the country was one of the scare stories of the moment. There were kids of twelve or so carrying guns around down in Croydon.

'But you guys are older…'

'Yeah we've always had an age bar at twenty-one but sometimes you've got to move with the times. It's all very well having all the old guys together but you can't stand still, you have to be thinking about the future of the club, the next generation.

'Besides which, it's good to get some new blood in. You've got to have young blood around, guys who are hungry to keep the club strong and looking after business.

'If we carried on like we are without bringing on new guys we'd just end up as a bunch of fat old bastards sat around on our lardy arses whinging on to each other about our cholesterol levels with a bunch of street kids running rings around us.

'This way there'll be new guys coming up through the ranks to keep the patch strong.

'Besides which, Charlie's special. He's a legacy. Don't get me wrong, we're not going to throw open the gates so any fucker can join, we've gotta maintain standards. People are still going to have to prove they've got what it takes to wear our flash, but we've gotta be realistic. We have to look at fresh talent and where it's merited give it a chance.'

'And Charlie's got that chance?'

'Well, like I said, Charlie's special. He's really got his old man's blood in his veins. Hey, you of all people ought to know that. He's the guy who put you here isn't he.'

I had to admit he was right.

'But Danny never had it did he? A chance I mean? You guys saw to that.'

'Well that's the way it goes sometimes. He knew what he was getting into. And we didn't do it to him, he did it to himself…'

'What d'ya mean you didn't do it to him? You're the ones that got him to drive the fucking van! You're the ones that got him to call the number, to send the signal to blow up the fucking van he was sitting in for Christ's sake!'

'He did it to himself when we heard he had called you. The moment he did that he was out.'

That chilled me instantly. It was simple confirmation that I'd been right, that Bob had been intercepting my calls and feeding them to The Brethren. What else did they know I wondered?

'War or no war, you guys are going to have quite a party tomorrow aren't you? You've got plenty to celebrate, what with topping the squaws and Charlie getting made up.'

'Yeah I guess we are at that.'

'So what was all that about with Toad? Why's it such a bigger thing for him than anyone else?'

'Oh, once he's patched, Charlie's going to take over as P up North.'

'Charlie?' I was shocked. 'But he can't just walk into that as soon as he's patched, can he?'

'It was part of the deal. Everybody knows that,' Wibble shrugged as if it explained everything.

'So I heard from Toad, but seriously Wibble, what is this all about? Is Charlie coming into his inheritance? Did Damage leave him the Northern charter in his will or something?'

He didn't want to answer that one.

'Anyway, whatever he says in public, Toad won't be happy about it,' I challenged.

'Toad? What d'you mean? About what?' he asked.

'About Charlie of course. Damage's son. The young pretender to the throne.'

'Oh that,' he said, 'Toad's fine with it, like I said, it was all arranged years ago. It's all part of the deal.'

So it wasn't just about getting his patch early. Once he was made up, Charlie was clearly being fast tracked within The Brethren for some reason, and taking over as Northern charter P was no joke. After all, part of

186

Damage's lasting legacy had been the entrenchment of the power of the Northern charter within the national club through its control of the business end of the club's affairs.

So what had been happening here? Could Toad really have just been holding the charter as a regent pending Charlie's vote?

And if so, would he really just step aside now that it was time, let go of the reins and hand it over to some kid, whoever's kid he was? How happy would he be to do that? And if he did, where would he stand? Even if he was completely loyal it could be a dangerous place, being a power behind the throne. Because to whoever was on the throne, anyone with power, with respect, however they acted, would always have to be seen as a potential threat.

In some ways, as Damage had pointed out to me long before, a healthy dose of paranoia was a necessary survival trait as a Brethren P. But as he had also acknowledged, it was a fine balance to maintain, since an obvious lack of trust in those around you alienated your potential supporters and corroded the strength of feeling that made up the bonds of LLH&R that wove them together; whilst obvious paranoia made you a threat to everyone else with any standing in your charter or club and the natural reaction to any threat was for the threatened to seek to destroy it utterly.

'It'll be OK,' Wibble said, as if reading my mind, 'Charlie knows he needs Toad's local cred with the guys so he'll be working hard at keeping him onside.'

'Maybe,' I said, unconvinced. 'So what if that was the deal? That was then, this is now. Times change, people change.'

'Besides which, Toad's his uncle anyway.'

I must have looked surprised.

'On his mum's side, not Damage's. So it's all in the family.'

'Yeah, like that's a guarantee,' I sneered. 'You ever watch The Sopranos? Yes OK, Damage was respected but he's been gone a while now. How do you know that Toad hasn't settled into his role? And what about the other guys in the north, how d'you know they're going to be cool about some freshly made up kid coming in as new head honcho?'

'Well that's true enough, but I guess Charlie will just have to persuade them won't he?'

'Persuade them? What's he going to say to do that then?'

Wibble grinned at that.

'Say? Nothing. You have to show people in this game, not tell them. Words are just empty bags of air. Who's going to believe them?'

'But you can't be serious about putting a kid like that in charge of a charter can you? Particularly not now?'

'Why not now?'

I was lost for words for a second or two.

'Because you're at war aren't you? And what, your cunning plan is to put a twenty-one year old who's been made up the day before, in charge of your key powerbase? Is it just me or does that sound nuts?'

His grin just got wider as he I spoke.

'Not really, not anymore,' he replied.

I was confused.

'Why not? What do you mean?' I asked.

He shrugged.

'That's it, we've won.'

'What d'you mean you've won? You've just taken out two of their guys that's all. They'll be back at you soon enough.'

'No, we've not just taken out two of their guys. We've taken out their top two guys. There's a difference.

'And it won't just be them will it?' he continued, 'this is wartime don't forget, neither of those two will have gone anywhere without at least one, maybe two bodyguards each, possibly more.

'So if we're lucky we'll have taken out maybe half a dozen of them including some of their toughest guys.'

'Even so…'

'Don't you get it?'

He held up his hand to count on his fingers for my education, 'Number one, we've decapitated them. No one will be in charge and whoever's left in either club will need to sort out between them who's going to take over.

'Chances are they'll fall apart again if they can't agree between them sharpish who it's going to be.'

'Divide and conquer?'

'Something like that.

'Number two, we've done it to both sides and they won't know how we knew to do it. They'll be running scared, wondering what went wrong. A grass is the obvious explanation and each side'll be suspicious it was someone in the other club.'

'So it's divide and rule?'

'Absolutely. Number three, we've taken out some key members. You know how the clubs work, and the goat fuckers and zombies were no different. They've got to have about half a dozen or so full patches to have a charter otherwise you can't control your turf. Get too much bigger than that and you start to have infighting so you split some off into a new charter to take new turf.'

He made it sound a bit like amoebas. I had a silent mental vision of a culture multiplying and spreading across the face of a petri dish.

'And between them they had five charters which means they've probably only got around thirty, maybe forty or so full patches. And if we've taken out half a dozen then they're down by what, fifteen percent or so in one hit?

'And in a war where they're fighting against two clubs with a combined strength of about a hundred and fifty between us, that's serious.'

'Number four, the war will be hurting their trade. We're national, our business is still going on around the country. They're regional, all their shit is concentrated in one area and while this war is on they'll all be in full lock down.'

'It'll be hurting.'

'So they'll soon need to come out to keep their business going, and that's when we'll be out there, hunting them down, one by one.'

*

There was a knock at the door.

Wibble peered at a small CCTV set hanging on the wall just above the light switch before throwing the bolts to open up. Even so, he kept his gun in his hand as he did so.

'Ah good, he's here!'

Bung had arrived back.

189

'So, shall we do it now?' Bung asked once he was inside with the bag he was carrying.

'Might as well,' said Wibble, 'everyone's gone and they won't be coming back.'

'OK then, I'll get set up.'

Bung plonked the bag on the table and unzipping it brought out an ordinary desktop electric fan, an extension lead and a part filled black plastic bin bag while Wibble resecured the door behind him.

Plugging the lead into a socket just behind the door he trailed the flex to the middle of the room, connected up the fan and then untied the top of the plastic bag.

'I hate this,' said Wibble conversationally, 'it always makes me sneeze.'

Bung switched the fan on, turned it up to maximum and lifted it up in his right hand.

As it whirred dementedly, he plunged his other hand into the open bin bag. Lifting out a cupped handful of dust and crap, he thrust in front of the fan's wire guard and then, blasting the dust into the air as he did so, began to work his way methodically around the room.

'We get it from a car vacuuming service down at Tesco's,' Wibble told me conversationally as Bung tugged at the trailing extension cable so that he could pull the fan and his bag of fluff down the corridor and towards the room they had used as my cell. 'It's run by some Polish guy. He's got a connection with the club back home so he saves it for us when we want some.

A minute or so later the noise of the fan cut out and Bung reappeared with an empty bag.

You didn't have to be a genius to work out what he'd just done. With the dust from out of tens, if not hundreds, of cars now silently and gently settling throughout the flat across every available surface, the scene was now completely contaminated as far as any DNA trace evidence was concerned.

'Well, what do you know?' said Wibble sounding pleasantly surprised, 'This time it hasn't got to me.'

'Yet,' said Bung with a smirk.

'Well that's true,' said Wibble playing the martyr.

There was just too much of it to be any use in picking out any individuals and hoping to tie them to the flat. So as and when they found this place, assuming for a moment they ever did, the cops would be reliant on more old fashioned technologies. They would be looking for fingerprints, but of course The Brethren had all been wearing gloves all the time. I thought again about the objects that were forced into my hands, including the gun. Anything I had touched like that would have my fingerprints all over it.

'OK Chief,' asked Bung. 'Do you want me to handle this?'

'No, it's OK I'll look after it, you go see…'

And Wibble walked him to the door giving him instructions as he went and clanging the steel security doors shut behind him.

So then it was just back to the three of us again in the flat.

Wibble, me, and Bob still lying oozing onto the floor.

*

'Why me?' I asked after a while.

It was a question I'd been asking myself for a while.

Obviously I hadn't been brought in for PR purposes. That story had to be complete bullshit.

'Because you knew Bob and Bob knew you,' Wibble said as though it was the most obvious thing in the world. 'You were his choice not mine.'

'Choice, what choice?'

'He wanted someone outside to know, someone who could be a witness if anything went wrong. You were part of his insurance policy, his back up. You were just one of the safeguards he wanted to have in place when he made contact.'

'Whatever the risk to me?'

'He didn't give a flying fuck about that. Why should he?'

So my guesses had been right after all. Wibble had only brought me in as a way of getting to Bob. I had been what, go-between? Hostage? Witness? All of them or something in between?

I had been there because Bob had wanted me there, to have a liaison point, a source he could trust, and Wibble had agreed they would bring me in and use me.

For Bob I was part of his security, if anything went wrong he had hoped my presence and press links would make it more difficult for Wibble to do anything about him.

'Having you around, it was just part of the way to get to Bob. You were just a risk worth taking.'

For Wibble, for a while, I was part of the price he paid for maintaining Bob, and then in the end, I was the bait for Bob, luring him into a situation where Wibble could deal with what could otherwise be a dangerous loose end.

'Well what now?'

'Well, now then,' he said facing me and holding the bag with the pistol casually in his hand, 'we've got another decision to make haven't we?'

13   Out

Monday 23 August 2010

There was a flat dark grey sky and the smell of damp and turf smoke outside again when I opened the door, while the rain was an insistent and insidious fine continual drizzle.

It'll be nice when they put the roof on it, as she always said whenever I moaned about what she called the soft weather.

I shuffled as quickly as I could round to the outhouse at the back where we'd installed a shower, trying to keep under the roof's overhang and out of the long cold wet grass as much as possible.

Inside, I washed. The little electric shower had been an absolute bastard to fit when I'd got it, but it made all the difference in making the place habitable. It had been raining now for about three days solid and the flow of water in the spring that fed the tank had stirred up the usual level of peaty sediment, so that the water coming out of the tap was the colour of cold tea and was quickly staining the tile grouting to a yellow brown.

A mile and a half out of town and up a winding mud and gravel farm track off the road, the cottage was an old traditional single storey, slate roofed, stone flagged, whitewashed Irish farmhouse. Beyond the gate held shut with string, the path led through an overgrown garden to a small porch to hang up waterproofs and keep the worst of the weather out. Inside there were just two rooms with a central chimney for the kitchen-cum-living room's peat range and the wholly inadequate little stove in the bedroom. Outside there was a stone built outhouse with a pile of dried turf cut by the owners the previous summer, and an outside loo at the end of the building, which now backed onto the newly installed shower facilities.

Romantic, unless and until you actually had to try living there.

A young guy in Belfast had inherited it the agent had told me. It had been his uncle's hidey hole or something, although anything less like a secret passion palace it was a bit hard to imagine. Anyway the current owner never used it, except very occasionally for a quick break and didn't have any cash to spend on doing it up so while he'd had it listed as being for rent no one had ever wanted it.

Not until I had come along that is.

For me, it was ideal.

It was anonymous, but not too low profile or that would raise suspicions and questions in itself, particularly here, where people were very good at not asking questions. Derry was only a few tens of miles away across the border and the boyos' white painted Mac-mansions paid for by the troubles with their high walls and parked Mercedes had sprouted around the landscape.

Here, up my quiet ungraded track, well off the road in the wild Irish countryside of Donegal, I had no neighbours.

I liked it here, there was the space, the emptiness, the lack of people. When it was dry some evenings, as it had occasionally been over the summer, I could sit outside playing music; Leonard Cohen, Radiohead, sometimes even Bauhaus if I could stand it.

*

With my cap jammed down on my head and fastening my jacket against the rain as I pulled the door shut behind me, I set off along the track to the road and the walk down into the village.

I walked in once a week or so to pick up the papers they kept for me.

'Hi there,' I said as I walked up to the counter of the village stores, 'here for the news.'

'Now here you are then,' the shopkeeper said reaching under the counter and producing the week's bundle.

'D'you have a piece in this week?' he asked.

'Might have,' I said, 'I'm not sure till I check.'

We had more or less the same exchange every week as he stuffed the papers into a plastic carrier bag so I could keep them dry, or as dry as possible on the walk home back up the hill. It was a routine.

I had thought that I had to tell him, and them something, as not telling people anything would lead to even more questions and right now, questions were the last thing on earth I wanted. And I'd thought that saying something that was close to the truth would be easier to carry off than an absolute fiction.

So I had told the agent I was a freelance writer, after the peace and quiet to work on a book, which was kind of the truth as it happened, but not the whole truth obviously. And now everybody locally knew it too.

There was a howl as I splodged my way through the puddles along the track and then an outbreak of ferocious sounding barking as I reached the gateposts, a noise that didn't seem to be disturbing the cows grazing in the field opposite one iota. Robbie, our Old English Sheepdog came bounding down the path, a muddy dreadlocked bundle of fur and teeth. He was soft as shit with us but big and nervously loud and territorial when it came to anyone else swinging off the track and starting to undo the twine holding the rusty iron gate shut. Which was just what I had wanted when I'd found him almost a year ago just after I'd arrived, lost or, more likely these days, abandoned, howling in the pound; alarm and deterrent in one furry package.

She was sat at the kitchen table as I walked back in. The folder with its typed pages open in front of her, the inevitable mug of tea cupped in her hands.

'Have you read it?' I asked.

'Yes,' she said, looking up at me with an odd expression in her eyes.

'So what do you think?' I asked.

She seemed to consider this for a moment.

'Well I have to say, I just don't get it. Why are you still alive?'

I sighed.

That was the easy part.

*

'So what happened?' she asked.

We were lying in bed. The fire had burnt down in the grate and I needed to organise some more turf, but snuggled up here with her under the warmth of the duvet, and with the wind howling around the outside of the cottage, venturing out into the dark was the last thing I wanted to do right now.

So I told her.

I talked her though my last conversation with Wibble.

The last one I'd had, and which I sincerely hoped, would be the last one I would ever have.

14 These colours don't run

He had picked up one of the cheap looking kitchen chairs and carried it over to just opposite me. He swung it round so it was facing away and plonked himself down astride it, legs either side, so his face was a few feet from mine, his chin resting on his clasped hands and his elbows resting on the straight top of the chair back.

'Look, before we go any further,' he said, 'I want you to understand one thing. I'm not stupid, so don't make the mistake of ever trying to treat me as if I am. Is that clear?'

I nodded.

I had never thought he was stupid and I certainly wasn't going to make that mistake now.

'Now I know you're not stupid either, am I right?'

I nodded again, more gingerly this time.

'So I'm guessing that you are going to have taken steps to protect yourself. Once you started getting involved with us that is.'

I didn't know what to say at this point but it didn't seem to matter, Wibble wasn't actually waiting for or even seeming to expect a response from me at this point.

'Look,' he said making himself explicit, 'I know you'll have a whole load of incriminating stuff on us. Files, papers, notes, tapes, pictures, all sorts of whatever, right?'

I shrugged as best I could in my trussed state. There was no point in denying it.

'And now you know all this shit as well,' he continued, as if in appreciation of my honesty he was going to be honest straight back.

So I would have protected myself he rationalised. He was just setting out his assumptions, what he would have done in my place.

Whatever I had found out and put in the paper, there would be other stuff that I would have found, stuff that I would know but couldn't have published, either because it didn't fit a story, or because I didn't have the evidence as such to back it up. Stuff however that, even if I didn't have proof, would be stuff that was useful to the cops. And if I was going to protect myself, what I would probably do is keep a full file somewhere, a file with everything I knew or thought I knew, a file to be opened in case of my suspicious death; a file in other words to hold over the head of anyone who might be thinking about organising a suspicious death.

I didn't say anything to disabuse him of this conclusion.

'There'd be everything you've ever had about us, going all the way back, the stuff from Damage, the tapes of your conversations, everything. Am I right?'

I nodded.

'Of course you have,' he said. 'What else would I expect you to do? You'd be an idiot not to do something like that to protect yourself wouldn't you? We've just agreed that neither of us are stupid haven't we?'

I just stared back at him, waiting to see where this was going.

'I think we understand each other?' he insisted.

At that I just nodded, 'I think we do.'

'So,' he continued conversationally, as he began to outline his options as he saw them and setting out their logic almost to himself at first, just as if he was running through an everyday mental list. 'I could get some of the guys to torture you, work you over until we get you to reveal what you've done, what you've put where.

'But then I'd never actually know for sure would I? You can get people to say anything with enough time and pressure, but you never know whether they've actually told you the truth, or the whole truth, or just what they think you want to hear. So I'm not a big fan, it's too uncertain, although obviously it has its place.

'Not when there are other ways. Other things that have more certainty.

'You know what we're capable of and prepared to do.'

I nodded, I knew just what they could do. I'd heard and now seen enough to know that.

'We could just snuff you,' he continued in a perfectly calm tone, 'but then we're back at the file problem aren't we? We just don't know what you've got put away that could come out and hurt us.'

So it sounded as though killing me and what might then bite him on the arse were just moral equivalents, nothing more than a choice of inconviences when it came down to it as far as Wibble was concerned.

'On the other hand we could just kick you out…'

'But then how do you know I won't talk?' I interrupted, not quite believing what I was hearing coming out of my mouth. Almost too surprised to try to box clever and bargain for my life, or perhaps looking back on it, just clever enough. Protestations that he could trust me not to tell anyone, not to talk would have been a waste of time. There was no way Wibble was going to rely on any crap I might say at a moment like this when I could be saying anything just to save my own skin.

No, Wibble didn't operate like that. Wibble operated on the basis of interests and fears and what makes people really tick. Wibble wasn't going to let me go on the basis of anything I might say. What was it he had called promises? Empty bags of air.

No, Wibble was going to make his decision based on realities, of threats and opportunities, on his judgement of risks and rewards, for him and for me and how these would make each of us act.

This wasn't a time for emotions or sentiment or pleading.

This was a moment for cold headed hard rationalism I realised. That and the right answers and circumstances were all that were going to keep me alive and get me out of here. I needed to be part of a real conversation with my potential killer, about the realpolitik of my situation and his potential interests in its potential outcomes.

'How do you know I won't just go to the cops with what I know?' I challenged, engaging with him in the process.

'Well firstly, why should they believe you? After all you're on their files, you heard what matey boy here put there,' he said, nodding casually at the blood stained mess that had been Bob, 'and now he's going to disappear. For the moment.'

He caught the look on my face as I realised what he meant.

'He'll be going somewhere nice and safe where he won't be found, and that gun with your prints on it? It'll be going with him, that and oh, I don't know, how about a note in his pocket asking him to come over to this flat? The one that'll also have your dabs on it.

'Not to mention all the other tasty bits of stuff,' he said with a grim grin tugging the baggie with the bomb's detonation telephone number out of his pocket and dangling it between two fingers in front of my face.

'But the question you then need to ask yourself is, are they going to stay there, or are they going to reappear some day? Are you getting the picture?'

Oh yes, I was getting the picture alright. The cops turning up Bob's murdered body with hard evidence linking a gun and a crime scene back to a scumbag journalist with evidence on their files that I was some kind of tagalong wannabe Brethren, probably out to prove myself. That was going to take some talking my way out of.

'And secondly?' I asked.

'Well I'd have thought that would be easy, after our little chat a while ago wouldn't it?'

I guess it was. He could only be referring back to that afternoon, a few weeks and a lifetime ago now, when we had sat in the sunshine at the garden table out back of the London clubhouse, and he'd calmly and comprehensively catalogued everything they knew about me and mine.

Yes, I could see where he was heading with this bit of the picture he was painting.

'We know where your family is. We know where your friends are,' he answered, as if laying out for me the arguments he had been rehearsing to himself in his head. As if saying them out loud, spelling them out to me, helped him to refine his own logic and where it was taking him in his world of interests and pressures.

'And the question you need to ask yourself is, would shopping us really be worth the risk?

'Is it really going to be safe if you grass us up to the cops? For you, for them?

'Even if the cops nick a load of us, they won't get the whole club, there'll still be some of us out there, and then beyond Britain there's a whole world of our brothers we can call on for help. It'll take months to come to trial. Months when you and your testimony will be target number one.'

He prodded Bob's dead body with his foot. 'Do you really think we haven't got any more people we use within the cops, that this was it? Do you really think the cops can keep you, your family, your friends, every one of them, safe until a trial is over?

'And even after that, what then? How long do you think the cops will keep it up once you've given your evidence?

'You have to ask yourself how long after the verdict is in will the cops stay interested? And then ask yourself, how long do you think we'll be prepared to wait if necessary?'

He went on remorselessly, 'And even if the cops keep you all safe, what's it going to be like? You might be prepared to spend the rest of your life on the run but are you going to do that to your family? Are you really going to put them all through that, for the rest of their lives?'

It took a moment for me to realise he had stopped speaking.

'What's this?' I asked confused, 'what about *Three can keep a secret?*'

I held my breath as I heard the words out loud. What I had just said without thinking about it? Did I want to die?

He looked thoughtful as he considered. Then it seemed that at last he had reached a decision.

'Yeah well, sometimes,' he answered, 'just sometimes, maybe three can keep a secret better if two are alive rather than one.'

I shut my eyes with a silent prayer of thanks.

'Well,' he continued, 'if I tell my guys you're dead, then so long as you disappear and no one hears a peep out of you, you're going to be safe aren't you? No one's going to come looking for a dead man are they?'

'And if no one hears from me about any of this then you'll be safe as well? Is that it? Is that the deal?' I answered bitterly.

He gave a satisfied smile, 'Well yes, now you come to mention it. Now isn't that a happy coincidence?'

'Isn't it just.'

'Just so long,' he emphasised, the smile switched off as suddenly as it had come, and a cold look in his eyes, 'as nothing, and I mean nothing, ever comes out to suggest that you might still be alive. Nothing about this, nothing about what you've seen, nothing about anything, ever. Zilch! Got it?'

I nodded. I got it. 'Understood.'

'Good,' he said, for all the world as if we had just concluded some ordinary business deal. But then in his world perhaps we had. Perhaps it was just me who wasn't used to bargaining for my life.

*

'But why kill him?' I asked nodding down at Bob by my feet. 'That wasn't just about setting me up was it?'

'Nah,' Wibble shrugged as though it was of very little importance. 'Don't flatter yourself. He got too greedy, too demanding, he outlived his usefulness, he knew too much, he became a threat, he was playing all ends against the middle, us, the cops, the Mohawks, selling info on all of us to the others. Take your pick,' he said off-handedly.

Then Wibble stopped and looked at me quizzically for a moment, as if wondering how far he wanted to go with something.

Then as if he had made up his mind he asked, 'Do you remember you asked me once who would have known about what was going down at the meeting? The peace deal?'

'Yes.'

'Well outside of the club, the only other people who would have known were the cops, his mob,' he said, giving the body a prod with his foot.

'Would they? Are you sure? How?'

'Well we know they are investigating us, they use bugs, they try and get people into the club. Sometimes we spot 'em and then it's a choice. Do we leave them be and just use them? Or do we sort 'em out?'

I didn't want to ask what 'sort 'em out' meant as I could guess all to easily what it might involve.

'And you made sure news got back.'

Yeah, I made sure Bob here got to know about it.'

'How can you be so sure?' I asked.

'Because I was the one who told him,' he said flatly.

As I sat there, slack jawed while I took this in, all I could think of was to ask, 'Why?'

'Well, somebody had to make the calls.'

Calls, I wondered. How many calls? And what about?

'But why did you tell him?'

'Because I thought he would make trouble with it.'

'Why would he do that?'

'He was a cop of course,' he said sounding surprised that I'd even had to ask, 'investigating the clubs. If times were peaceful, what's he got to show for his investigations? Diddily squat and we're all out getting on with our business so he's not shining in the force. And by the same token, how much do we need to pay a bent cop when times are sweet? Why should we, what's in it for us?'

Not a lot, I could see that.

'But when the shit hits the fan, all of a sudden there's more action around. More stuff for him to do on the force, higher profile investigations, all that shit.'

'And there's a bigger and better market he had for his stuff with you guys.'

'Yeah sure.'

And of course it just made perfect sense when he said it.

'The more uncertainty there was, the more we would need the information he could sell.'

'And the more you needed it…'

'The more he could reckon on raking off us for it,' he confirmed.

'What did he mean when he asked Noddy if the offer was still open?'

'Capricorn had used him to put out feelers…'

'A last ditch attempt to avert war?

'Yeah, they wanted us to call Thommo's boys off.'

And Bob had brought this message to Wibble. I couldn't quite believe what I was hearing. Not speaking to the cops about anything was such a fundamental rule amongst the clubs that I wanted to be sure about what he was saying.

'So you knew he was going to make trouble with the info you gave him? About the meet and The Rebels being there?'

Wibble seemed pleased that I'd joined the dots. Of course he was the one that had told the cops.

'Yeah, well I guessed he might.'

'That much trouble?'

He laughed, 'Well no, not quite that much.'

'Did he do it deliberately?'

'Yeah I reckon so. He knew what he was doing. The cops would have had sources in the goat fuckers and the zombies. He would have known that they were in the process of patching over to the squaws. He'd have known they'd want to blow onto the stage with a spectacular. And our run up to Cambridge is right into the turf the goat fuckers have always claimed was theirs so it wouldn't have taken a genius to work out what was likely to go down and where.'

No it wouldn't have, I decided. And that would have gone for Wibble as well. He might not have anticipated that the Mohawks would be patching over The Capricorn or Dead Men Riding, but he would have anticipated some trouble.

What was it Bob had said about Damage? He'd forever been going on about the *pax Damage.*

Damage had won the peace, had been his point, and that was what had settled his rep within the club.

Damage's were a big man's shoes to step into. So big that it had taken three of them to do it at the time but that wasn't something that was going to last for ever.

How do you step into a big man's shoes? You have to earn your own respect, your own rep, by doing something different.

So if Wibble wasn't going to forever be living in Damage's shadow, then Wibble would have to do something different. Just continuing Damage's peace wouldn't be enough.

Wibble would have to win a war.

There would have been just one slight practical problem with that as a plan for consolidating his powerbase and position from Wibble's point of view.

Which opened a whole new can of worms.

To win a war, there had to be a war to win.

*

There were so many questions that were churning around in my head and demanding answers, right now, about the events of that day back in Cambridge when the rockets exploded, that I was having trouble thinking straight.

It was a crazy idea. It was too big a risk even for someone like Wibble to contemplate.

After all, how far could Wibble really hope to try to control events once a war had started?

Everything would then be in play, nothing would be certain from then on.

The Mohawks' attack could well have immediately resulted in a challenge to his leadership from someone like Thommo. But for how it had actually turned out, wouldn't a war have given Thommo the ideal opportunity to try unseating Wibble using the pitch, 'We need a real boss in charge now, not some kind of weak-arsed compromise choice?'

But it hadn't happened like that, had it?

Instead, the way it had turned out the war had bought time for Wibble's leadership.

In fact, going further, the war would have actually made it difficult for Thommo to start a challenge to Wibble, not just because of the way Thommo's boys were involved, but in general, because the natural reaction of the club under attack would have been to enrage their truly ferocious elemental sense of loyalty to the club and each other.

When one Brethren fights, all Brethren will participate was the club rule.

So God help anyone inside or outside the club who got in the way of that.

No, the only risk for Wibble to his position from a Thommo challenge was if the war had gone badly. But then again, if the war had gone badly, given that Thommo was responsible for leading the fight locally, how strong would Thommo's credentials have then been to launch a take over bid?

That couldn't be right, could it? That the outbreak of war was actually a win/win situation as far as Wibble was concerned? But the more I thought about it, the more I started to think that it was.

Fact – the war was actually good for Wibble. It was just what he needed to show the club and any private doubters what he was made of. It was his opportunity for him to show he could lead the club.

Which begged the question, how much had Wibble known about the planned attack in advance?

Fact – from what he'd said he was obviously expecting some trouble. He'd told me as much and…

Fact – he'd actually deliberately leaked the information about the event to Bob because he thought it would get back to Capricorn and Dead Men Riding through him and cause some trouble.

So really, the only question was, had he known it was going to be so serious?

The choices weren't appealing.

Perhaps Wibble didn't know anything about what was about to go down that day. He might have been expecting there to be some aggro at some point, perhaps even a ruck, but not the sort of attack that actually happened, in which case he would have been as surprised as anyone when the assault came.

But given the build up of tensions, and with the show being on Cambridge turf just next door to Capricorn, Wibble surely had to know there was a risk of real trouble that day. He didn't seem the type to be in denial or to think that something on that scale just couldn't happen, but then if Barbarossa seemed to take a suspicious bastard like Stalin by surprise even after all the warnings the Soviets had received, didn't that prove anyone could make a mistake?

The final possibility was the truly chilling one, which was that Wibble had known full well about the Mohawks' plans to attack that day and their likely scale; but had calmly and deliberately let the event go ahead and accepted all the casualties that would ensue, without warning anyone else in the club what was about to take place. Now I was starting to sound like one of those American nutters who say Roosevelt deliberately let Pearl Harbour happen.

Bob was the key here I realised.

I knew Bob had contacts with the other clubs' leaders, Noddy and Leeds Kev, his last conversation with Noddy had been evidence of that. But whatever relationship they had with him I reckoned they were unlikely to tell a copper what they were planning were they?

But he also had other sources in the clubs I was sure of that. It had to have been him who called Wibble after the Cambridge crew bomb to say that the Mohawks leadership weren't getting together the way Wibble had expected.

So what would Bob have known about the planned attack in advance and how much had he told Wibble?

Bob was the key to the puzzle.

But Bob was dead.

Two can keep a secret, I thought to myself bitterly.

*

So was that it? Was this war Wibble's Thatcher moment?

It was starting to look like it.

A war would unite everyone underneath him, it was no time for division and anyone who showed anything but absolute loyalty to the club and its war at such a time would be risking more than just their colours, so it would remove any immediate threat of a challenge.

There was a risk that it would give an opportunity to a challenger if the war didn't go well. Someone could say that it was time for a change at the top, that The Brethren needed a real leader. But it would be a tricky pitch to make, particularly for someone already known to have a grudge, as it risked being seen putting personal interests before the club and being divisive in the face of the enemy.

If Wibble won the war, he would be safe with his reputation ensured across the club.

Even as a combination of two regional clubs, the enemy would be relatively weak in numbers compared to the full strength of The Brethren's national presence; let alone in combination with The Rebels. So whatever happened, the club stood a good chance in winning any war.

And it was a war moreover that he and his supporters didn't need to do much fighting in. Since because of the way that it started, Thommo and his Cambridge crew had to take that job on.

So for Wibble, once it was on, really it was a safe little war.

It all came back to Bob again.

There had been a peace overture before. Capricorn had put out a call via a trusted contact, with a message for The Brethren, call off your dogs in Cambridge before it's too late.

But it didn't happen.

Bob?

Bob had been the channel.

We want you to use the place you met them before.

Wibble had known that Bob had used the safe house to meet with Noddy and Leeds Kev before. It had been where they'd given him the message to take to The Brethren.

Bob knew all the clubs and was known to all the clubs. He was the obvious choice to use as a last ditch envoy.

Bob. That was why they knew him. That was why they knew the house. That was why they thought they were going to meet him there.

Meet me where we did before, you remember?

That was it. I knew.

And who would Bob have taken a message like that to?

Well there was only one answer to that wasn't there?

And he was straight in front of me talking to me.

Wibble had had the peace message from Bob before the war finally erupted.

But how long had Wibble had the message for? Trouble had been brewing for a few months in retrospect.

And then there had been the Leeds shooting. The local clubs would have been on edge, waiting for The Brethren's response. They'd already lost both a member and a business and now they were waiting to hear what the verdict was going to be, peace or war?

And what did they get?

A drug debt collecting Cambridge charter full patch Brethren turning up in the heart of the zombies' territory and throwing his weight around as he came to lean on somebody for money.

It had to have been the final straw. Dead Men Riding and Capricorn had taken it as their answer and it had all kicked off from there.

And to make all that happen, all Wibble had to do was to have deliberately ignored the message for long enough to have let it happen.

Cry 'Havoc!' and let slip the dogs of war.

Damage had brought and won the peace.

So Wibble had brought and won the war.

I was sure of it.

*

'So what happens now?'

'Now? About the squaws?' he seemed surprised that I needed to ask.

'Now we wipe out the rest of them, hunt them down, strip their colours, we might even have some of them strike for us, the ones we think have something, and we'll split up their turf with The Rebels.'

'How?'

207

'Oh we've already sorted that. The Rebels'll get Leeds and around about for the clubs, the security work. It gives them the dealing territory.

'We'll take East Anglia and the goatfuckers' routes. We'll keep them open and the shit coming in, only now it will be our shit.

'So it all works out fine in the end. The Rebels get some good paying turf, we take out a competitor on the supply side. Everybody's happy.'

'And you've established your own reputation and one of your rivals got taken out into the bargain?'

'Yeah, sweet isn't it?' he smiled.

I risked the guess, more for confirmation than anything new really.

'Just hypothetically, the war was good for you wasn't it? You couldn't lose unless you really lost it, in which case it wouldn't have mattered anyway would it?' I asked.

'Well to quote something else old Damage was very fond of saying, *you might very well think that*,' he said, reaching forward and prodding me in the chest, *'but I couldn't possibly comment*, and more to the point, you couldn't possibly write it could you?'

'No, no I couldn't,' I admitted as he stood back and looked down at me.

For all sorts of reasons.

*

'Why don't I tell you a joke?' he asked.

'A joke?'

'Yes a joke. Don't sound so surprised, you'll enjoy this one.

'There's this dictator right? And he's on his deathbed so they call for a priest to read him his last rites.

'So this young priest gets called in and he's put in a chair by the side of the dictator's bed and nervously he starts to prepare him for death, asking for God's blessing and all that sort of stuff.

'*Do you forgive your enemies*? asks the priest.

'*Oh I have no enemies*, the dying man replies calmly.

'*How do you know that*? asks the priest surprised that such a powerful figure like this could be so sure.

'*Oh that's simple*, the dictator replies, *I had them all shot.*'

It was funny, I'd give him that. But it was funny with a message. A bit like a lot of things I got used to someone else saying to me, a couple of years ago now that seemed like a lifetime.

'Damage told you that one didn't he?' I asked, taking a chance. It had to have been him, it just sounded too much like Damage for it not to be. And from Wibble it sounded like some kind of a test.

I just hoped to God that I'd passed.

He nodded, 'Yes, yes he did.'

There was a strange look on his face, one that I couldn't decipher. Then with what might have been a small sigh, as if over some little regret, he added, 'He was a good teacher, was Damage.'

A veritable *Prince* amongst men I thought but did not say.

And Wibble had been a good student by the looks of things. If a charter gets out of hand, the answer is simple, liquidate it and turn the liquidation into an opportunity to be made the most of.

Damage would have been proud of that one.

*

'So?' he said as though he was waiting for some kind of answer.

'So?' I asked.

'So do we have a deal?' he said.

'We need to make a decision one way or the other since we're going to need to start getting organised,' he said coming back to the point of our cosy little chat.

'The plod'll be able to trace the detonation call within a few days I guess. As soon as they find the remains of the phone they'll know that was how it was set off and start looking. They'll be able to zero it back to here easy enough through triangulation, they can work out a bearing from the local masts that have relayed the signal. And when they find here, they'll find the blood, they'll find the bullet, they'll find your dabs.

'But what they won't find is a body, or these,' he said picking up the white red and blue Tesco's carrier bag from the coffee table containing the gun and my phone, and the baggie, 'at least...'

'Not if I keep my mouth shut.'

'Not if you disappear you mean.'

'And where will they be?' I said nodding at the bag which looked heavy with my future.

'Oh I'll be keeping them safe, you can bank on that. But they will if...'

I nodded in agreement. 'What choice do I have?'

'None, and that's the way I like it,' he said with satisfaction.

*

Having decided what he was going to do with me, to my surprise, Wibble didn't seem to be in any great hurry to do it. I realised that as I sat there, bound to my chair and listening to him barking orders down the phone on a number of calls over the next hour or so, I just wasn't at the top of his list of priorities today. As far as Wibble was concerned, I was just one more loose end he'd needed to tie up and now he'd done so.

He seemed to have got over any irritation he'd felt at my question and between the events he was coordinating we even had time to talk a bit more.

*

It gave me more time to think through the implications of what he'd told me. And the more I thought about them, the worse they looked.

Ever since the Cambridge crew bomb it was obvious that Wibble had taken advantage of the situation to settle internal club business.

But now, knowing that Wibble might actually have deliberately started it, since it was more than a simple sin of omission in allowing the war to start, I was presented with another possibility.

That Wibble had planned all this, everything that had happened, right from the start.

Fact again – from Wibble's point of view the war had killed two birds with one stone, which just seemed too much of a coincidence for comfort.

Because not only had he established his reputation and leadership across the club, Wibble had also culled the local Cambridge charter, destroying Thommo as a threat.

And without the war, without Thommo's apparent fuck ups, he'd have never been able to take him out like that. Now he'd done it and the whole club would just applaud him for cleaning house.

210

Wibble had just applied one of Damage's old P principles. If you are going to hurt someone, destroy them utterly and absolutely so they can never, ever, recover to threaten you again.

So Wibble hadn't just looked to take on his rival Thommo and his Cambridge crew piecemeal. He hadn't wanted to disband them, strip them of their colours and hound them out of the club. No, that was too casual. Instead in one surgical strike of absolute violence they had been wiped out to a man.

Then it was done, and done for good.

Why had I been so slow in working it out?

Wibble hadn't just started a war, that's what he had just told me.

In doing so he'd deliberately set Thommo and his crew up to take the fall as well. It wasn't just a side effect or a happy accident, it had all been part of the plan right from the start.

The essence of power is control, Damage had taught me that. Don't be reacting to other people's actions, had been his rule he said, instead have them react to yours. Make your enemies come to you, to fall into your trap.

It was so obvious once you saw it. Wibble had evidently been a good student.

Fact – Thommo and his Cambridge charter had been a threat, even I had seen that.

Fact – their charter territory ran up against Capricorn and Dead Men Riding, the clubs which would come together to form the new Mohawks club.

And if these clubs were the likely enemy then the attack when it came was likely to be on Thommo's crew's territory and with any luck as far as Wibble was concerned, they would suffer casualties. Whether they did or not, as the local Brethren charter it would be up to them to step up to the plate to take revenge. It was a club and charter honour thing straight and simple. If you couldn't control your territory for the club, then you didn't deserve to wear the club's colours.

So once the war had started Thommo was faced with a choice, to go it alone or to appeal to the rest of the club for help.

Thommo's problem was that neither choice would look good. A pair of regional clubs they may have been, but once Dead Men Riding and Capricorn had combined into the Mohawks their numbers outstripped those of the Cambridge crew many times over so going it alone would be a problem.

But as I'd heard that day on the field, Wibble had beaten Thommo to the alternative of all out mobilisation for war involving all The Brethren's UK charters, by spelling out a local responsibility.

It's your shit.

You want to be a P in this club? Well then it's your responsibility to take care of these local cunts, unless you need us to come in and do it for you?

Worse he'd done it in front of The Rebels.

We'll let them handle it, so long as it gets handled right and quickly enough.

And he'd even made it clear that there would be support offered if Thommo needed it.

If these guys need any back up both clubs will step up.

Now if Thommo asked for help he'd be accepting Wibble's offer and admitting he couldn't cope with the situation on his own.

The situation had immediately turned into a nasty trap for Thommo.

I could see that for Wibble, by contrast, it could all have been quite amusing.

Going forward once he'd got Thommo into that position he could even be all charm and concern if he wanted to play it that way. Looking back I was surprised that he hadn't been more solicitous of Thommo as a way of lording it over him and giving him the needle with very public offers of support and concern from the rest of the club, that Thommo would have had no choice but to reject through gritted teeth.

Wibble could have been as 'love-to-help-offer-is-there' as he liked, in the full knowledge that Thommo couldn't possibly accept it without losing all hope of ever challenging Wibble.

Instead he'd gone the hard nosed approach.

So you started this. So you need to finish this, and soon. Or if you can't handle it, we'll come in and do it for you. Is that what needs to happen here?

But either way I guess, the overall effect was the same. Thommo had been on the hook and squirming with no obvious way off.

And it wasn't just that the attack was on their territory of course and that his crew should have been able to keep the local junior clubs under control.

Then he'd been able to pin responsibility for the provocation on Thommo and his crew as well. He'd been able to show the rest of the club that it was Thommo's fault that the squaws had ever formed on the mainland in the first place, not Wibble's.

That was why Wibble had had Bob leak the information about the previous run-ins to me knowing that I would print them.

I don't know where he got that.

I don't give a flying fuck where he got it, that wasn't the question. Is it right?

It gave him the excuse to call the council of war, to put on record in front of the other key Brethren players, and The Rebels, Thommo's responsibility for letting the Mohawks form; and in doing so to pile more pressure on for Thommo to solve a problem that he could never tackle without the one thing he would never have but Wibble did, an inside track on the Mohawks.

In effect Wibble had forced Thommo into a position where he had to take enough rope to hang himself.

Particularly if the Mohawks had sources that let them anticipate and counter every move that Thommo made.

It was a complete fucking ambush! The squaws must have known we were coming...

He hadn't known it when he had said it but I now knew that he had been absolutely right. The Mohawks had been tipped off about the planned raiding party and were able to ambush it and beat it back.

Because of course, someone knew someone who had an open channel through which to pass messages to the Mohawks, didn't they Wibble?

Then Wibble and his Freemen contingent, the old Damage loyalists I guessed, could come in as the cavalry. They could liquidate the troublemakers who had stirred up all this shit and then couldn't deal with it, without anyone else in the club doing anything other than applaud; and then defeat the Mohawks and win the war, new territory and new business, and come out with a consolidated powerbase.

There'd been a snitch alright I thought, but it wasn't in Thommo's crew.

Thommo and his boys hadn't just been snitched on, they'd been stitched up good and proper.

*

'You did it didn't you?' I asked eventually. Whether it threatened our deal or not, and frankly given what had gone down so far I doubted it would, I had to ask the question.

'You set Thommo up for all of it, right from the start.

'You knew there would be a war and you manoeuvred Thommo into having to take it on alone didn't you?'

'Yes,' he said calmly.

'Having The Mohawks form on your watch would be bad for your rep as P for having allowed it to happen.

'But using Bob and me you had Thommo and the Cambridge crew take the fall for allowing that to happen as well didn't you?'

'Yes.'

'Why?'

There was a silence.

'It wasn't just that he was a rival was it? It was more personal than that. There was some history there, some agenda wasn't there? Whatever it was, there was more to it than that wasn't there?' I pressed.

He looked at me for a moment in silence and I held my breath as I waited for him to speak.

Then at last it came in a flat dead tone.

One word.

'Damage.'

'Are you saying Thommo had Damage killed?'

I got his best blank stare. Did that mean there was no answer to that, or was it his version of you might very well ask that but I couldn't possibly comment?

'Is that all you're going to say?' I asked.

He shook his head, 'Look chum, it's over, finito, got it? We have a deal and Bung's on his way back. You're going to walk in a few minutes so I wouldn't push it if I were you.'

But he wasn't me. And even now I just didn't know when to shut the fuck up for my own good.

'But before I go, there's just one question.'

He seemed genuinely amused at this turn of events, 'A question Mr Journalist? Now? After all we've just been talking about and what I've just said? Do you really think that's wise?'

To tell the truth, well no I didn't, but having gone through all this shit I was probably feeling a bit light-headed.

'It's just one question and I… I… have to know.'

'Know what?' he asked calmly, although I guess he suspected what was coming.

'Did you kill him? I mean not you personally. Just, was it you? Did you organise it? Or was it someone else?'

'Who? Damage?'

I nodded and locked my gaze on his face.

He stood looking down at me quietly for a moment as our eyes bored into one another.

'You really, really don't know when to quit when you're ahead do you?' he said in an undertone.

'No,' I said, 'I don't. And now there's no reason not to tell me is there? I mean you know it's not going to go anywhere. No one else is ever going to know. Not with where we are now.'

He stayed silent.

'This is just for me,' I said, 'this isn't for anyone else; this is just me wanting to know.'

'You know,' he said at last, 'I don't think I'm going to answer that.'

He turned on his heel and headed across the room to where he had left his mobile phone.

It looked as though I was never going to be any the wiser as to whether Wibble had done it or not.

And if not Wibble, who then?

Someone obviously had done it. I was right back where I had started in many ways.

Was it someone in the club? A rival, a challenger?

Was it someone outside the club? If so who? And why?

The Rebels, *pax Damage* or no *pax Damage*? Another club? Or someone entirely unconnected?

And if it wasn't him, did Wibble actually know who had done it? Or did he just have suspicions?

But the way things were, I had run out of chances to ask.

*

'Well, that's it then isn't it?' he said brightly looking back at me, and then picking up a vicious looking sheath knife that had been lying out of my sight on the kitchen table, he turned and advanced on where I sat trussed into my chair.

'What the fuck's that for?' I asked nervously, as he advanced towards me. In terror I wondered if he had suddenly changed his mind, had he heard something that had made him decide that he was better off with me dead after all? Had he just been toying with me all the time?

'You've got something of mine,' he said as he stopped in front of me, 'and I want it back.'

Reaching down, he jabbed the point of the knife under the side seam of the support patch where I had sewn it on and slashed downwards, the razor sharp blade slicing through the threads that I had so painstakingly stitched sitting at my kitchen table a lifetime ago now.

With a few deft strokes, he had cut the support patch off my jacket and taken it back.

As he walked away with it I was surprised about how naked and yes, rejected, I suddenly felt.

I was out. And not in good standing.

And I was upset at how that made me feel.

15   LLH&R

'And this LLH&R stuff?' she asked, 'What's that?'

'It's a motto, to those on the inside it's what they're all about.'

'So what does it stand for? And why did some have it and not others? Was it significant?'

'It's a biker saying. It stands for Love, Loyalty, Honour and Respect,' I told her quietly, thinking about the words, 'and I don't know but it had something to do with Damage. It was on all the RIP tabs that Wibble and his crew were wearing, so something only the Damage loyalists wore in his honour perhaps?'

'Or a badge to show whose side they were on?'

'Could be I suppose. You know looking back I don't remember ever seeing any of the Cambridge crew with them. I think at the time I just assumed it was only those who had known Damage personally or been in the Freemen with him who wore them but now I'm not so sure.'

So are they all, all honourable men.

'Anyway, it's what they live by.'

'Christ.'

'Or at least say they do.'

*

'Is that it?' she demanded quietly from where she was curled up against me under the covers on the bed.

'Just about.'

'But I still don't understand,' she said sounding puzzled. 'If you knew so much, why did he let you go?'

That was something I had thought about a lot myself ever since that day when I had walked out of the flat with looped gaffa tape still stuck to the cuffs of my jacket and around my ankles. It had taken a while to come to terms with it, with everything that had happened, and with what it would mean for the rest of my life. But when it came down to it I had to face up to a simple truth, and one that had determined whether I was going to live or die that day.

I was more dangerous to him dead, because of what might come out from stuff I'd left behind, than alive and silent. It was that simple.

'And that's it?' she gasped as I said it out loud, 'Mutual blackmail? That's all that's keeping you, us, safe?'

'Just about,' I admitted.

'Jesus!' she exhaled, 'so what happens if he changes his mind?'

There was no way of sugar coating this. It wasn't fair. I'd had enough in my life now of leading people into places, dangers that they weren't aware of. I couldn't do it to someone else.

'Then I'm not as safe.'

'And how do you know he hasn't?' she asked.

'I don't, and what's more, I won't, not unless and until someone has a go at me. And by then it might be too late.'

'Christ!' came a low whistle out of the darkness. 'And that's why you are hiding.'

'And that's why I'm in hiding,' I agreed.

There was silence for a while which it wasn't my place to break.

Then eventually she spoke again, 'So why are you telling me this? If you need to keep yourself a secret I mean. Why tell anyone this?'

'Because I have to. It's not fair not to and I won't, can't, put anyone else in unwitting danger. I did it once, and it got him killed, and I just couldn't do it again.'

She snorted in derision, 'Don't be so fucking wet. If you mean your man Danny then you're just soft in the head. You didn't get him killed; he did that himself when he decided to get mixed up with these guys.'

'And as for your man the polis. What kind of a fuckwit do you have to be to set up a patsy for your own murder anyway?'

Well, I thought to myself in the darkness, it was a point of view.

*

'So are we safe here?' she asked quietly, 'now, I mean.'

I was pleased she had said the 'we'. That meant a lot to me now that she had heard what she had heard.

'I think so,' I told her after a moment's contemplation about what I could really tell her, 'at least as safe as we'll ever be. I covered my tracks getting here, and I deliberately chose Ireland not the mainland, as it should be safer.'

'Why's that?' she wanted to know.

'Because The Brethren like the other big six clubs aren't here south of the border. The main Irish 1%er clubs came together a while ago because they wanted to keep their independence. They wanted to keep the Irish bike scene out of the international politics of the big clubs.'

'*Ireland her own, from the earth to the sky,*' she murmured.

Yeah, well that's the romantic way of putting it I thought. Either that or it just keeps the local market for the local guys.

Whatever the reason though, what it meant was that there wasn't either a Brethren charter or a beholden support or striker club on the ground that might be actively looking for me. Which was about as much as I could hope for. While it lasted.

But still I reflected as I lay there staring up at the darkened ceiling, despite the beard I had grown and the careful way I had kept myself to myself the last twelve months, I couldn't help but still be jumpy. I still felt a chill run down my spine if I ever heard the rumble of big bikes in the village.

'But it doesn't make sense,' she said eventually.

'What doesn't?'

'So what is it that you could know and could have squirreled away about them before they caught you, that yer man Wibble would be so concerned about?'

'That's the funny thing, I had to admit, 'in some ways I'm not sure...'

'Because the bombs, the killings, the really heavy stuff,' she interrupted, 'from what you're saying, you only found out about once they already had you. If that was what he was thinking about, then from his point of view wouldn't killing you have been the easiest and most certain thing to do?'

She was right, it was something which had been gnawing away at the back of my mind for a while but which I'd been doing my studious best to try not to think about. But now she'd put it to me so bluntly, there was no escaping it. She was right and it was a real worry.

'I can only guess that Wibble thinks I know something...' I ventured.

'Or that you have something else he wants,' she countered.

'Then why let me disappear?'

'Who says you really have?' she challenged, 'Listen, they couldn't have got that you would be at the yard that evening from Danny's call could they, even if Bob had intercepted it? Because Danny didn't say anything about the place on the phone did he?'

'No he didn't. He just sent me the text asking me to be at the call box.'

'So how did Charlie know that you were going to be at the yard? He was waiting for you for feck's sake wasn't he?'

'Well yes…'

'Then someone must have known,' she concluded.

'Well Danny…'

'Ach no,' she scoffed. 'You said yourself he wouldn't, he was too scared. He'd got himself into something too deep and was just looking for his out wasn't he. Do you still think that?'

'Well yes…'

'Then it must have been someone else mustn't it?'

She was right, 'But who?'

'The kids in the café,' she said, 'it's got to be.'

'Who?'

'Look, you know Bob was having the bikers' phones tapped don't you? And that would go for Danny as well as the others.'

'Yes.'

'And the one thing Bob could have got from intercepting Danny's text was to find out that he was making contact with you?'

'Yes, the…'

'Well your boyos knew that all they had to do was put the tabs on you or him. Have you followed to work out where you were going and send someone in to have a listen in.'

'The café. Right?'

I thought back to that brief exchange in the phone box between me and Danny. I had never asked him where he had called from I realised. It had really only been a few words. 'Well yes, I suppose…'

'And you said that when you got there to meet Danny, the place was empty wasn't it?'

'Except…'

'Except for a couple of street kids who came in just after you, and had enough time and cash to stand there in the corner of the room playing the fruit machine.'

'They weren't there all the time…' I protested.

'Most of it? Enough to have overheard what he was telling you if they'd been listening?'

When had they left? I hadn't really noticed at the time, it hadn't seemed important. All I really remembered was glancing up at the ring of the bell on the door as they headed out into the dark shortly before Danny and I broke up. Could they have heard enough to know what Danny had been telling me?

I had to acknowledge to myself that the answer was yes.

'Because if they could use street kids there to spy on you over in London without you ever realising, who's to say there isn't someone over here keeping an eye on you now?'

It was a chilling thought that was going to fester.

It was stupid really not to have thought of it.

Like Wibble had said, there were so many ways they could come at me if they wanted to. Turning up on bikes would just be too obvious.

That was the thing. I would never know. And if they did it right, I would never have known.

And I knew, that was going to be my life from now on.

*

And as it happened, I did have a piece in the paper, sort of anyway.

Inside on the table I had left the paper open at the article I'd been expecting to see.

It was buried away on page seven.

The Guardian

Monday 23 August 2010

Journalist Still Missing One Year On

Police have issued a new appeal for information in respect of missing journalist Iain Parke and Inspector Robert Cameron of the Serious and Organised Crime Agency.

It's now a year since Guardian crime correspondent Iain Parke's mysterious disappearance which police have repeatedly linked to the suspected murder of Inspector Cameron who disappeared a few days later.

At the time they both vanished each had been investigating the Brethren/Mohawk biker war which had broken out after the missile and gun attack on The Brethren MC's annual Toy Run on the weekend of the first and second of August last year, at which six people died; and police sources say they are still convinced that there are links between the two disappearances.

It is known that the two men were in regular communication in the period before they were last seen, including calls which were traced back to having been made from a flat in North West London. Police believe this property to be linked to the biker gang and blood, bullets, and both men's fingerprints were subsequently recovered from it when searched.

Despite an extensive investigation, no body or the weapon that had been fired in the flat have yet been found and police have continued to remain tight lipped about what information their files contain about these discussions and each man's activities at this time.

This has led to some speculation that Iain Parke, who had apparently been becoming increasingly involved with the gang while conducting an investigation for this paper, was either also acting as an informant for the police, or had lured Inspector Cameron into a trap at the flat on behalf of the gang; although both suggestions are strongly denied by this paper.

Author's note: fiction and respect

As with the previous book in this series, all characters, events, and in particular the clubs named in this book, are fictional and any resemblance to actual places, events, clubs or persons, living or dead, is purely coincidental.

Once again I have also had to ascribe certain territories and names, and in the case of The Mohawks, a patch description, to my fictional club charters.

For all of these inventions I apologise to the 1%ers in the areas mentioned, and any clubs with similar names or patch; and also, for obvious reasons, to anyone involved in the nightclub security industry.

No disrespect is meant; just what I hope is an enjoyable story.

None of the views expressed are those of the author.

> There is a tide in the affairs of men,
> Which, taken at flood, leads on to fortune.

Julius Caesar, William Shakespeare 1564–1616

Also available from www.bad-press.co.uk
by Iain Parke:

The Liquidator

Dangerous things happen in Africa.

People disappear.

Everybody knows that.

But as an outsider, Paul thinks he is safe, even from the secret police, whatever he starts to find, or wherever it leads; despite the turmoil leading up to the country's first multi party election and with a diamond fuelled civil war raging in the failed state just across the border.

But when Paul finds himself and his friends trapped holding a potentially deadly secret as the country begins to implode, what will he be prepared to do to protect himself and those around him in order to escape?

Download the first chapter to read FREE at www.bad-press.co.uk

ISBN 978–0–9561615–0–5

Available for Kindle at Amazon and as an ibook for Apple

The Brethren Trilogy

A real page turner…

American –V magazine

The first book in The Brethren trilogy:

Heavy Duty People

Your club and your brothers are your life.

Damage

Damage's club has had an offer it can't refuse, to patch over to join The Brethren.

But what does this mean for Damage and his brothers?

What choices will they have to make?

What history might it reawaken?

And why is The Brethren making this offer?

Loyalty to his club and his brothers has been Damage's life and route to wealth, but what happens when business becomes serious and brother starts killing brother?

Download the first chapter to read FREE at www.bad–press.co.uk

ISBN 978–0–9561615–1–2

Available for Kindle at Amazon and as an ibook for Apple

Coming in 2012

Heavy Duty Trouble

The final explosive book in The Brethren trilogy

Made in the USA
San Bernardino, CA
14 December 2013